despite the transgression

down

whatever path awaits

a story

        must be told

                    a canvas;,

paints running down ...

                    a pool of red

pulling ...

PHOENIX ROSE

A NOVEL

BY MICHAEL BAILEY

Published by Written Backwards
www.nettirw.com

Second Trade Paperback Edition

ISBN: 978-1-7327244-1-9

"Deep into that darkness peering, long I stood there, wondering, fearing, doubting, dreaming dreams no mortal ever dared to dream before."

– Edgar Allan Poe, *The Raven*

Phoenix Rose

Prologue

"Have I told you about my problem?"

Dr. Milton watched Hillcrest rub the scars covering his arms. The meshed marks of self-mutilation glowed purple-blue under the fluorescent lighting. Dressed in whites, his patient waited for an answer to this complex question.

Notepad on his lap and a pen in hand, Dr. Milton studied Hillcrest with concern. He studied his facial expressions and watched as nervous fingers danced along his forearms. Suicide patients were complicated to work with and often explosive—at least in his experience—and each word, as a response, had to be precisely placed.

The doctor clicked his pen before saying, "Yes. Yes you have, William." It was such a strange name, William Hillcrest. Somewhere he had heard it before. Just saying the name aloud sparked déjà vu.

"You told me about your … *condition* yesterday, as well as the day before." He was careful to replace the word *problem* with *condition*. "Please, continue."

Hillcrest's shoulders were slumped, his head drooping to the ground. He glanced up to his doctor with sunken eyes. A hand rose to touch old bruises circling his neck. He pressed at them gently. It was enough to make him cringe.

Dr. Milton jotted down notes while his microcassette recorder hummed in the small room.

"You see, I have this problem," the patient said. "And, by the way, this is our second session together, doctor. You are mistaken."

"I see …" said Dr. Milton, although he couldn't see anything. It was just a kind agreement to get the man talking again. He thought, *I can't seem to remember things from one day to the next.*

"I can't seem to remember things from one day to the next," said Hillcrest. "It's like I wake up each morning not knowing what I did the day before. As if I'm reborn." He adjusted in his seat and wiped the redness under his eyes. "And there's nothing I can do to fix it."

"What is it you have tried, William?" It was one of those dangerous questions, also an important one.

The patient extended his arms. On his wrists were dozens of slash marks. His veins appeared gray and there were pockmarks by his elbows.

Although he had seen it all the day before, Dr. Milton leaned forward for closer examination. He tried not to wince, but it was difficult to look at. He leaned forward in his metal chair and caught a better glimpse of the patient's neck, which was bruised of course, but contained rashes near the throat. Rising up from the collar of his shirt was a rose tattoo, the petals deep scarlet, everything else black. It was a feature he hadn't noticed in his last few sessions so he wrote the discovery on his notepad.

"Only our second meeting," his patient said again. He began counting on his fingers as if to track the days and then said, "Anyway, I mean I try to kill myself and it doesn't seem to work."

That's terrible, Dr. Milton thought. He flipped back a few pages in his notepad and each was blank. He flipped back a few more, perplexed. It was an empty notebook.

Hillcrest continued, "I don't even remember doing any of this." He pointed to his wrists and forearms. "They can't possibly be from the same incident. Look, these lines are new." He traced some of the darker scars with his fingertips. He then pointed to a few apparently older marks. "And these … these are at least a month old. They are lighter than the others and don't look like they were as deep, yet I don't remember inflicting any of them."

Dr. Milton flipped through his notepad, wondering where he misplaced the one he had used in their previous sessions. "What do you remember?" he said, attempting to show he was paying attention despite the distractions.

"I remember waking up on the couch one evening. It must have been around eleven or twelve o' clock." Hillcrest's eyes connected with the white floor tiles. He seemed to trace their outlines.

The doctor looked at the patient folder. HILLCREST, WILLIAM. At least he had the correct file this time. He returned his attention to the patient.

"My depression tanked and I made my way to the bathroom. I looked at myself in the mirror a while before drawing a bath."

Dr. Milton was again distracted by the thoughts of a former patient who experienced similar issues with reflections; he thought the reflection was not his own, but a complete stranger staring back at him through the glass. He had attempted suicide as well.

"I took a box of razorblades from the medicine cabinet to slice my wrists. I set them on the tub near the faucet and undressed. Why do you think people get naked before kill-ing themselves?"

Their eyes met as each looked up from the floor.

"Well, some believe it has to do with rebirth. As one is born into this world, one must therefore leave. Others think it is a form of humiliation. To have such a low sense of worth, humiliation is all that remains. Think of a typical armed robbery. A person goes into a gas station and holds the place up at gunpoint for cash. This person usually ends up with the place surrounded with a store full of hostages he or she never meant to acquire. He has two choices: one is to surrender, leaving through the front door; the other— let's just say sometimes the guy shoots up the place and leaves through that same front door in a body bag. Does this make sense?"

"Which path would you take?" asked Hillcrest

"I would prefer the surrendering approach."

"I mean, with the suicide patient."

Dr. Milton smiled and said, "My answer is the same. Please, continue your story."

Hillcrest relived the memory, but had heard it all before.

"There's not much left to my story, really. I sat in the tub for a couple minutes. Lit a candle and watched it melt. Cried. And then I opened the box of razors."

Dr. Milton brought the next words from memory, *and it was filled with paperclips.*

"And it was filled with paperclips," said Hillcrest, "as if someone, or me even, knew I was going to kill myself and had replaced the blades with paperclips beforehand. I never thought to kill myself until I walked into the bathroom and saw the mirror."

And you saw the reflection of a man holding a gun to his head, thought the doctor. *No, that was the other patient. Focus.*

"It was spur of the moment."

"Maybe your subconscious knew what you were planning."

Dr. Milton had a hard time looking away from the rose tattoo on his patient's neck. He drew a sketch of it on the next page of his notepad, outlining the petals heavily.

The microcassette recorder made an audible click.

"Excuse me a moment." He flipped the tape over and with a similar click the hum continued.

Hillcrest took a moment. He held his face in his hands.

"This is how it always happens. I try to kill myself, but fail. Yet, I must succeed in some part because eventually I either end up cut or overdosed in the hospital. I don't remember any of it. I only remember the failed attempts— like with the paperclips."

On the middle of his notebook, surrounded by a plethora of random words and phrases from the session, was a detailed rose. He had drawn flames at the base of it for some reason.

"Are paperclips significant to you in any way, William?"

How could they be, he thought.

"How could they be?" Hillcrest sighed. "I mean, sometimes it's paperclips, sometimes it's toothpicks, sometimes it's safety pins."

"And you never check the container in advance to make sure the blades are there?"

Dr. Milton knew it was a stupid question the moment it left his mouth. He shouldn't have asked such a question. It was too late to pull it back.

"Of course not!"

Hillcrest became anxious again, his fingers twisting within his shirt. He leaned over, toes balancing him in place. His heels bobbed up and down, knees twitching.

Patients often rocked. It was a self-calming gesticulation, or a maternal instinct of sorts. He read about it once. It showed instability. He had to reel him back in before he fell apart.

"There's no way you could have known. I shouldn't have asked you that, William."

Silence separated them.

"It's almost as if someone—or my subconscious, as you said—wants me alive, and it's going out of its way—or my way—to protect me from anything harmful."

Thoughts from his previous session with Hillcrest flooded his mind. *I could have used knives. I could have swallowed pills. I could have used the gun on my headboard to blow my freaking head off.* He clicked his pen off and on, off and on. The thoughts were vivid. If patients could rock themselves, psychiatrists had the right to click pens.

Hillcrest repeated those exact words.

"I could have used knives. I could have swallowed pills. I could have used the gun on my headboard—"

"—to blow your freaking head off."

"Have I told you this story before, Doctor?"

"This is at least the fourth or fifth time," Dr. Milton said, but not unkindly, "as well as what you just said about your condition. I love hearing your stories; otherwise, why would I be here?"

He could tell Hillcrest was about to inform him this was their second session, but he scratched his head, puzzled.

"This is interesting, William. You have all these poten-
tial, life threatening objects around you, yet you insistently
choose the one that is tampered with … if I'm not being
too—"

"Not at all."

"Have there been any similar instances?"

He knew there had been. He could vaguely remember
details about the gun incident, as well as the misplaced pills.
He listened anyhow and took his notes.

"It's usually the razorblades, but once I had it in my
head to overdose. I grabbed a couple orange prescription
bottles from the medicine cabinet above the sink. Most
of them were a few years expired. There were painkillers
and maybe antibiotics." Hillcrest laughed, despite the seri-
ousness. "I remember sitting on the bed. After struggling
with the stupid child-proof / adult-proof / idiot-proof
lids, I began pouring them in my mouth, directly from the
containers. I chewed a handful, at least, without even caring
what they were. When those were gone, I grabbed more."

But, inquired the mind of the doctor.

"But, they were only sugar candies."

"Sugar candies?"

He knew they were sugar candies.

"The chalky kind. Smarties, or something. I hadn't really
paid attention to their flavor. How should I have known? I
didn't give my tongue much of a chance to tell they were
not pills."

"You are indeed lucky," said Dr. Milton.

"Why?"

"Because it shows in your records you have never overdosed."

"But, couldn't I have? Maybe it just hasn't been recorded. I'm not trying to gain credit, but you never know."

"It is possible, but with the manner in which you take your pills—or candies, in this case—if they were prescription medicines, you would either be dead, or would have come close to dying at some point in your life. You would have surely gone comatose. However, I believe you have *never* overdosed, William."

The patient thought for a second before asking, "Could an OD cause a dysfunction of memory, such as with my condition?"

"It is a possibility."

But it was deeper than that. Hillcrest's problem would have developed from some sort of trauma, some kind of abuse or struggle he was forced to endure. *What else could explain it?*

"Tell me about the gun," asked Dr. Milton.

Hillcrest took a deep breath and sighed.

The gun on the headboard, Dr. Milton thought preemptively.

His patient said those same words, and then, "—was loaded, of course. Where was I going with this?" Light sweat dotted his brow, a ring of perspiration forming around his collar.

"You were telling me about the bullets," he informed, "or you were about to."

The patient gave a bewildered look.

Dr. Milton imagined a bathroom mirror speckled with blood, bone fragments and brain matter. And again thoughts of his former patient crossed his mind; it was all familiar. *Death can be so different, yet so alive sometimes.* He brushed those

words away, as he would with dust on a mantle. *Why mantle?* And then he remembered.

"So I stood by the fireplace mantle, smiling at the portraits on the wall, and pulled the trigger. Nothing. I pulled it again … click, the same thing. I pulled six times in a row and nothing happened."

Mike & Ikes instead of cartridges.

"Can you imagine pulling the trigger? Thinking with each pull that *this* could be the one; *this* could end my life. That's what I was hoping for—the end of my life, for the end of my torture, my sadness—and with each pull of the trigger I was denied this. You try to end your existence because you feel you are a disappointment to everyone you love and everyone you hate …" Hillcrest paused, his body shaking. Tears glossed his eyes. He placed a hand over his rose tattoo and said with a rasp, "I want to die, but the world doesn't want me to die."

The soft hum of the recorder filled the room.

"I am like a phoenix and each time I die I am born again."

Dr. Milton wrote: PHOENIX, and next to it added: ROSE. He circled the words and thumbed back a few pages to his drawing of the flower in flames.

When Hillcrest spoke again it gave Dr. Milton the chills.

"From the ashes a rose."

PART ONE

LIFE OF 'ODD

ONE

The sun was about to die.

"It's getting dark," Roy Kenseth told his oldest boy. He used a pitchfork to lob hay into the stable and noticed the finches and mockingbirds had stopped chirping.

Roy was born and raised a cowboy, yet he was not a burly man. He stood five-ten, a hundred and seventy pounds, kept a stubbly face, dirty hands and fingernails, wore boots and a flimsy hat.

"Is this enough hay, Dad?" Charlie was a ten-year-old version of his father. He bent down and measured the depth.

"How deep is it?"

"About a foot," said Charlie, yawning.

"Just about right, then."

It was a small stable. The two of them were able to walk over the hay floor to press it flat in a matter of minutes.

The barn was the centerpiece of the Kenseth farm in Brenden, Washington. Once red, it was now a dried-blood brown. Metal white-tipped fence posts, painted red and green, stood like matchsticks around the ten-acre property. Naked oaks, like hands, reached skyward throughout the lifeless yellow fields.

The rest of the family joined them in the barn, bringing more propane lanterns, one held by his wife, Susan, the other by their daughter, Cindy. She carried the swaying lantern, nearly scraping the ground with its base. Towels were draped over her arms. Next to her was Todd, their youngest. He carried a bucket of water with a bar of soap floating in it. Only three, Todd looked like one of Cindy's toy dolls carrying a sack of cement, his face straining with effort.

"Can you keep an eye on these rugrats?" Susan placed her lantern down at the rear of the stable. She grabbed a lead rope from a hook on the wall.

Roy nodded and tipped a finger to the brim of his hat as she ventured to one of the pastures around back.

Todd set the bucket down by the stable gate. Water sloshed everywhere. The bar of soap swayed in the bucket like a buoy.

Cindy set the lantern next to Charlie. She stood an inch taller than her brother, despite being a year younger. The two often fought, but usually over petty things. Once, last spring, they fought over who could run the fastest. They had run from barn to tree and tree to barn repeatedly, arguing over who had won, who had cheated, and who was dumber than the other. She and Charlie were inseparable.

"Why do we need hay, anyway?" Cindy asked. She looked to Charlie, who leaned against the handle of a pitch-fork. It nestled under his arm like a crutch.

He sneered at his sister. "To keep dirt out of the horses 'jina."

Roy laughed, although he knew he shouldn't have.

"No it's not," said Cindy. "Is it, Dad?"

"Uh, huh," said Charlie.

"Enough, you two, or you both go back to the house."

"Yeah, stop," Todd said, which got Roy smiling again.

"It's to help keep everything sterile and to make cleanup a little easier afterward," he told his children. "So yes, Charlie was partially correct, although I have no clue where you got *jina* from."

Todd stared into the lantern and reached for the glass.

"Todd, that's hot."

Todd pulled his small hand back as if the thing would bite. Perhaps it did, because he stuck a finger in his mouth.

"That's why we don't use shavings or grass or alfalfa or anything else. Hay is much cleaner and easier," said Roy.

Cindy asked why it was easier. Charlie asked why it was cleaner.

Roy had a single answer for both of them. "Are you messier after playing in a pile of hay, or after one of you has rolled around in the dirt or played in shavings?" Both somehow understood the logic and quieted down.

Then Susan walked into the stable leading the pregnant horse. The mare's sides were ballooned out to twice her normal girth. She had carried eleven months and tonight was her night. The whole family would watch her give birth.

"Joey Bean," said Todd. The kids had wanted to call her Jelly Bean, but Todd was too young at the time to pronounce his Ls and so the name stuck.

Five gallons of fluid gushed out of Joey Bean the exact moment Roy finished wrapping her tail with plastic to make the birthing easier. She was upright at the time, her muscles twitching and contracting.

Cindy started to cry. Her entire lower half was covered

in the horse's thick fluids. Some got onto Charlie, but he hadn't noticed, and dared not to laugh or to poke fun at his sister. Both wore blue jeans. Cindy's looked as though she had been wading in the creek behind the house.

Joey Bean, confused, circled round, Susan still holding the lead rope. The horse spiraled to the ground like a cat preparing for a nap. More fluid escaped as she did this. Her head plopped onto the hay. She was breathing hard, her nose perspiring.

"I've got her," said Roy, meaning the horse. He took the lead rope from Susan and knelt beside the mare. He rubbed her long face. "There are more towels in the house. Why don't you run and get those, Charlie. Don't just stand there looking at your sister. Help her. It could have been you standing there."

Without hesitation, Charlie ran to the house.

Susan took Cindy by a wet hand to the edge of the stable where Todd was playing in the soapy water. She took the bar of white soap and handed it to her daughter.

"Is this why … you had … us bring …" Cindy said between sobs, "the bucket of—"

"It was meant for the horse. But I'm sure Joey Bean won't mind if we use it to help clean you up." She dipped her own hand into the sudsy water and wiped at Cindy's face and then her arms.

Cindy turned the bar of soap over and over in her small hands, but didn't do much else. Her sobs were beginning to slow as her mother cleaned the rest of her.

"Why does Joey Bean need a bucket of soapy water?"

Cindy asked, calming.

"Well, to help Joey Bean deliver the baby easier, we need to soap up her ... her area around where the baby horse will come out. Remember when you got your finger stuck in that metal piece of pipe—the rusty one you found in the yard? Remember how we used soap and water to get your finger unstuck?"

"Is the baby horse stuck in Joey Bean?"

Susan laughed. "Not exactly. The baby is being *grown* in Joey Bean, like you were grown in me."

"In her belly?"

"Yes, in her belly."

"How does the baby get there in the first place?"

"That's for a later time."

"Then how does the baby come out. Is that where we put the soap and water—on her tummy?"

"You'll see."

A small fire burned in the distance, glowing yellow-orange against the mountainside. Roy would have to remember to put a call in later to report it. A meteor shower overhead shot lines through the sky. No one but Roy seemed to notice these spectacles. All eyes of the Kenseth family were glued to the baby horse.

Hooves protruded from the mare.

"Stand back," Roy said.

Joey Bean propped onto her front feet, and pushed with her hind legs to an awkward stance. As she did this, the nose of the foal poked through against the protruding front legs, hooves facing downward. It all seemed to take too long.

Fifteen minutes passed, and then thirty.

The horse staggered and fell to its knees, and finally onto its side, legs stretched.

"What's wrong?" Susan pulled Todd close, remembering his difficult birth.

"The head should be fully out by now."

The kids grew scared, but stayed.

"Something isn't right," said Roy.

Joey Bean lay on her side, huffing in and out. After minutes of tense breathing, her uterine contractions became more intense as the slimy neck and front feet of the foal were exposed.

Then Joey Bean stopped pushing.

She looked up to Roy with a hopeful, glossy eye. Flies buzzed and burrowed into that large, black marble as she panted, her chest heaving up and down, nostrils flaring. Mess everywhere. The foal half inside her.

"What's wrong?" Susan's words came out cracked and dry. "It went faster with the other horses ... do something, Roy. Please, do something."

Roy rushed to the mare's rear legs and began pulling at the foal's front legs, which broke the membrane. He slipped once and grabbed again, this time pulling part of the neck and anything else he could hold onto. Using his legs for support, Roy pulled, slipping and sliding in the mess, until finally the foal slid out in one mammoth lump.

Roy lay exhausted with the baby horse. He nestled it on the hay-covered stable, breathing as rapidly as the mare. Various fluids covered Roy's body, but mostly blood. Too much blood. The umbilical cord was on top of him, still connecting the two animals like a weathered garden hose.

A minute later, the foal struggled in his arms, stood on shaky legs—breaking the umbilical cord—and took its first steps of life.

TWO

"*A bead of light shines with the rest of the stars in the moonlit sky, not twinkling, but brilliant against the darkness and with sharp points reaching in every direction like a hand-drawn star. It dances playful circles around wispy clouds before descending to the ground, where it stops near Joey Bean's body. The light it casts varies between pallid and blinding.*"

What are you?

The white sphere floats gingerly. "I am Loah. Are you afraid? I can take another shape."

Have you come to take me away?

In a soothing voice Loah says, "I am here for another. You shall stay, my friend, but only for a short while. Your kin shall stay for a longer while—for many full moons."

Who will come to take me away?

"*Nuveli.*"

Is Nuveli Death?

"*No,*" *says the form.*

Are you Death?

"*No. We are just two of three. We often cross paths, for sometimes life offers us hand-in-hand, but we are neither life nor death. That role is for the balancer, one whose name is derived from death. I am the protector. The one coming for you is the guide.*"

Will there be pain?

"*There will be pain,*" *says Loah.* "*A short, but intense pain.*

For a while you will reject guidance and you will suffer unto that pain. Eventually you will succumb and be free from all pain. I must leave you now."

To protect another?

The white sphere of starlight is gone.

A gunshot breaks the silence and everything turns black. Not a single star peeks through, not even the full moon. Joey Bean is alone. Intense pain flowers warmth through her head. Her legs kick in spastic jerks, one making contact with something hard, a rock on the ground perhaps. After a second shot, it all goes away.

A second star-like entity hangs freely in the air with a reddish hue and an intense pulse that beats like a heart.

"Greetings," it says. "I am Nuveli."

THREE

Roy turned his attention to the mare. Blood pooled around her lower half, the amount of it rising steadily. Her breathing slowed. Water gathered around her eyes. Her belly, once round and full, now clung to her ribs each time she exhaled.

"Joey Bean is dying," he said to his family.

It took them a while to interpret what he had said. They were still excited about the foal.

"We should call her Daisy," said Cindy.

"Daisy's a girl's name," said Charlie, "You can tell it's a boy." He pointed to the newborn.

"No it's not," said Cindy. "That's part of the unbiblical cord, stupid!"

The older kids continued to argue as Susan joined him at the mare's side. Their youngest, Todd, was asleep and leaning his head against the stable wall, snot bubbles erupting from his nostrils.

"You want me to call the vet? Maybe there's something they can do." Susan placed a hand on his shoulder.

Roy inspected Joey Bean carefully.

"No." He waited for a second opinion. "There's nothing that can be done. She's going to die either way. Might as well be me that puts her down."

Susan buried her head into Roy's shoulder. They had raised Joey Bean from birth.

"There should've been the afterbirth by now," Roy said, trying to keep himself steady. "After birth, much sooner than now, there should be …" he trailed off, putting a single hand into his pocket. He looked at the tips of his boots. "And if we could help her, if she lived through this, she could get *Lamintis*, or *Metritis*." They were medical terms Roy knew firsthand from growing up on a farm, terms you didn't want to find yourself saying if at all possible.

"Will you go inside and get the rifle?"

Susan stiffened and brushed tears with a dirty sleeve. Dirt smeared across her face. Roy rubbed it away with his thumb, leaving a clean spot that revealed just how dirty her face had become this last hour. She leaned down to Joey Bean and brushed the white diamond on her brow.

"Everything will be all right," she told the horse. She then walked over to Todd, still asleep and angled uncomfortably against the stable wall, and shook him awake. "Honey, let's get you to bed."

Todd rubbed his eyes as he followed her to the house.

Roy met with Charlie and Cindy and put a firm hand onto each of their shoulders.

"Where's Mom going?" asked Charlie.

"Are we going to bed now? I'm tired," said Cindy.

"Your mother's going inside to fetch the gun."

"The 30'06?" asked Charlie.

"No."

A set of horrorstricken faces stared up at him.

"You see," said Roy, and then he paused, looking for the words. He looked to the west to the flame on the mountainside. You had to squint to really see it. A bright stripe of light split the sky above it—a falling star. He pointed to Joey

Bean in the hay. She was breathing heavier now. "You see, sometimes the mother horse—"

"Has to be put down," finished his son. "I saw a show about it on *The Discovery Channel*. Like in olden times when a work-horse broke its leg. They'd have to put it down 'cause the horse was no good, and it was best for the horse."

"Yes. And sometimes a mother horse has complications when delivering and has to be put down, but not because she's no good to anyone, but because she's in a lot of pain."

"It's not fair," said Cindy. Tears welled from eyes and streaked down her round cheeks. "Don't kill Joey Bean."

Roy put an arm around her but she brushed him away. "Is it fair, Cindy, if an animal is suffering, and is *for sure* dying, to let it suffer until it *does* die, for days and days when there's nothing anyone can do?"

"No."

"And don't you think Mom and Dad love Joey Bean just as much as you and would do anything to help her?"

"Yeah."

"Joey Bean is in a lot of pain right now. She's hurting all over. If I knew a vet would help, I'd call one out, but she can't be saved. It's too late, honey."

"Would you put Mom down if she was suffering?" Cindy looked up to his hard, rough face.

Roy thought for a moment before answering. Cindy deserved an honest answer.

"If Mom was in as much pain as Joey Bean is in right now, and I knew there was nothing humanly possible that could make her feel any better, then yes, I would."

He thought about it longer and realized that what he told her was the truth. If it came to it, he would. If Susan were a vegetable on life support, he'd surely pull the plug. If Susan had lost as much blood in comparison to the horse, and her life was hanging on by a single thread that refused to break and, of course, if she wanted to go, then he would ease her suffering and cut that last remaining thread of life.

"And Mom would want her husband to do such a lovely thing," said Susan, joining them. Todd was still at her side, barely awake. "I couldn't leave Todd all alone in the house; it just didn't feel right."

She held out the heavy rifle to Roy. Humped over one of her arms was a holey blanket he recognized from the shed. "Come over here kids." Cindy latched onto her leg. "You too, Charlie."

"I wanna be with Dad when he does it."

"Absolutely not," said Susan.

"Dad, can I?" Charlie's eyes were full of mixed emotion.

Roy took the gun and the blanket from Susan and remembered when he was a boy and watched his own father put down a horse for the first time. The images flashed through his mind like a nightmare. He was six at the time, but could remember every last drop of blood and speck of flesh as the bullet entered the horse's head. It had happened in slow motion. He put down his first horse at ten. Charlie's age. What a horrible set of feelings those were: to love something so tenderly and to have to watch it die … to have to help it die. And now he'd have to help Joey Bean die, and his son wanted to be there to see it.

"Go with your mother, Charlie."

Charlie didn't argue. He joined them and cried with his little sister. Susan stood strong for a moment, looking off into the distance, and then she led them to the house.

Roy stood over his horse, rifle in hand. He waited until they were out of the barn and then placed the blanket over the mare's long and pleading face. An empty black eye stared up at him through a tear in the material; in it he could see the orange moon peeking through one of the barn windows. Something deep down told him killing the horse was a mistake.

Aim just inside the ear. Make sure you don't only knick the thing or there will be hell to pay. These were his father's words. They cycled through his mind as Roy peered down the barrel, trying to hold it steady. *We'll miss you, Jelly Bean.*

The creaking of the barn door broke the silence.

Roy jerked.

The horse jerked.

The rifle blasted.

Joey Bean had lifted her head the moment Roy pulled the trigger. She took a bullet just above the temple. She bucked and writhed, somehow making it to all fours.

Todd was running toward them, arms outstretched, Susan chasing him.

Roy tried settling the horse but he was knocked to the ground, landing in a mixture of urine and afterbirth. The rifle flew out of his hands and into the hay.

The space inside the stable quickly shrank as the horse circled and whinnied and bucked with the last of her strength. She circled round and smashed one of the stable walls before finally settling to the ground. Roy grabbed the rifle, loaded a new round, and finally put Joey Bean down. The shot echoed in the barn.

Behind the fallen horse lay Todd, bloody and mangled from ironclad hooves.

FOUR

Todd is above the land, circling in a downward spiral through the black sky. Todd has wings outstretched like a hang glider, black and pterodactylesque. Below him is a wheat field with a circular shape pressed into it. Todd glides lower as the flattened circle grows larger. Running through it are two wolves. Todd tries to yell out to them, but produces an earsplitting shriek. The wolves disappear into a wall of un-flattened stalks, leaving a pair of squiggly trails behind. Todd falls until the ground is upon him.

He lands and folds his wings. In the center of the circle is a single rose. It pulses blue in the darkness. The edges of each petal crisp and turn black and as two of the petals part, light glows from the gap. The flower breaks apart into ash. The stem shrivels and falls. Left behind is a small bead of blue light floating majestically above the ground. An aura surrounds it like the lunar ring before an approaching storm. The full moon above glows in similar fashion.

What are you? *Todd asks the blue light.*

The light speaks back to him. "I am Thade."

Are you here for me?

"I am here for another."

Why are you here?

"Is my form acceptable? I can change shape to your liking." *The entity flickers with anticipation.*

Todd pictures a horse in his mind.

The light in Thade explodes into millions of smaller speckles of light and changes into a thoroughbred constructed of countless blue constellations.

Joey Bean.

"I thought you would like that," says the horse.

What are you and why are you in my dream?

"I am here for another." Its long head turns to the fresh trails in the field.

One of the wolves?

"If that is what you call them. I am Thade, the balancer." The head of the blue horse looks again to the trails in the field, as if eager.

What do you balance?

"Life."

How do you balance life?

"How did you fly down here?" The horse appears to smile. *"Imagination and reality share a thin veil. I must be going. As for you … your fate is now in the hands of the protector, Loah."*

Are you Death?

"With life there must come death, and with death, life. That is the balance in this world. The pure shall not leave in death, but be guided to other worlds. If one must be guided, another must be protected to live, and if one must live, there must surely be balance with death."

Loah is my protection.

"In time your questions will be answered," says Thade. *"I must leave."*

The shape of the horse condenses back into a miniature ball of brilliant blue light. It shimmers before shooting off into the darkness. The wheat field darkens because of its absence.

Todd tries to wake himself, his arms now the arms of a three-year-old boy, his wings gone. He tries to change them back but fails.

Loah?

"I am here," says a voice from nowhere in particular.

Todd looks to the moon and notices the star next to it is not a star at all, but an unusual speck of white light. It outshines all the other stars with sharp flares pointing every direction. Growing larger, it floats as if held by a string.

"You have many questions," says Loah.

Who needs guidance?

"Did Thade not show you that shape?"

He showed me Joey Bean.

"Then you already know the answer to your question." The ball of white light shimmers in amazing iridescent.

Why can I not control this dream? Why am I so mature? I'm only three. Who were those wolves?

"You are different than any other I have met, Todd."

Loah is quiet for a while before saying, "A soul is not bound by physical restriction. Age, maturity, handicap ... these are all physical traits. Your soul is the same as when you first entered this world. It is simply a matter of remembering."

Todd looks to his hands.

"There is a saying I am fond of: once one has seen the face of God, he loses faith; there is no longer a purpose for faith."

There really is a God?

Loah laughs. "That is for you to remember. As for why you can no longer control this dream, well ... that is why I am the protector. If I let you wake up now, you will die."

FIVE

"Todd!" Susan Kenseth screamed when she saw the bloody imprint on the broken stable wall. She ran to her son's lifeless body.

Blood pooled between broken pieces of his skull. Spongy brain rose from the red.

Susan picked up his limp frame with care, cradling his head. She rocked Todd in her arms. "It'll be all right," she said. "Everything will be all right."

Roy ran to the house to call 911.

"They're on the way," he said when he returned, "and they said not to move him."

"I'm not letting go of my son."

A lot of Todd had soaked into her shirt. She held a clean towel to his head, attempting to stop the bleeding. It was dripping when the van arrived.

It was hard to let him go, but she reluctantly handed him over to one of the paramedics.

They wrapped Todd's fractured head with gauze and strapped him to a child's stretcher. After lifting Todd into the ambulance, they began hooking IVs to his wrists and injecting needles into his thin arms.

She tried joining them in the van, but a hand pushed her back.

"I'm sorry, ma'am, but you'll have to ride separate."

"I need to be with my son."

"I'm sorry, but you can't ride in the ambulance."

"You don't understand. I need to be with my son. I need to be with Todd." Susan pushed back and tried to squeeze past him to one of the seats.

"You'll have to ride separate," one of the paramedics said, holding her firmly by the shoulders.

"I need to be with my son!"

Susan beat him on the chest and pushed her way through.

"James, I need some help," he said.

"Kinda busy," the other said, holding a bloodied glove.

"You let me ride with my son!"

"Just let her in," said the paramedic working on Todd.

The back doors slammed shut and they were soon on their way to Brenden Memorial.

Roy stayed with the kids, but not for long. He called Katherine Jensen next door. In the middle of the ninth ring, an older woman with a raspy voice answered.

"What in Sam Hell …?" the voice said before yawning.

"Katherine! It's Roy, next door. I need your help."

The other end of the line was quiet except for the noises of an older woman knocking things over in the dark.

"It's almost half past tomorrow—"

"Todd's been kicked in the head by the horse!" It came out sounding like one gigantic mouthful of a word.

"I'm on my way," she said and hung up.

He met Katherine halfway and explained everything. She placed leathery hands onto each of his children. Her silver hair gleamed brightly under the moonlight. Shadows found homes in the wrinkles of her old, dark skin.

"Come with me, you two," she said.

"I want to stay with Dad," said Charlie.

"Your father has a busy night ahead," Katherine said in a grandmotherly voice. She yawned, bringing bony fingers to cover her mouth. Her liver spots looked black, her thin skin almost transparent.

"Thank you, Katherine," said Roy after giving the old neighbor a hug. "You don't know how much this means to me and Suse."

"Don't worry about a thing." She coughed a smoker's cough. "Best be going to bed, kids. Take care of your baby, Roy. And I don't just mean Todd neither. Give me a call in the morn'n."

Roy watched as she disappeared with his two eldest children. He felt nervous until they were all inside.

"Tell me he's going to be okay," Susan said to the paramedic. She stood at the rear of the vehicle and smacked her head against a storage bin when the van lurched forward. She balanced with outstretched arms until she was sure they were off the gravel driveway and onto the main road. There was one final bump as the ambulance tires connected with the asphalt. She sat onto the red vinyl seat and stared at Todd. He was looking right at her, but was somehow looking past her as well.

How could he have so much blood?

The white gauze the paramedic applied quickly turned red. Susan knew he was doing his best to stop the bleeding, but wondered how it would even be possible to apply the pressure needed without injuring him further. She watched his eyes bounce from monitor to monitor as he checked various numbers and pulsing lines that meant absolutely nothing to her.

Susan closed her eyes and clasped her hands together. She hadn't prayed for years, but said the following under her breath: *If you are there ... Look after my son. Help him live through this. Send him an angel. Help him pull through this. Save Todd.*

She opened her eyes and found the paramedic staring at her; it was a somewhat hopeless expression.

"How long till the hospital?" he asked the driver.

"Twenty minutes. Maybe more."

Susan could barely hear him over the engine.

"We won't have that much—" the paramedic said before cutting himself short.

"Improvise," said the driver.

The man standing over Todd bit his bottom lip and nodded. He looked again to Susan.

"Your son is losing a lot of blood."

Susan rolled up her sleeves.

He pointed to a small refrigeration unit on the floor and said, "We've got plenty. We're one of the few ambulances that carries blood. Do you know your son's blood type?"

"AB Positive," she said.

"Good. Put on a pair of rubber gloves from the open drawer behind you."

Susan pulled them over her bloody hands.

The paramedic held out compresses with his free hand. It was an inviting gesture.

Susan scooted closer and took it from him, awaiting instruction.

The paramedic switched gauze again, somehow never removing pressure from Todd's skull and made sure Susan paid attention.

"I need you to hold these bandages, exactly like this, while I get blood ready. Can you handle this? If not, I need to know."

Susan nodded.

"You're going to need to apply some pressure, but not a lot. You'll get the feel of it. Try to avoid movement as much as possible. Pretend you're holding a vase full of water. Do this until I can relieve you. I'm sorry to have to ask you—"

Susan interjected not with words but by rushing between Todd and the paramedic, and putting her hands in place of his. She applied pressure as he slid his larger hands from underneath. Blood quickly rushed to the gauze, but slowed as she applied pressure.

Like holding a giant cracked egg with the yolk oozing out. She closed her eyes and imagined holding a vase, water sloshing just below the lip. As the ambulance dipped and swayed and bumped along the highway, her hands never moved, only her elbows repositioned. Not a single drop of water spilled out of her mental vase. She felt Todd's pulse under her fingers.

"You'd make a fine paramedic."

He moved in to take over and placed his hands directly over hers. When he applied pressure, Susan simply slid hers from underneath. She sat closer to Todd than she had when first entering the ambulance. Somehow she felt more bonded to her son.

"Where the *hell* are my keys?"

Roy checked most of the house and turned over two rooms. He checked the key ring a second time, but was unable to find a spare, and searched the path leading to and from the stable.

He checked the truck ignition, the seat crevices, the dashboard, the floorboard. No keys. He had to get to the hospital, even if it meant breaking the steering column and hotwiring the truck.

When he reached into his jean pockets for his pocketknife, he found the keys. Roy slapped his forehead and started the truck. The old Chevy pickup chugged before idling, and revved hard as Roy stepped on the gas. Gravel flew wildly as the back tires spun and caught friction first with the driveway, and then the paved highway. With much effort, the old pickup accelerated. The speedometer needle hammered back and forth between 30 and 80. The tachometer was broken and stayed at 0 RPM. It felt like seventy, maybe even seventy-five miles per hour. Roy didn't dare push the aged truck over eighty. It shook badly however fast he was driving.

He thought of Todd and pressed the gas pedal to the floor. There were complications with his birth. Katherine Jensen watched Charlie and Cindy during the hospital stay. Like the foal, Todd had required assistance coming out. They had cut Susan open in plenty of time, but he required resuscitation before he could breathe on his own.

"You need to stop thinking these things," he said to himself. "Everything be fine. Everything is going to be—"

Roy lost control as the tires of the old truck ran over something in the road. The truck swerved left, then right, bouncing the cab up and down. One of the tires blew. The truck tried to pull left on its own, but Roy slowed down and turned onto the shoulder.

When the truck came to a stop, Roy pounded on the wheel.

"Fuck!"

He jumped out of the cabin and kicked gravel.

The left front tire was trashed. Only a ragged doughnut of rubber remained on the rim.

Roy found a section of metal piping lodged into the wheel well. The other end of the bent four-foot pipe stuck out from the bottom of the truck. Holes were drilled through each end of the pipe and tied through them was a type of rope normally used to hang laundry. The ends of each were frayed. Roy assumed the two broken pieces once connected.

"My son's dying and I have to deal with this."

Prying it from the undercarriage, he swung it violently into the black that encompassed the road.

The moon, now below the horizon, left the night dark blue, like the uniforms of the paramedics. He was close enough to the city that the stars had fizzled out.

An hour later, after struggling to get the spare on with a flashlight wedged in his mouth, Roy lowered the truck to the ground using a nearly useless jack. He grabbed the shredded tire and rim and threw it off the side of the road as well.

Roy peeled out as he got back on the highway. Blood-ied knuckles gripped the wheel tight. The truck steadily

rose back to around eighty miles per hour before the cab resumed shaking. The glowing cityscape grew closer and closer as he barreled down the highway, his fingers tapping against the wheel.

Visions of Todd filled his head: blood everywhere, his body limp and thrown to the side like one of Cindy's dolls, Susan in the stable trying to hold him together like some kind of shattered ceramic.

The ambulance doors opened and medics rushed to join the already crowded space. Susan got bumped back onto the vinyl seat, the edge buckling her knees. They unlatched Todd's gurney with a series of mechanical snaps, lifted him out of the van in a single motion, and snapped him onto a rolling gurney.

During Susan's next breath, Todd was rolling away from her through the Emergency Room entrance, the medical team running him through glass double-doors and down endless corridors.

Susan was able to keep up for the most part, but as he vanished behind the swaying Operating Room doors, Susan fell to the linoleum floor. She brought her hands to her face as she kneeled on the cold surface. They had taken Todd away from her. Tears raced down her cheeks in parallel rivers. She kicked a leg out, knocking over a yellow WET FLOOR / PISO MAJADO sign.

Her chin sinking deeper and deeper into her chest, Susan cried. She lifted her head and screamed at the florescent lighting in an echoed sadness that reverberated through the empty halls.

"Is Todd gonna be all right, Mrs. Jensen?" Charlie asked. It was the early hours of morning. Living on a farm, it was routine to wake up around sunrise. Those who slept in past seven were called lazy.

Katherine Jensen was lazy and would have preferred to sleep in until eleven or even twelve if she hadn't the kids to watch over. She knew they'd be a handful. But what kids weren't little handfuls at nine and ten years old? She had been a wild one almost seventy years ago when she was their age. She smiled an old, peaceful smile at Charlie and said in her morning voice, "I'm sure your brother'll be just fine. No need to worry none."

Her voice needed a couple cups of black coffee before it would sound right. Katherine wasn't a smoker but sounded the part. "You kids want some breakfast?" It sounded like brayfist. "I scramble a mean dish of eggs."

"When's Todd coming home?" asked Cindy. Her expression held a set of shimmering puppy eyes. Her hair, frayed in clumps, still gave home to bits of hay.

Charlie looked just as bad, greasy hair shot into the air.

"Is he coming home today?" Charlie asked.

Katherine poured herself a cup of coffee. "Sit with me a while." She sat the kitchen table and they joined her.

They were eager to know when Todd would return, how Todd was doing, if Todd was going to be okay, when they'd get to see him, and such. They looked to Katherine as if she were a wisdom tree handing out leaves of knowledge.

Katherine looked solemnly at Charlie, and then to Cindy. She sighed. "I spoke to your mother this morning.

She called 'round four o' clock. Still no word on your brother's condition. We gotta sit tight till some kinda news comes our way, she says. Your father got a flat on the way there last night. Took him over two hours to meet up with her at the hospital. They stayed the whole night."

Cindy whimpered.

Charlie stared at the white doilies on the tabletop.

"Your brother'll be just fine."

Roy found Susan in the waiting room when he finally made it to the hospital. She looked terrible. Red lines like warrior paint streaked down her face. The front of her blouse covered in blood. There was no word on Todd, she told him. She didn't even ask what took him so long. On her lap was an insurance information form littered with unfilled boxes. She had made it to the box marked PATIENT'S FIRST NAME and stopped. She couldn't even write her son's name on the page. She tapped her pen against the metal clamp on the wooden clipboard that held the form as she stared at the door leading to Todd.

"You should get some sleep," Roy said, taking the clipboard from her. "I'll wake you when the doctor comes out."

She ignored him.

"You can lean on my shoulder."

"Can *you* sleep?" she said monotonously. "I can't sleep, not while Todd's in there and I'm out here. If you want to sleep, go right ahead, but don't expect me to wake you up."

"Suse …"

She turned toward him and started trembling. "You didn't hold your son's crushed skull in your hands. You didn't see the blood in the ambulance. You didn't have to wait here alone for two hours."

"I can't stop trucks from getting flats, Suse. I would've run if I knew it would've gotten me here faster. I changed a tire at half-past midnight down an unlit stretch of highway with only a flashlight and shit for tools."

"You left me here … alone, for almost *two hours*, Roy!" She looked at him with disgust.

"I am only capable of so much. The kids are at Katherine's for the night. I'm here now."

"What about tomorrow night? And the night after? And the night after that? This isn't a *'take the kids in for their tetanus shot'* kind of thing. You can't just slap a Band-Aid on it and let 'em play, Roy. Todd got kicked in the head. By a horse! His head is cracked in at least four places. I saw his … I held pieces of his skull in my fingers. I felt his pulse."

"What do you want me to say?"

Susan's temper turned to sorrow. Her face conformed quickly. "I … I want to make this right again. I want to be able to turn back time, to go back and shoot that damned horse. No—it's not Joey Bean's fault. She was dying, confused. When you shot her, she just wasn't ready to go."

"It's no one's fault." He put a hand on her knee and another on her shoulder. He wiped a tear running down her left cheek. It was followed by another.

Susan took his hand into her own and brought it to her lips, kissed it. They held each other for close to an hour, neither of them saying a word.

Roy was nodding off when Susan asked him, "What about the foal? Who's going to take care of the foal? Oh, God. Joey Bean."

"I'll call around in the morning."

"It *is* morning."

"Then a little later in the morning. The foal can wait that long for food. She'll be fine. I led her into the corral before I left. She's not going anywhere."

"What about Joey Bean?" And then in a more concerned voice she said, "What do we do with a 1,200-pound dead horse?"

"The kid's are doin' fine, Roy," said Katherine's voice through the phone in the lobby. "And don't you worry none about Joey Bean. Got her covered with a blanket."

"I can't thank you enough." Roy's voice was cracking. It was roughly eight in the morning and he hadn't slept.

"Still no word on Todd?" Katherine asked. In the background, sibling voices feuded over something trivial.

"Nothing yet, although Suse says another hour of waiting and she'll break the Operating Room doors down and find out herself."

Katherine laughed. "Want me to call the vet? See if they can't get someone down here to look after the colt?"

"Colt?"

"Yeah, I went out early this morning to have a look. Congrats, Roy. It's a boy!"

"I never even thought to look."

"Never had the chance to look is more like it. You had yourself a busy night. I'll give 'em a call if you like."

"Who?"

"The vet. Someone needs to take care of him," she said. "He looks hungry. And he's still all gooped up. Needs a good cleanin'. Maybe I'll go out there with the hose a little later and—"

"You've already done plenty, Katherine."

"Need me to get you the number at least?"

"Nah, just watch over the kids. I may swing down to help take care of things after we hear from the doctors."

"You stay with your son, Roy. He needs you now. Suse needs you. You come down here and I'll turn you back around where you came from. Where you at?"

Startled at the power behind those words, Roy was dumbfounded. "Where am I at?"

"Which hospital?"

"Brenden Memorial."

"Well, if you want the kids come visit, just give me a ring and I'll drive 'em down there."

Roy hesitated. "Sure."

He hung up and dialed Information.

"City and state, please," said a soft female voice.

"Brenden, Washington." He waited for the operator to return.

"What can I help you with today?"

"I'm looking for a veterinary clinic. I've got a dead horse and a foal to take care of."

"I'm sorry to hear that. In Brenden, sir?"

"Close enough," he said. "Wait? What day is it?"

"Sunday."

"Try Seattle. Nothing local will be open today. I'll take the first one that comes up. Any who handle horses?" He wasn't sure if she would be able to help. He had never called Information before.

"Well," she said, her tone revealing she was at least

trying to help, "there's an Equestri-All Veterinary Clinic in Seattle. Other than that, there are about a hundred different vets. Want me to patch you through?"

"Yes, that would be great."

The line went silent and then started to ring. On the second ring, a woman answered.

"Equestri-All. This is Jessie."

"Hey, Jessie."

Roy froze. He thought of Todd—crushed against the stable wall, bleeding from his head down. He replayed Susan rushing to their son while he stood paralyzed, unable to cope with the horror. It was his own damn fault this had happened. It was his decision to put down Joey Bean.

"Is anyone there?"

"Yes. Sorry. I'm looking for some help."

"What can I do ya for?"

Roy broke down and told her everything: his horse giving birth while his family watched, the complications, Roy pulling out the foal, the mare dying and in pain, how he tried putting her down with the rifle but had messed it up, his three-year-old son getting kicked in the head. Roy was in tears, confessing to some stranger named Jessie. He told her he was at the hospital.

There was a long pause.

"Let me get this straight," said Jessie. "Is the mare still alive?"

"No. I shot her a second time. Joey Bean's dead. The neighbor watching over my other children covered her with a blanket."

"We won't be able to help with the mare. You'll want to call the city dump for that, unless you plan on burying her somewhere on your property. A lot of horse owners do. You might want to rent a backhoe and read up on it. We can help with the foal. You can either bring it in for care, or we can come out to you. The latter's not cheap, sorry to say."

"I can take care of the colt," said Roy, "but I can't while my son's in the hospital. It might be best if you come out to the farm."

"How long has he been without food?"

Roy glanced at his watch. "About seven or eight hours." It felt longer than seven or eight hours.

SIX

Todd sees only white rings of light that pulse like a heart; they rivulet outward like a rock thrown into a pond.

Loah?

"Yes," says the voice. "Are you ready?"

It is a frightening question.

To die?

"To live. It is not your time for balance. There must be three and you are only one."

Will I see you again?

The light of Loah begins to fade as an electronic heart beats synchronous to his own. Silhouettes of men break through the whiteness. As they become more focused, Todd sees they are wearing masks and looking over him.

The light of Loah is nothing more than the bulb in the light fixture over his head.

<h1 style="text-align:center">SEVEN</h1>

"Todd is dead," Roy expected the doctor to tell them.

Was it possible for Todd to live? *Of course not*, his mind told him. *Your son was dead the moment the horse kicked him.*

Roy ignored the thoughts and shook Susan as he approached. If she had slept, it was only for a nod or two. Her tired eyes were wide awake when she saw him.

Roy held Susan's hand as they rose from their uncomfortable seats.

The doctor was Indian, but not the type of Indian Todd used to pretend to fight off the farm. He wore a baby blue doctor's mask over his face, strapped with elastic white bands. He resembled a butcher. *Perhaps he* is *a butcher*. The doctor was spotless in his white getup, not a drop of Todd's blood on him. He wasn't even wearing gloves.

Roy looked at Susan. She was covered in Todd, as if someone had roller-coated the front of her outfit with a tray of rust-colored paint.

"I'm sure you are both curious about the condition of your son," the doctor said. He reached out his hand. "I am Dr. Deggar. I am one of the many doctors working with Todd."

"Tell me my son is going to be all right," Susan said.

"Todd is in critical condition, I must ill-inform you."

Roy put a comforting arm around Susan.

"There are complications. His skull is fractured in places and broken in many others, but we have stopped the hemorrhaging. He is no longer bleeding, Mr. and Mrs. Kenseth. His frontal lobe, however, sustained damage that is irreparable. If and when he pulls through, there will be brain damage … of an amount that is uncertain at this time. Where the animal's hoof made contact—this section of the head and face …" the doctor illustrated by grabbing the top left section of his own head, "took most of the impact. That is where most of the damage to the skull is located. We have spent many hours repairing what was repairable. I assure you, our doctors are doing fine work. For now, we must wait for your son's vital signs to improve. Nurses are giving him fresh blood as we speak, as well as medicines to bring his blood pressure down. His heart rate is unsteady."

Hearing the doctor say "fresh blood" made Roy queasy and lightheaded.

"Your son is in a coma. It is the body's natural way of handling this intense situation life has put him through. He is not in pain. If not for the coma, Todd would not live. His body would be unable to handle the stress."

"Will he wake up?" Susan asked, her voice raspy.

"*Will*, Mrs. Kenseth, may have a lot to do with it. Todd is currently kept alive by machine. He is "plugged in" you could say. He cannot live without this aid. You may have heard the term "pulling the plug?" It is much like that, but more sophisticated. It is more like switches and computers nowadays, but we hope it will not come to that."

Susan buried her face in her hands.

"Tell me your honest opinion," Roy said. He lowered his voice. "Do you think Todd can pull through this? Will one of us have to pull the plug?" They were straightfor-ward, crude, and to-the-point questions, but that was the only way Roy worked. Straightforward answers required straightforward questions.

You couldn't even put down a horse, his thoughts interjected. *How can you even think of helping Todd die?* It was a matter of quality, anguish versus suffering. *A vegetable for a son is no son.*

"Will he live?" Roy asked.

The doctor smiled timorously. Hope was missing behind his eyes. "That is up to Todd, Mr. Kenseth."

Katherine insisted cleaning the young animal. "It ain't no hassle," she told Roy over the phone. "The kids will help. It'd be good for them."

Cindy held a bucket of soapy water. Charlie grasped the end of a yellow hose as if ready to put out a fire. Together they could start a car wash.

"Are you sure this is how you clean a horse?" asked Cindy. She had mixed expressions as she followed Charlie to the corral where Roy penned the colt the night prior.

Charlie hooked up the hose to the water faucet and turned on the pressure. He pulled the handle on the nozzle to test it against the back of Cindy's head.

"Hey! Mrs. Jensen, this isn't the way to clean a horse," she said. She squeezed her wet ponytail and snarled at her brother.

"Couldn't be certain," said Katherine. "I never had to do such a thing. Should do just fine for a baby horse. Used to warsh my own kids this way." She smiled. "Only fooling."

The colt's hair was pressed against its body from the

dried fluids of its mother. Dirt clung to him as well. His eyes were closed, exhausted from the busy night. He had curled up like a kitten, his stomach heaving.

"Best if we suds him up first," Katherine told the kids. "Get as much done before he wakes up and gets to his feet."

"He can already walk?" asked Charlie.

"Horses walk just minutes after birth, like stilts on slip'ry ice. Funny thing to watch. My boy Hal took forever to learn to walk, God rest his soul. I thought he'd never get off all-fours. He liked crawling around. I bet the two of you came runnin' out of Suse."

Katherine grabbed the bucket and led Cindy into the corral. Charlie followed with the hose pointed to their backs.

"Ain't he precious?"

Both Cindy and Charlie made faces.

"He looks gross," said Cindy.

Charlie added, "Looks like he was pooped out."

Katherine couldn't help but laugh. "You'll understand when you have kids. Course, if you ever had a baby this size, you may think twice before saying such a thing."

The colt was roughly the size of a Labrador retriever, legs over two feet in length and a head like a football. His eyes, now slightly open, were two black marbles he'd grow into over the next few years. Not quite awake, the newborn hardly moved as Katherine splashed sudsy water over its lengthy body. Cindy helped, rubbing her hands over the clumpy hair. They brushed most of the dirt away before the colt rose.

"Give him some room," Katherine said. She held Cindy back with an arm. "Let him walk around a bit and get comfortable."

Charlie stood ready with the hose.

"Easy on the trigger finger, Charlie. Don't wanna blast a hole through 'em."

Charlie squeezed the nozzle. A trickle of water dripped out. He kept it that way for a while.

"Maybe a tad more," said Katherine. "Need at least to get the poor thing wet."

Cindy laughed at her brother, who then, without trying, blasted a hard stream at the young horse, causing it to flinch and nearly fall. Charlie eased up and created a shower type affect with the nozzle.

"That'd be perfect, Charlie."

Katherine walked next to the colt and rubbed him down with her hands. Cindy joined in and the two of them were soon soaked. The horse tried to shy away, but they were able to keep him steady. They dried off with the towels Katherine had hung over one of the fence posts.

The colt walked around in strange patterns within the corral, still unused to its legs.

"Now it's precious," said Cindy. Water dripped from her hair.

"I guess so," said Charlie, shrugging.

"Only one thing is missing," said Katherine, looking innocently to the children. "Charlie needs to get wet, too."

Cindy's eyes widened almost as largely as the colt's.

As Cindy chased her brother down for the hose, Katherine observed the colt. *I bet you're as hungry as the Donners.* "Just have to wait a little longer," she told the horse. "The vet will be here soon."

"What do you mean we have to make a choice?" Susan stood over her son. "There's no *choice* we have to make. This is our *son*, Roy. The only choice we have is to wait for Todd to wake up. He *will* wake up."

"All I'm saying is that he may not. *If*—and this is the world's smallest *if*—he does not, what do we do then?"

"We wait," she said firmly.

"And what if a week passes and still nothing?"

"We wait another week, and then another week.

"Do we wait a month, a year … longer?"

Prepare for the worst and be grateful for what you get. It had been her mother's way of thinking. Expecting the most from life is what really brings you down, when what you get in the end is close to nothing, or nothing at all.

In a broken voice she said, "We need to handle what comes our way *when* it comes our way. I am optimistic about our son. I wish you felt the same."

Roy reached for her hand. "I want nothing more than Todd to be okay."

She pulled back and sat close to where Todd lay. She put a hand onto one of his skinny legs. "Maybe you should go home and look after the kids. Take care of things around the house. Take care of Joey Bean."

Susan had no idea what they'd do with her body.

"We'll need to rent a backhoe," Roy said to the tiled floor. "Find a nice corner somewhere on the property and bury her there."

"Joey Bean was a good horse," Susan said to Todd.

"It wasn't her fault this happened," Roy said.

Susan looked at Roy. "It wasn't your fault, either."

"You'll be fine by yourself? And you'll call if anything—"

"Of course I will. I have Todd, and this EKG thing on the wall to keep me occupied. I can't help but stare at it and wonder if this is all that keeps us alive—these stats and vitals. What do they know about life?"

As if in response, the EKG beeped, followed by a low hissing sound as the machine automatically took Todd's blood pressure. His pleuth, whatever that was, paced along at a high rate. Todd's pulse, the most important vital of them all, held her attention.

Roy pulled up to the house in time to see Equestri-All busy at work with the young colt. There were two vets: one young, one old.

"Dad!" Cindy ran to the truck, her ponytail bouncing back and forth. Her hands smacked the door. "Look, they're letting Charlie feed the horse with a bottle."

Roy's window was rolled down. He leaned out.

"I see that. And hello to you."

"Mr. Foger—he's the old guy—says they need to take him to *their* home for a few days, maybe longer. Is that true?"

Roy looked across the yard to the blanket-covered mass of Joey Bean. "I'm afraid so, sweetheart. I'm afraid so."

"Me and Charlie and Mrs. Jensen gave the him a bath. It was gross but he's all clean now. Then we had a water fight. Is Todd okay?"

Little did she Cindy know, her little brother was being kept alive by machines at the hospital. He might never come back home, might never be a part of one of their water

fights. It would be a long time before he could come home, and he'd be mentally impaired if he did.

"Todd's going to be in the hospital for a while. We'll know more soon."

Roy decided he'd tell his children about Todd's condition when he was compelled to tell them. They were growing up much too fast already.

"Where's mom?" Cindy asked. "Are you listening?"

"She's at the hospital with your brother. Now, are you going to let me out of this truck, or am I going to have to start living in here?"

Cindy backed up. "At least you'd have a bed to sleep in."

Roy didn't laugh but thought the joke was clever. He got out of the truck and followed her to the corral.

Katherine was waiting for him. She appeared weathered, showing her age, her skin like sun-baked leather.

Two veterinarians stood over Charlie as he nursed the colt with a bottle. The newborn suckled vigorously. Charlie's arms were around the animal in a fatherly embrace, one hand under the chin and the other holding the upended bottle.

"Your boy's a real pro," said the older of the two. He looked like a rancher himself and sported a pair of riding boots. The few remaining hairs on his head were as white as the moon the night before. His partner was a scrawny young man, possibly is son.

"Well, speak of the devil," said Katherine. "How's Todd? Tell us its good news, which is why you're back here so soon. Either that, or Susan's had enough of 'ya."

"They have him hooked up to a machine." He pulled her aside and spoke softer. "He's in a coma. At least that's what they told us. I haven't slept so everything's jumbled. They have him critically stable or something like that. I'm just here to get away from it all. Suse is supposed to call if his condition changes."

Katherine's face saddened. Her wrinkles stood out in bold stripes. "How long they think he'll be sleeping?"

"Not sure. Could be hours, days, weeks, months, maybe forever. The doctor said it's up to Todd. If he shows any improvement, they'll try to get him functioning on his own again with some extensive surgeries. Right now he's being kept alive. Turn off the machine and you turn off Todd."

"Bless his heart. How's Susan holding? Must be hard on her."

"Susan and I had a long talk. If Todd wakes up, there's going to be brain damage. Maybe a lot. And that's *if* he wakes up. We've decided to have the doctors operate anyway. Later tonight if possible. The way I see it, and the way Suse sees it: if he's going to live, the procedure has to be done. No matter what. No matter the cost. Someone already came up to us to talk about pulling the plug."

Roy had thought long and hard on the subject, even before the doctor had approached them with the idea. *Would I want the same done for me? Would it be suffering?* Roy would want someone to pull his own plug if it came down to it, plain and simple. *Quality of life.* But with Todd, he had to stay at his wife's side. He'd try for Todd's life no matter the consequence. It burned him up inside, but that's how it had to be.

"Could be why they're waiting so long to operate," Roy said. "To see if we think it's worth the trouble. Maybe it's best to just let him go."

Rick's Rentals was a bust; so was their major competitor, a CAT rental service not far from the farm. He finally found one at a small mom and pop shop called Rent-4-Less. They had one backhoe available as long as he had it back by six.

By three-thirty they had a gravesite—approximately seven feet long, four feet wide, and nearly eight feet deep. The hole was located in the corner of the pasture closest to the barn, closest to Joey Bean. Roy would have rather buried her farther away, but there was just too much horse to move. The hole seemed crater-like and had taken most of the afternoon. It was all hard work, but at least it took his mind off Todd.

Joey Bean's body was a good ten feet from the hole.

"Any ideas?" he asked Charlie.

They both stared at the hole.

"Maybe we should've dug the hole closer."

"A little late for that."

"Well," said Charlie, "we could *pull* it—"

"It would take a lot of men to pull something that big."

"… with the backhoe."

They both looked to each other and visualized it. Roy imagined a rope tied to the backhoe framework on one end, hog-tied around the legs of the horse with the other end. Who knew what Charlie imaged, maybe the arm of the tractor dragging the horse as it rolled her over and over in awkward rotations.

"With the backhoe," Roy said.

By five, he and Charlie were raking the ground smooth. He was a tough kid. Didn't even cry while they were burying her. A large mound of dirt and rocks lay to the side, roughly the mass of a horse. Cindy used some of the larger rocks to outline the site. They made a simple wooden cross and painted Joey Bean's name on the front, followed by the date she died. They even transplanted one of the rosebushes from Susan's garden to the middle of the grave. Roy cried and couldn't help but think of Todd when he heard his daughter say, "Goodbye, Jelly Bean."

EIGHT

Three men stand over Todd's body, one with a pair of glasses hanging from the tip of his nose as if held on by glue. The center doctor, upside down to Todd, works a set of stainless steel instruments in his white, rubber-gloved hands. They reflect light beaming from the giant lamp over his head. The other two doctors pay close attention to each motion he makes with his blood-coated tools.

Todd feels nothing, his body numb. He tries to read the middle doctor's name and cannot for two reasons: one, his badge is upside-down and backward; and two, he is only three and hasn't learned to read upside-down and backward.

The middle doctor pokes at a section of Todd's head and the three masked men fade away. Todd's world turns white.

"Welcome back," says Loah.

NINE

"Susan Kenseth never smoked a day in her life. One time, back in high school, she was offered a cigarette—what she liked to call cancer sticks—for a drag, but she had refused. Secondhand smoke was bad enough. *Let them all get emphysema,* she remembered thinking back then. *Let them all get lung cancer. Not me.*

A young woman was smoking outside the waiting room. She looked eighteen or nineteen. Susan saw her through the window. She looked like a young mother. Susan imagined her with a child of three or four, maybe Todd's age. She also imagined one of those cigarettes perched between her own set of lips. They eased stress, or so she heard. Susan's mouth watered for one, her throat already prepping for that familiar smoke—second-hand, anyway—to fill her lungs.

Susan's father used to refer to smoking as "fresh air." He'd say it each time he'd sneak outside for a cigarette. He'd later return with an awful cough and spit something crude into the sink. Susan remembered it clearly. She also remembered him waking in the middle of the night to cough out what sounded like his lungs before heading outside for more "fresh air." He died from some form of lung cancer shortly after he started coughing blood.

A latch clanked loudly in the waiting room and the glass double-doors opened like barn gates. They hissed closed

behind her. She rounded the corner and saw the young woman standing there.

She offered a cigarette with an outstretched hand.

"Thanks, but I don't smoke, but can I stand by you for some friendly second-hand?"

The young woman nodded and brought it back to her lips. She blew out smoke in a thin stream from the corner of her mouth. Four earrings, mostly hoops of various sizes, filled her left ear, two studs in her right. A belly button ring was revealed from the midriff, as well as half of a black dragon tattoo; the other half hidden behind a pair of low-rider jeans. She looked too young for all this.

"Started smoking when I was twelve," said the young woman. "And I haven't been able to quit since. Well, not really. I guess I've quit about a hundred times."

Susan breathed in the smoke. It brought back memories of her father. She needed that connection.

After returning the backhoe, Roy sat at the kitchen table waiting for popcorn to finish popping in the microwave. Charlie and Cindy sat with him and argued over stupid little things: whose turn it was to take out the garbage, who was making fun of whom, when Mom and Todd would be back from the hospital. Cindy said tonight. Charlie said it would be a week. Roy tried to ignore them as he waited for Susan's call, hoping her voice would offer good news for once. He was avoiding the hospital. He was also avoiding Susan. The doctors. Todd.

The microwave beeped and they both raced for it. Charlie won, which meant Cindy had to get the bowl. They managed to get most of it in, but the rest toppled on the tablecloth like oversized, yellow snowflakes. A meek smile formed on Roy's otherwise glum face as he watched his silly children. They sat on separate sides of the table, hands battling for the same pieces. It reminded him of his own childhood. Popcorn flew in arcs across the table.

"You two need to settle down."

"She started it," said Charlie, pointing a finger.

"He threw first," she said as a popcorn fluff hit her in the forehead.

"I don't care who started it."

Another piece flew over the table.

Chair legs screeched over cheap linoleum as Roy leapt from the chair. He batted the bowl of popcorn. It flipped in midair, contents raining downward. The bowl landed near the end of the table, spun a few times on edge, and clunked to the floor. He closed his eyes in frustration.

The room turned quiet.

The phone rang and he jumped. Roy let it ring three times before answering.

"Hello, this is Roy." He was hoping for a telemarketer, wrong number, anyone other than Suse.

She's calling to say Todd is dead, he's in a better place, he's no longer suffering, or even, *the doctor said it was in our best interest to put him down, like Joey Bean.* But it wasn't Susan's voice that answered. It was Katherine Jensen.

She had told Roy earlier in the day, when he was burying the horse, that she'd watch the kids another night so he could go back to the hospital.

"Holdin' up?"

"Somewhat," he said, glancing at the chaos of popcorn.

He had packed two suitcases—one for Susan, one for himself. They were at the front door, his truck keys on top so he wouldn't forget. He had also grabbed a wad of bills from the emergency stash above the stove and put them in his wallet, enough for the two of them to survive on cafeteria food for a few days.

"I wouldn't wait too much longer before headin' there. Want me to come over so you can head out?"

No, he wanted to say, but couldn't. He had to go to the hospital. It was inevitable.

"Give me half an hour to shower and get the kids ready. If you don't mind coming over to get them—"

"Not a problem. I'll be there in thirty to pick 'em up. Tell them we can pop us some corn and watch a movie."

Roy set the phone down.

"Sorry, guys. Don't worry about the mess. I'll clean it up. Why don't you two run upstairs and get ready for bed?"

Their shoulders slumped.

"Get some clothes ready for tomorrow. Katherine's going to sit you again tonight. She's set on watching a movie and making some popcorn."

"My name's Julie."

"Susan," said Susan. She felt as if she could crush the delicate hand within her own. "What are you in for?"

"My daughter, Hannah. Tetanus shot," Julie said. "She's three. They're running some other tests, so it'll be a while."

"Good tests?"

Susan breathed in smoke; the smell calmed her.

"Fertility," she said and took a drag. After smoldering

the spent cigarette, she retrieved another. "You sure?" She held the pack out to Susan.

Hesitating, she succumbed. "Why not."

Julie tapped one out of the pack, lit up, and used the end of it to light one for Susan.

Susan held it between her index finger and thumb like a joint, inhaled, swallowed, and coughed. "I haven't had one of these in years," she lied.

"Well, don't blame me if you get cancer." She waited for Susan to finish coughing before asking, "What about you? What are you in for?"

"My son, Todd. He's also three." Susan took a long, hard drag and slowly leaked it out, not swallowing the smoke this time. "Last night he was kicked in the head by a horse."

Julie laughed, taking it as a joke. She looked to the road to an ambulance speeding by with its lights on. Not until she turned back to face her did she notice Susan was serious.

A shaky hand held her first cigarette.

Susan was headed to a payphone in the lobby to call Roy when a nurse tapped on her shoulder.

"Excuse me," she said, "Mrs. Kenseth?"

Startled out of her semi-daze / semi-desire to call her husband, Susan turned around.

"The doctors would like to speak to you and your husband in room seventy-eight. Ready to see your son?"

"I don't know where Roy is. I was about to call home to see if he's left the house."

"Why don't you go talk with the doctors and I'll try to track your husband down."

"The home phone number's—"

"It's on the paperwork," the nurse said sympathetically. "Your son's down the hall and to the left. Seventy-eight."

The phone rang seven times before anyone picked up.

"Kenseth res'dence," said Katherine's old crackly voice. She sounded freshly woken. It was half past eleven in the evening.

"Yes, this is Meghan of Brenden Memorial."

"How is Todd? Tell me he's fine as any three-year-old."

"Are you a relative? I'm trying to reach—"

"All'most."

"I'm trying to reach Roy Kenseth. Is he available?"

A long pause. "Isn't he there at the hospital?"

"Mrs. Kenseth is here. We're looking for Roy," said the nurse. "We've paged overhead here a couple of times but he hasn't turned up. If you hear from him, let him know he and his wife can see their son now. Susan's already—"

"Tell Suse Katherine sends her love," said the old voice. "I'll do that."

"And the kids. They want Todd well, too. Tell her that her other two are no problem at all. And the horses are taken care of—well, Roy'll tell her that, I guess. How is Todd?"

"Sorry, but I'm not authorized to hand out that information."

"Following that hippy-hospital legal stuff still?" A loud yawn followed.

"Yes ma'am."

On the road to Brenden Memorial, Roy's mind wandered. He hadn't slept much following the accident—maybe an hour or two—and his body was letting him know it. He was physically and mentally drained.

The left-hand side of the road appeared twice as illuminated as the right. As a car approached from the opposite direction, its headlights flickered once, filling the cabin with high-beam. In his rearview mirror Roy watched two red eyes of taillight fade. Looking again to the empty road, Roy knew what was wrong—why he was straining his eyes, why this not-so-friendly passerby had high-beamed him. As his son Charlie would have said, Roy was driving pirate style, a blown right headlight in lieu of a black patch.

Just what I need. He flipped on his own high beams, only to find the right still inoperable. For a while he drove with one luminous beam, but gave up and switched back after a couple cars flashed him.

What else can go wrong tonight? he thought, and then hit something standing in the middle of the road. It caved in the right front bumper and fender of the truck. The hood dented as the windshield splattered in blood. The truck swerved across lanes as Roy tried gaining control over the vehicle. He inadvertently switched on the wipers, smearing thick red arcs across the glass. In front of him, a red mass flew out of sight. The truck screeched to a halt on the shoulder.

"What the … please God be a deer."

Roy stayed in the cab for close to a minute listening to the wiper blades, his heart frantic. Sick to his stomach and legs shaking like wet noodles, he stepped out of the truck to check the damage.

It wasn't the first time he had hit a deer, but it was definitely the messiest. The grill, and the radiator behind it, was speckled in red. Blood painted bold strokes over what was left of the bumper, hood, and the dented right front fender. A piece of bone, maybe from one of the creature's legs, was jammed into the empty socket of the headlight that hadn't worked. He checked out the road, tracing the last hundred feet or so, until he came to the point of impact. It appeared as if someone had dropped a red bucket of paint along the highway.

Not realizing it before, Roy felt something running down his cheek. The area was sore to the touch, but luckily not bleeding badly. He wiped the cut using an oily rag from his toolbox while giving the truck another brief look-over. It was still drivable, but extensively damaged. Disgusted, Roy examined the road, swinging his flashlight from one side to the other. Wheat fields surrounded him, but he couldn't find what he had hit.

It began to rain, a hard downpour. Roy was drenched by the time he made it back in the truck. Water on his jeans soaked into his underwear and pooled around his shoes on the floorboard. He put the car in Drive and shivered as he drove, his hair a wet mop.

A long while later, he pulled into the hospital parking lot, with a badly beaten but otherwise clean truck. The rain had washed the mess away.

TEN

Todd stands without shadow in the whiteness. A single black dot, like a hole punched through unpainted canvas, captures his attention. But it isn't a hole, as he soon realizes, but a stationary object that draws near, slowly at first, and then exponentially faster. It advances with a whine like the brakes of a train and takes a rectangular shape as the noise intensifies until it's deafening, and then stills as the black object stops just a few feet away.

Todd is no longer alone.

Floating in front of him is a mirror as large as a refrigerator. Wooden trim surrounds the obsidian glass; etched into it in a strange script is a single word: SPIEGEL.

Todd doesn't cast a reflection. Loah joins him and a reflection of white light appears next to where his should be. Confused, Todd circles around the mirror, reaches over and under it, searching for the cables holding it in place. When he gets to the back of the mirror, he can see right through it, like a window, and there is Loah. A different word is etched into the wood above the clear glass: FENSTER.

Todd rejoins Loah on the other side.

"There are no tricks. Look with your mind."

Todd instantly sees an older version of himself staring back. Deeper into this looking glass he sees his father, his hair no longer brown but peppered gray. He's in the barn with a book on the ground next to him. Rundown, he tosses back a beer. Charlie is with him, but he is now in his early teens and asks for a taste. Maybe in a few *years, says his father, and he downs the rest before handing it to him. Through the mirror, Todd watches light shimmer on the sip left in the bottle. It looks warm, foamy, and mostly backwash. A bitter smell travels through the mirror.*

Is this a mirror or a window?

"It is a little of both."

ELEVEN

Susan stood over Todd with wet hair from the downpour dripping onto the small hand she held in her own. She tried to remember him as an infant, squeezing her fingers while he slept. He looked peaceful as he lay on the hospital bed awaiting surgery, his chest rising and falling. The damage witnessed earlier was well-covered by the tape and gauze around his head, his neck held immobile by a brace with wire and thumbscrews. The skin around his eyes and nose and part of his jaw were purple and blue under the lights, his right eye just a bit lower than his left. Stitches ran up his brow and disappeared behind the bandages. *There will be complications*, the doctor had said. *Brain damage*. She imagined Todd much older, years behind his peers in school. Possibly three forever as his body grew without him. In a wheelchair, perhaps, or arm braces as he stumbled through life. *Will he ever smile again, laugh again, talk with coherence?* Susan gently squeezed his hand, and it was like holding something cold and dead. She wrapped his fingers around her thumb but they wouldn't hold on. She looked to his other hand and the device attached to it connected to a wire running to a machine on a cart that recorded his vitals. The machine next to it beeped. She watched his pulse on the monitor, the only thing telling her Todd was still alive. She looked to the outlets on the wall and the many devices plugged into them as she thought of what the doctor had said about pulling the plug and she had to look away to keep from crying again. *Will he live?* It was such a hard question to hear Roy ask the doctor, as if already giving up on him. *It was up to Todd,* the doctor had said. She remembered the timid smile on his face and its hopeless revelation. "Where are you, Roy?" she said aloud, but no one was there to listen except Todd, but Todd was just a broken toy patched back together again with a blank expression on his sad, bruised face. She thought of Todd running away from her as they left the barn so Roy could put down the mare, Todd's arms reaching out as he ran back inside to see Jelly Bean one last time as he called out her name and Susan trying to grab for his arm but he was too fast and had slipped away and …

PART TWO
UNDER THE MOON

FANG

Horror is the world in which I live. I can say this because I was mauled by our neighbor's dog when I was a child.

She was known to pace the good-neighbor fence. A grim mix of German Sheppard and wolf, a monster. Dark shadows marked her place as she followed my movements through the fence that early August morning. I remember the sliver of light from the early sun that split each plank. I remember her drooling, growling, and licking her chops, hungry for the flesh of a child. Young Billy looked delicious.

It rained the night before and smelled of ozone, the yard full of mud and glistening leaves. The moon was a faint disc against the sky. A few stars still glimmered as if only holes poked through black tarp.

The screen door leading to the patio was unlocked, so I went outside wearing the T-shirt and shorts I had slept in the night prior. Mish-mashing my toes through mud and soppy leaves, I ventured farther into the yard. I remember looking up to the moon and wondering why it wasn't blue as Mom had said.

Then I heard Fang. That's what I always called her. The growl started low and intensified as I made my way closer. By the time I reached the fence, her growl was mortifying.

Through the cracks, I could outline her shape. Her stance indicated that if the fence were not there she would pounce. I didn't dare touch the fence, and it would have meant my insanity to put my fingers through one of the knotholes, but something drew me closer—the odor perhaps, that wet dog stench.

Fang's growl deepened, grew louder, wetter. With every step I could feel my heart pound, my legs shaking.

I got to where I could see through the fence. Between glimmers of light escaping between boards, I found myself staring into the black depths of hell that were her eyes and they glared back hungrily. Viscous globs of drool plopped on the leaves below her mangy paws, dripping from her curled-angry mouth. Her hot breath, visible in the early morning air, puffed like steam through breaks in the fence. Fangs protruded from her mouth like a vampire, ready to draw blood, ready to feed.

Time ran from us. Leftovers from a meteor shower streaked the sky white.

I looked back into Fang's eyes and growled. I don't know why. It came out a bit high-pitched at first, and then lowered as low as my young voice could manage. Then I barked and growled some more. I stomped my feet around and kicked mud. I became the wolf; she was *my* prey.

Fang turned silent and angled her head with curiosity.

I continued to growl and bark and strut to show her what I was made of. Fear and I were distant cousins.

Fang slowly backed away. Her silhouette disappeared into the shadows.

For that moment, I was the victor.

Broken wood splintered the yard around me as she smashed through the fence. I could only see her face as she pinned me beneath her body. I swatted at her neck,

her chest, and that enormous gaping jaw. Teeth snapped together, saliva and blood spanning the endless rows. They ripped at my flesh.

Adrenaline pumped through my blood, but only dulled the searing pain as each bite tore a part of me away. Her evil eyes bore down, her mouth a red smile of delight. I cried aloud under Fang as she ate me alive.

And then everything in my world turned black.

It took over two weeks in the hospital before I was well enough to return home. Friends and relatives sent cards, balloons, even flowers, all to wish me a speedy recovery.

I can still taste the horrible hospital food. It was rubbery and, for the most part, tasteless. The only thing worth savoring was dessert: watered down Jell-O served in tiny plastic cups. Food came in those avocado-colored containers resembling flying saucers. Every time I removed the top of the container I expected something alien underneath—a squid-like creature, tentacles, or antennae poking out from a spongy mound—but it was always the same tasteless meal. I never looked forward to the food, no matter how much my stomach rumbled.

Visitors stopped by during my stay, mostly relatives I barely knew and would never see again. I learned that is how family works—only gathering when something drastic happens: funerals, weddings, extensive surgeries. Once or twice in a lifetime families regroup, but mostly they stay distant and become buried in everyday life, resurfacing only for life's highlighted moments. My incident with the neighbor's dog was such an occasion.

One hundred thirty-three stitches: eighty seven on my neck and face, twenty-two on my wrists and forearms—from fending off the animal—and twenty-four across the middle of my chest. My body, for most of my younger years, resembled the downtown Brenden train depot. The wound on my chest wasn't from Fang's teeth, but her claws as she ripped at me; those on my neck and arm were from her teeth. I was apparently a tasty dish. *Filet-me-young.*

Ulna and radius bones were broken during the attack and my interosseous membrane, the fun substance between them, was shredded like cabbage. Muscles, such as my biceps, brachialis and coracobrachialis were nothing more than tenderized pork loins. Most of the arteries within me needed extensive repair. I cracked my left humerus and three ribs, but I didn't find any of it funny. No other broken bones, fortunately.

Bruises and contusions turned my skin plaid. It hurt to urinate. It hurt to do a lot of things.

Doctors were able to repair my jugular, otherwise I'd be dead. It was one of those unique but ever popular "another millimeter to the right and he would have surely died" sort of things. It must be something doctors say for patients to see them as saviors. Maybe doctors tell stories of patients nearly missing certain death because all the other patients died. Maybe doctors don't like telling those stories.

Blood was the major factor in God sparing my life. Or was it his curse? Either way, blood transfusions saved me. It seems that when a child is ripped apart by a vicious beast, one can lose blood at a rapid rate. Blood, I have learned, is life. I've learned to love and to respect blood. I often order my steaks medium-rare so I can see the blood, taste the blood, suck in the red juice hoping it might keep my heart ticking a while longer. A longing for immortality.

Somewhere in my struggles for life—according to my

mother's recounting of the tale—my body was unable to handle the stress so it went into shock, blocking me out of this sick world. Blackness. It was a place far from white. From the moment this dark place overtook me to the moment I woke up in the hospital, I have no recollection. What I have now are only the memories of my mother passed down to me as one would pass down a watch from generation to generation.

What I do remember, in lieu of this blackness, is an evil dreamworld—a world of pure, unimaginable horror. There I discovered what I used to be and what I'd eventually become.

As the story goes, my mother woke up to my screams. At first she thought it was only a dream of her own and she began dozing, but maternal instincts kicked in. Love in its purest form tossed her from bed. She rolled hard onto the floor, rose and shook the empty blankets that should have been my father. He was already at work working hard at hardly working. She raced out the bedroom door, down the hall, through the kitchen, and into the backyard. And so she found me, no longer screaming, but flapping loosely like a rag doll. Neck, head, torso, legs; every part of me was lifeless.

Grabbing the shovel leaning against the side of the house, she ran at the dog and swung it around. I'm not sure if the shovel made a hard metallic sound as it came crashing down onto the monster's thick skull, but it adds flavor to the story. Fang cowered, and then clamped back down onto me. This is where my mother states my neck was punctured. Arcs of blood spewed from my neck like a broken sprinkler, or so she said. She delivered another blow to the dog and it released. A third blow—again to the head—sent the dog whimpering.

At first she thought I was dead, my limp body to blame. She sat there rocking me to sleep, *forever this time*, she probably thought. But then she remembered something from nursing school: the dead don't bleed; when life stops, so does the heart. My limber body continued to bleed all over the place.

She slapped a hand around my neck and somehow drove me to the hospital with me on her lap—one hand on the wheel, one hand on my jugular. How she ever managed to even get me into the car I'll never know, let alone how she managed to drive the car.

While I was in the Emergency Room she called my father. He arrived when my condition turned from critical to critical but stable.

Surgeons stitched me together like Frankenstein's monster.

Neighbors

Days after my encounter with Fang, my condition changed to stable. My mother decided to pay a visit to whom we suspected were Fang's owners. She nearly beat down their door with her rage. She could always tell the story best, but I'll give it a shot.

They were the Johnson's, a religious family with nothing going for them but popping out kids while retaining the annoyance of being overly pleasant. One might approach you on the street, smile and, in an upbeat tone, ramble off, "It's a beautiful day if I ever saw one." Rain could be dumping to the ground, hail could be rumbling down, yet the Johnson answer would be optimistic. That's how Mr. Johnson answered the door that day after my mother nearly beat it down on top of him.

I can imagine their conversation …

He smiles gingerly. "What can I do ya for?" he says, or something similar. I imagine his mustache crinkling.

My mother, in hysterics, brushes past him and enters the house, uninvited, of course. She scouts the room.

"Why, my house is your house," he says, "make yourself at home. I'm making some iced tea. Should be ready in a jiffy if you'd care for a glass."

"Where is the bitch?"

Mr. Johnson shows a questionable look before saying,

"If by that you mean Margaret, she's at the grocery store with the kids. Ran out of those instant mashed potatoes we've grown to love. Shoot, I should have asked her to pick up an extra bunch of garlic; we might just be out."

"The dog! Is she outside? I'm going to kill it."

"Well, I'm sorry to tell you this, Liz—"

"Elizabeth. Please call me Elizabeth." Friends called her Liz.

"Well," he starts again, "I'm sorry to tell you this, Elizabeth, but we don't own a dog. Only got us a couple of cats and our little rascal, Steven. Speaking of which, how's little Billy doing these days? Still staying out of trouble?"

"No dog? No hundred and fifty pound beast, grayish-black, maybe some breed of husky?" She looks at him with lawyer eyes.

He stares back like soon-to-be road kill caught in the trap of an oncoming car. Something clicks and Mr. Johnson—Steven's dad, as I have always known and called him—displays insight. "You must be referring to that stray we keep seeing around here. It was here last weekend. I thought it was a coyote at first until I saw it up close and personal. Scared the living tar out me. Nearly chased me down for breakfast."

"Well, that stray *did* chase Billy down," my mother says. "Put him in the damn hospital. Tore him apart."

At this point in the story my mother would say she cried as she thought of me in my hospital bed, patched up and sewn together. I don't believe my mother was ever capable of shedding a tear. She was much too strong.

"Oh my dear lord. Here, Elizabeth, have yourself a seat," he says with annoying comfort. "I'll pour us a few glassfuls of that wonderful iced tea I was telling you about."

My mother looks around the flower-curtained room. Family portraits hang everywhere, as well as awards and placards from his children. She doesn't find a trace of the Johnsons ever owning a dog, not even in the pictures. She checks the couch for hair and realizes they have cats.

Mr. Johnson returns with the drinks and sits down at the loveseat across from her. He hands her an iced tea and watches as she finishes it off in a single long shot. He takes a sip of his own and sets his drink on a coaster.

My mother holds the empty, condensation covered glass between her hands as she looks out to their patio.

"Is Billy going to be alright?" he asks. "I'll be certain to let Steven know. He and your boy play like brothers."

"Stable, for now," she says. "I've lost count of the stitches. He will have nightmares his entire life."

"I'll pray he doesn't," says Mr. Johnson. "The whole family will, every night before supper."

There is a silence for some time before my mother recounts the morning to him, retelling the dog attack between yards while they were asleep in their beds dreaming utopias.

"That's just dreadful," he'd say now and again, or, "Bless that brave boy's heart."

ALLERGIES

Most of my teeth grew in crooked, some in dual rows. By thirteen my mouth was full of metallic devices: retainers, braces, springs, spacers, and many trial orthodontic devices. I often had train tracks running the gaps between my teeth, much like the scars left on my neck from my encounter with Fang. I was quite the project.

Cavities were a problem. So was Novocain. I was deathly allergic to the stuff. Nitrous Oxide was the only thing they could give me—happy gas. I thought of Steve Martin in the movie version of *Little Shop of Horrors* whenever I got the stuff. I also thought of his crazy practices whenever I sat in the waiting room. I was one of his metal-filled monsters.

One time a group of cavities found their way into my bottom row, farthest in back. This was my first trip to the chair and my first time seeing a doctor of any kind besides those that pieced me back together after the accident.

If Fang was the first monster I ever encountered, then Dr. Dellup would have to be the second. Dr. Dellup seemed gentle at first, dressed in peaceful white with a bright, perfect smile of his own. Inside I knew he was the devil, a mad, twisted man who loved yanking out children's teeth. At first I succumbed to his "relax, everything is going to be fine" way of presenting himself. To his side was a beautiful blonde woman, his siren or whatever the nymphs in *The*

Odyssey were called, who reeled you into the rocks.

The doctor leaned me back into a chair and lowered me down. It took a while for him to get over my face. Most people reacted this way. Most people couldn't handle the patchwork of skin and the jagged scars. He looked at me through thick glasses that made his eyes twice their actual size. I watched his assistant help him into a set of latex gloves. Dr. Dellup cracked his knuckles before fixing a light blue mask to his face. As Miss Helper pinned the spit-towel to my shirt, the doctor tilted his head the same curious way Fang had prior to attacking.

He leaned down and said through a muffled voice, "Let's see what we have here. Say ahh …"

I opened and watched my reflection in his glasses. My tongue filled most of the view. From my peripherals I watched Miss Helper hand him a blunt object. From his glasses I could see it was only a mirror with a long handle. He moved it around like a spoon, knocking it against every tooth. *This isn't so bad,* I thought. She handed the doctor a second tool, this one smaller. He took it in his opposite hand and it came into my reflective view next to the mirror. I immediately saw the sharp point and flinched as it poked my tender gums. The two metal tools danced around in my mouth, clinking and clanking. My reflection looked like a box of leftover Chinese food, these two tools a pair of chopsticks. Sweet and sour sauce formed around my gums.

The doctor must have sensed my nervousness because he said, "Only a moment, not to worry," as he prodded.

When he got to the bottom row in the back, he took his time and jotted down notes on the chart by his side. He poked gently at first, but then really dug the pick into them.

After what seemed hours he sat upright and said, "It looks like we've got us a few cavities. Three of them."

We? I thought.

The doctor pressed a button and my chair automatically up-righted. His assistant unclipped the spit-towel hanging from my chest and put the tools into a container filled with clear-blue liquid. My mouth felt violated.

Dr. Dellup returned to his chart as my seat halted.

"I'm scheduling an appointment two weeks from today." He smiled behind his mask. "We'll have these cavities taken care of in no time." And then came his trademark words, "Won't be a problem."

The lady at the front desk handed me a sucker, as if stating the obvious.

Two weeks later I plopped into the same dentist chair with a smile, but the atmosphere was different. R.E.M.'s "Everybody Hurts" played in the speakers overhead.

Dr. Dellup craned a gigantic sun of a light into my face. All I could see was blinding white. Not until the doctor leaned over me did my vision return.

Out came the mirror and without asking for an 'ahh' this time, my mouth opened. I saw it all from the doctor's glasses and their twin reflections. I waited for the pick. A needle twelve inches long was there in its place. It may have been smaller, but my imagination saw it this way as he grabbed it with both hands and stabbed it into my mouth.

I never felt the needle, only warm fluids. Heat ran through my gums and partway into my neck. Soon my entire head was a numb watermelon. The room spun. Something wasn't right. For the next few minutes I sat alone. I couldn't remember Miss Helper placing the spit-towel onto my chest, but there it was, as well as a tray to my side with metal instruments lined neatly across a white towel. A hammer, chisel, and hacksaw were also there, or so I imagined.

A slurping vacuum hose hung from my bottom lip. My tongue and gums were sucked dry and prune like. The bitter taste of a chalky substance lingered. The sound of a high-pitched dentist drill followed. I blinked and it was there, along with a device spraying water when needed—cold water, slurped up by the leech on my bottom lip. I could tell when the doctor drilled because the sound of the instrument would increase in pitch. One-by-one my teeth were hollowed. My jaw flexed each time the doctor applied the intense pressure. Spray, drill, slurp … over and over again.

Apparently I was allergic to Novocain. My mouth was numb; otherwise there would've been pain, lots of pain. It wasn't just my mouth, but my entire head, neck and left arm that were numbed. I was too afraid to say anything. I watched patiently with an intense throb in my head as each tooth was packed with silver. Hours later the ordeal was over, the chair tilted upright, the soaked spit-towel removed, and I was on my way to the waiting room where my mother awaited my return. Sometime during my visit she scheduled a follow-up. Right there in the waiting room, I collapsed.

The second doctor I met that day was a man by the name of Edalb Deggar. He came from a country I hadn't heard of yet. He told me and my mother that I was allergic to Novocain. The lady at the reception desk didn't offer me candy.

AMALGAMS

The headaches started after my cavities were replaced with metal in the epic battle against my teeth. They lasted about three years. It started at the roots of my molars and migrated north to my ears and along my neck. I chose to hide the pain and the headaches behind a blanket of youth ignorance, but it got to a point where the headaches were constant. Aspirin didn't help. My body tired easily, and my mother started noticing. She also noticed my winces whenever a shot of pain jumped through me.

"Where does it hurt?" she asked.

I responded with the typical childish answer, "all over," and then added, "… my head."

"Where does it hurt the most, Billy?"

I pointed to my jaw.

"Your mouth?"

I nodded.

"Open your mouth for me."

She peered inside, tilting my chin up to the light. She looked into my mouth as if peering through the lens of a telescope.

I pointed to the back teeth and said, "heeuh," which she interpreted as 'here.'

"Your fillings? Your gums don't look red or anything … have they been hurting for a while?"

Nod (up and down).

"Did your teeth hurt when they put in your fillings, when they were drilling?"

Nod (side to side).

"What if I do this?"

She pushed on a few of the cavity-corrected teeth.

Water developed at the corners of my eyes.

"Definitely the fillings. We'll take you to the dentist first thing tomorrow morning."

The next morning, after sitting in the waiting room reading pile upon pile of expired magazines, I was once again propped back in a dentist chair. The light above me was semi-blinding. Miss Helper was there, but she was a different Miss Helper than before. She clipped a spit-towel to my shirt. At first I couldn't see Dr. Dellup, only heard him writing on his chart. His chair squeaked as he rolled it closer. His creepy smile replaced the bright light above.

It had been years since my last visit. This time I was anxious to see him at work in the reflection of his glasses, but they weren't there. He had either switched to contacts or had Lasik.

Miss Helper handed him a set of tools.

"Say ahh!" he said and helped my jaw open wider than I knew capable. Again, like chopsticks, he used his tools, clanking them against my teeth. He poked a tooth on the bottom row, and pain jolted through my face. The doctor apparently checked my silver amalgams as he wrote different notes onto his tooth chart. He looked puzzled.

After a lot of prodding, the doctor decided on X-rays. I was transferred to a different room where an orderly-dressed woman helped me attire a parka-type vest that could have

weighed more than I did at the time. Before each X-ray, she told me to bite down on an annoying plastic-coated thing that didn't want to stay in my mouth, gagging me with its sharp sides. It pinched tender sections of my mouth and the back of my tongue. It kind of worried me that the X-ray technician left the room for each image, as if the radiation would dematerialize her. All I had was the fifty-pound shirt for protection. What about my head, arms, and legs?

I returned to the dentist chair sometime later ... some *long* time later. The fluorescent board on the wall illuminated the charts clipped to it, revealing a skeletal mouth with outlined teeth and white fillings. The film was amazing. I never got the chance to ask if I could take them home.

They brought my mother into the room to look at the charts with us while the doctor explained to her that I was perfectly fine.

"You might want to have some blood work done," he said. "His teeth are fine. His fillings look good. Maybe a blood test will tell us something different."

Later that same day we made a visit to Dr. Deggar at the hospital. A nurse who looked like a female rugby player drew my blood. The needle siphoned my blood like the world's largest mosquito.

"We have to send it out," we were told. "It will take a couple days for the results."

We waited eagerly those two days. A phone call finally brought the news that I had high levels of mercury, silver, nickel and other metals in my system, and I should come in for detoxification as soon as possible.

'As soon as possible' happened the moment after my mother dropped the receiver.

The emergency room wasn't necessary, but I had to stay in a hospital bed the entire night. I was given various detoxification regimes such as nutritional supplements, intravenous vitamin drips, and other fluids to flush out the toxins in my body. I was put on what they called an elimination diet.

We learned a lot of new terms the next morning as the doctor explained to us that the silver amalgams had reacted to my naturally conductive saliva, which was causing an effect similar to having a battery in my mouth for a long period of time which, if unresolved, could have caused cytotonic effects—cell killing—and neurotoxic effects—brain cell damaging—further down the line.

My mother said only one thing: "That's a mouthful."

ADAM AND EVE

After replacing the silver fillings—another set of almost endless trips to the dentist—I began to feel better. The headaches disappeared, the pains gone and good riddance.

A week later I was back to normal and spending a portion of spring break at Steven Johnson's house. He was the neighbor kid I befriended when we first moved into the neighborhood, one of the few kids in school who didn't turn away because of my odd appearance. But he lived in Fang territory. Every time I spent the night, I dreamt the beast would return to finish me off. Even though I believed they had never owned such an animal, I couldn't help but ask Steven each time I stayed the night.

"Nope," he'd say when asked. "Only a couple of cats, Adam and Eve." They were indoor / outdoor, still merely kittens.

"You sure?"

"Absolutely-one-hundred-percent-positively-certain," Steven would answer. Sometimes he'd just say the hillbilly 'Yup.'

One time we were up until three in the morning playing video games. Steven was never allowed violent games, those that had the threatening MA-17 tags on the front of their casings, so he'd ask me to bring them. The Johnson's despised such evil. They banned their son from any type of game or movie that had anything higher than a 'for all ages' or G-rating. We waited until his parents were asleep and then traded turns in a single-player game. When my time was up, I handed the controller to Steven, but he was sound asleep, snoring slightly. I shook him, but he was out cold.

It was dreary knowing I was the only one awake in the house. My eyes were heavy bags burned dry from staring at the television for too long. A full moon lit the entire bedroom; rings circled round the floating sphere. A handful of stars broke through as if tossed into the gray sky.

As I continued to play, my eyes sore and unwilling to give in to sleep and my thumbs blistering red, the silence and loneliness began playing tricks on me. The moon seemed to never move, centered behind the framework of the window as if painted there. I heard miniscule noises from both inside and outside the house. I swear I heard a door open and close, but that may have been my imagination. No noises came from the game because the television was muted to keep Steven's parents fooled. From outside came other noises: twigs breaking in two, a soft wind, and cats growling. The growls were Adam and / or Eve; they went outside sometimes by means of a kitty door.

One of them hissed. The other—if even there at all—remained silent. One made a sound I never imagined a feline could produce, so I went to the window. I looked down with the cold glass pressed against my cheek.

Fang.

She had a growling kitten backed against the corner of the fence in the backyard. The other kitten was clenched within her lip-curled mouth. Fang also growled. Blood traced her teeth and enlivened her snarl. With either Adam or Eve in her mouth, Fang took a step toward the other fear-stricken kitten, which instantly turned hunchback with tiny fangs of her own showing. Her tail puffed like a bottle-brush, ears back, whiskers parted.

Fang lowered to the ground, ears pressed flat against her head. Her growl grew deeper, louder, and more cutthroat. She clenched tighter onto the poor kitten within its mouth and split the thing in two. A head fell to one side, its mangled body to the other. She swallowed the rest. Bloody drool dripped from the sides of her mouth as she stalked the other kitten.

I glanced back to Steven, but his chin was still pressed to his chest. My eyes pulled like magnets back to Fang. Somehow I wanted Fang to get the other kitten—to feed. I was rooting for the beast but I didn't know why. My eyes were drawn to hers as they would be drawn to a traffic accident. It was impossible to look away.

Fang took another step closer, her lips curled fiercely. Her hind legs shook. Her head parallel to the ground. Breath puffed from her snout—two streams of hot anger against the cold morning air.

Now, I thought.

The mammoth half-wolf launched into the air and pounced onto the second kitten, breaking its neck within its jaw. It happened in seconds.

I spoke to no one about what happened. What I had seen was too horrible to describe.

Late the next morning Steven asked if I had seen Adam or Eve, so I told him I hadn't. It wasn't really a lie. They were dead. How could I have seen them?

THE CIRCLE

Looking at the back of my hand, I can still see the encircled star, a scar from long ago.

It was nothing like the scars that covered the rest of my body from my encounter with Fang. Those had healed rather nicely. The jig-jags and zigzags where doctors had sewn me back together had simply turned white. The skin on my forearms, chest, and the lower portion of my neck were patch-work quilts, but I could easily hide most of the scars with long-sleeved shirts and sweaters.

My friends were cool about it. We played in Canford Park. It was our secret place. The five of us spent most of the summer constructing a fort in a giant oak tree and damming the creek next to it. We all worked hard. Sarah would carry boards, nails, plywood, and other materials with her red wagon. Richard designed the fort. He was the brains, and most of the brawn. Steven never did much, but he was there to help. Steven and I provided the grunt work.

There were five of us—a magical number.

We met on the playground when school got out, minutes after the last bell. We sealed our friendship with a number 2 pencil. Richard came up with the idea. I thought of the star: five points, one for each of us. Sarah thought of the circle. She always considered us a circle of friends. One by one, using the eraser head of a pencil, we rubbed the symbol into the backs of our hands.

It wasn't until after I was grounded that I learned it was a pentagram. My mother said it was a satanic symbol and stranded me in my room for a month. To us it symbolized unity. While my friends pointed their stars north, I pointed mine south because I thought it looked cooler. Part of my punishment was to learn about the symbol. My mother thought—since it would be with me forever—that I might as well have an understanding of its meaning.

The internet provided most of my research. I entered "pentagram" into a search engine, which yielded thousands of results. I clicked a few. Some pages supported my mother's understanding that the mark was satanic, the upside-down star representing the face of Lucifer; others proclaimed the pentagram was the most spiritual of all symbols. This intrigued me, so I read on and found what the symbol meant to me: a unity of all the forces of nature (earth, air, fire, water, and spirituality), these five cornerstones of our very existence, these points of the magical star, encircled and linked together for balance. There were five of us that day, and we thought we had created this symbol from our imaginations. Five friends. Five points of a star. Encircled and linked together with friendship.

This symbol may hold different meanings for different people, but to me it's spiritual, maybe even a bit magical.

I relayed my findings to my mother. She smiled, but chose not to comment. She had wanted me to discover something different.

A week after erasing the six or seven layers of skin from the back of my hand, scabbing started. The first layers were dark and bubbly. I picked them off, a sucker for blood. The next scabs were lighter in color. The last scab was transparent with a white pentagram underneath. I peeled it away as if peeling off dried glue.

Over the years the scar has lightened, but it is still there. Twenty years later a hint of an upside-down, five pointed star still remains inside a barely visible circle.

Mine was the only one to scar. Apparently my friends had only rubbed a few layers of skin away, afraid of the rumor that a scar would be left behind … for life. I had rubbed with passion until drawing blood.

RECURSIVE SICKNESS

Most kids hated me for my hair, let alone the marks on my face. Prior to high school I sported a moustache and goatee, my sideburns nearly connecting to my chin. Chest hair even sprouted early. Most of my male friends spoke with the angelic voices of preteen girls, while my voice deepened. I used to tease Steven, whose voice remained squeaky the longest. They'd tease me back, though, and called me Harry sometimes instead of Billy. I grew up faster than all of them combined, it seemed. Through all of it, they never teased me about my scars.

With these rapid bodily changes, I often grew sick, bedridden for days sometimes. No one could ever figure it out. A pattern as regular as the cycle of the moon. A CTscan one year showed odd signs of neurological activity, but other than that I was as healthy as any adolescent boy. My body would just turn cold and drop well below normal, but it always felt like I was burning up. My mother would say, "Honey, you need to bundle up; you're freezing." I'd throw the blankets to the side, sweating, shivering and shaking. She'd wrap them back around me like I was a burrito. Anything I ate came back so I could taste it again. Nothing settled my stomach.

We'd go through this process once or twice a year, same symptoms each time, same hot / cold arguments. No one around me ever contracted whatever I had in me. My illness was for me and for me only. Antibiotics did nothing. Aspirin helped, but little. Pepto only made me gag—cherry flavored, my ass.

After two days of feeling like something an owl tossed up, it would pass. I'd wake up better than ever, my temperature between 98.5 and 98.6, and five pounds lighter. We figured the five pounds was a composite of the water my body lost from sweat, and the mass my body lost from lack of nourishment and food expulsion.

Whenever I got sick, I felt full, my appetite nonexistent, as if I could vomit an eighty-ounce steak.

To this day, the cycle continues.

For the life of me I wish I could remember what happens those days I am sick, but they're only black moments of time, my mind a giant puzzle with a few missing pieces.

THE SILVERSMITH

I haven't spoken much in reference to my father. He was never really around as I grew up; my mother took over because of his absence and did a great job raising me. Dad was a workaholic. Every morning he'd leave at seven and wouldn't return until close to six, sometimes seven at night. He owned a paint shop downtown called Ronan's Paint Wheel, which handled automotive paint jobs. Most of the guys that worked under him were into cocaine, but they performed artistic miracles when it came to custom paint jobs.

He did his best for the important stuff: baseball games on the weekends (he rarely missed work on weekends except for when I played ball), family functions, camping trips, and important conversations with his son. It was he who bought me my first razor and showed me how to use it. He also showed me how to use miniature squares of toilet paper to soak up the red dots on my chin and cheeks.

I mention my father only because I missed him growing up. Yeah, he was there for some things, important things, but not *all* things, such as Fang tearing me apart. It was Mom who found me, which is probably why I am still alive today, but to have had him there alongside us, that would have been better. He would have assuredly run into the house, grabbed the shotgun (if we had one) and blown the grimy dog back to the hell from which it came.

More time from my childhood was spent with Mr. Johnson than with my own father. Steven's father was sort of a role model to me—an annoyingly pleasant, overly Christian one at that. One Sunday morning, after spending the night at the Johnson residence and after playing hours upon hours of forbidden video games in Steven's room, I found myself stuck going to church with them while my parents were vacationing. I can still recall how badly and how loudly both Mr. and Mrs. Johnson sang while Steven and I flipped through the hymn book adding "in bed" to the ends of all the song titles. Some of my favorites included "I Stand All Amazed," "He Is Risen," and some song about the Second Coming. I think I may have corrupted their son.

After a wasted three hours of my life we returned from church services, ate homemade brownies Mrs. Johnson prepared, and rummaged through some old family jewelry Mr. Johnson removed from the attic.

Everything Mr. Johnson took from the box smelled of old lady and old lady perfumes. There was even a stuffed doily filled with potpourri mixed in with the junk. He tipped the box on its side and various rings, necklaces, pendants and broaches tumbled out in a wadded mess, much like a ball of tangled Christmas lights.

We spent the next hour removing one piece from the next and sorting the different objects by category: rings in one pile, necklaces in another, and other odds and ends in a third. It was the slowest hour of my entire life and, like some of the jewelry, the dullest.

When all the ugly items were contained in their neat piles, I thought we were finished and asked stupidly, "Is this

the only box?" It was polite, yet unnoticeably and unintentionally sarcastic. Steven looked to me with an expression that read: *Are you kidding? What are you thinking, you dimwit?*

"Yep," said Mr. Johnson, as luck would have it. "Sorry to say, Billy, but this is all there is. Too bad grandma Johnson wasn't into gold, otherwise we'd all be rich."

Steven stood and asked, "Can we go upstairs and play now? Before Billy's mom and dad get home?"

"Sure, right after we pick through all the silver," Mr. Johnson said enthusiastically. There's some silver in these thar hills, is how it sounded.

"Why are we looking for silver?" I asked.

"Steven didn't tell you? When I'm not working at the store," (a mom and pop grocery store run by the Johnson's), "I craft jewelry. I like to melt down old pieces of … history, like these," he said, pointing to the three piles, "and turn them into *these*." He held out his hand for me to see. He wore a wide-banded silver ring on his middle finger. It was plain, except for the crosses strung around it. I didn't like it personally, but I wasn't really into crosses. A few scratches were the ring's only blemishes.

"If you help me sort this stuff out, maybe I'll make you and Steven a matching set one day, like mine."

How lame, I thought. I could imagine the three of us wearing matching bands around our fingers. It seemed creepy.

Not too long after the boredom, the three of us (boys, as Mrs. Johnson would often call us) busied ourselves melting silver over a Bunsen burner in the Johnson garage. Mrs. Johnson excused herself. She wasn't feeling very well, or looking well for that matter. I would have used the same excuse had I not been 'one of the boys' and feeling only moderately uneasy in the stomach.

Mr. Johnson heated up a simple chain necklace and also the back plate of an ugly broach (after splitting the silver portion apart with a hammer and chisel) in a small crucible. He handled it with a pair of tongs while sporting a smock, a pair of gloves and eyewear. He looked like an evil scientist. Steven and I stood away to watch as the ordinate objects melded into each other and became one. The liquid silver moved around the bottom of the dish like spilled mercury.

"Where'd you learn to do this kind of stuff?" I asked.

"Way back in college I took a course in jewelry-making. I have held a love for the hobby ever since. This stuff could burn a hole straight through your hand if you're not careful."

He must have added that last tidbit of information for show. He then poured the hot liquid metal into two ring molds and set the crucible aside. I noticed he had enough silver left over to make at least five more.

"What will you do with the rest?" I asked, wide-eyed.

Mr. Johnson closed the ring molds and removed his glasses.

DREAMWORLD

The blackness: the first thought I remember from the dream-world I entered following my confrontation with Fang, a faraway land between reality and fantasy somewhere between life and death. As the animal feasted on my limber body and slashed with her paws, my mind had entered foreign land, one from which nightmares are born.

The sky is midnight black and I am falling. Everything above me is frozen in streaked starlight—a meteor shower snapshot. My body is weightless as different objects dissolve from a blurred focus. The silhouette of a bat. Its deafening screech breaks the night as it overshadows me with its spiraling flight. The tree fort in Canford Park. I can make out each and every branch, leaf, two-by-four, nail. It bursts into flame before my eyes. A fireball held up by a trunk. The area surrounding glows from the explosion, an orange-red strobe. It flickers with audible cracks as leaves crisp and branches crumble.

Still I fall.

My body hits the ground, but without pain. My stomach growls with a deep and angry hunger. There is no food nearby, only my friends who are trapped in the burning branches of an unfinished fort. I lay on my back, motionless. I watch as my friends, one-by-one, leap from the giant oak. Glancing to the man-made pond in the neighboring creek, I see bully Ray Duschenne, body bloated and floating face up. His eyes reflect the early moon's ghastly white glow in two identical spheres.

My attention turns to Steven, who has fallen to the ground. His body breaks apart beneath him and shatters into microscopic filaments.

My hunger yearns.

Richard lands on his feet and begins to run.

Steven falls hard, his head smashing against a granite boulder. Silence engulfs the thud that should have come with the impact. His skull breaks and oozes black syrup.

Richard makes it five strides and is struck down by a flaming limb that cracks in two over his head. I watch as his skin melts. The hairs on his head singe to a charcoaled baldness.

His girlfriend Allie has yet to leap from the fiery tree, but she rapidly climbs down the knotted rope through the fort's trap door. She sees Richard and screams.

The shadow of the giant bat covers it all and screams.

And I hunger.

The tree continues to burn, a sun held up by the oak's massive blackening trunk. Shooting stars race across the black canvass of sky. The full moon, actually blue as Mom said it would be, floats majestically like an ornament. I see it and it sees me. All this happens as I lay on my back.

I look to my hand and black blood outlines the pentagram scar. It throbs with pain. I wipe away the blood and the image returns and burns even hotter. I look back to the tree and see Allie's tiny hands at its base; she covers her

face, sobbing. The pentagram on her hand glows white in the blackness.

To the heavens above I notice the bat is only a conventional bat—not some mammoth and mystical vampire—no larger than a seagull. It flutters above us and then flies away. The giant oak no longer burns. The dead and dying bodies of my friends—and an enemy—are gone. Only Allie remains. She is alone and sobbing under the tree. I rise and this dreamworld changes once again. All but the blue moon turns black, white, or a grayish mixture of the two; everything but the blue glow in the sky is a scene from an old black-and-white movie. It stays this way for a while until Allie's hands drop to her sides and her eyes connect to mine. I feel her heartbeat. I see the blood flowing. A red aura.

The symbols on the backs of our hands pulse to the synchronized rhythm of our hearts. Her eyes are two black orbs reflecting moonlight.

My stomach turns over.

Fang joins us with a brisk howl to the moon. She looks to me and then to the girl. She drops to her usual stance: hind legs up, back arched, forepaws outstretched, hair rising along her spine. Ready to pounce. Allie, her target, screams. Steam trails from Fang's nostrils. Adding more color to this black and white world, her eyes glow blue. Great droplets of slobber fall from her pointed teeth; they stretch long before reaching the dirt.

My teeth clinch as I realize young Allie Hart is about to die. I turn my hands into fists and crouch to the ground. Rage flowing through me like the injected Novocain from my first trip to the orthodontist. I am about to unleash a monster of my own unto the world, one that has been hiding up my sleeves like some kind of magic trick. Somehow I have to get to her before Fang. The fate of the world, *my world*, depends on it.

Fang's eyes attract to mine, and then back to Allie's. Fang is closer by a good ten feet and she is in the runner's stance. There is no way I can make it in time but I have to try. A branch from the tree pops and the race is on; we are both off, running to Allie, Fang on all fours, me on all twos. Sprinting, my lungs pump in and out with quickly thinning air. My thighs grow hot and feel as if they are bursting from their seams. We both gain on the girl, but Fang slips and slides and tumbles into a bush along her path. She gets up, but I am closer to the whimpering girl. Fang regains her lost ground quickly. We are both within striking distance. Saliva drips from Fang's snout. Saliva drips from my mouth. I hear the beast breathing and she hears me the same.

I leap first and tackle young Allie to the ground. Fang misses her target and keeps on running, never looking back. She shrinks into nothingness as her sleek but furry form runs into the blackness. The girl is under me, trembling, sucking air in short bursts.

Overhead is a shriek and with it another shadow that blankets us from the blue moonlight. It is the bat. It circles above us.

Blackness overtakes me again and steals my memory in the process. When it passes I am alone. There is no sign of Allie Hart, no sign of Fang, and no sign of the bat. The burning tree is also gone and so are the bodies of my dead friends. I am no longer in Canford Park at all. No, I am far from Canford Park.

It is a wheat field in which I stand. A dead field. Acres

of crop stretch around me as far as I can see. Thickets poke out from my socks and jab my skin. The ground underneath is muck, sucking my shoes into the ground. Each step I take sounds like the lunch lady in elementary school plopping ice-cream-scooped balls of mush onto my plastic tray. The stalks around me are waist-high and sway with the breeze, creating a hollow hum as it sings to me.

The ground beneath snaps and gurgles from the dead wheat and muddy soil. I leave a slithering trail of broken stalks in my wake. A rattlesnake tail shakes in the distance like a maraca. I walk past it and the sound fades into the rest of the silence.

A rock trips me to the ground and I tumble. Chills run up my spine as I discover the secret alcove I have stumbled upon. For the past few minutes I had walked unbeknownst with the stalks no longer beating and slapping against my sides. Around me now are flattened wheat stalks, smashed by some*one* or some*thing*. Soon I discern that I am in the middle of a phenomenon I had only prior seen on the television, and once read about in the *Brenden Daily* a few years back: *a crop circle*. Tracing those words with my lips, I look around at the marvelous spectacle. Stems lay flat in a spiraled counter-clockwise rotation. The epicenter is directly underneath what I had tripped over. The flat cylindrical circle is luminous.

The rock isn't really a rock, but a human skull. Black sockets stare up to me, the nostrils only slits, and the jaw—a horrible elongated jaw—broken, smiling an evil smile that is much too long to be human.

I kick it aside and it breaks in two pieces: jawbone and skull. The pieces come to a stop at a rosebush growing in ashes. The plant looks burnt. A lonely stem holds a single magnificent flower. Its petals bleed with crimson.

I stare at this beauty, no longer afraid.

Fang growling breaks me away from this attraction and brings fear back into play. I feel her hot breath down the nape of my neck. Drool drips down my back. A shadow covers us both, the shadow of the mysterious bat. I feel the ground beneath us as the earth begins to tremble.

I turn around to face Fang. Our eyes glow blue.

The next thing I remembered was family, strangers, and oddly named doctors looming over my hospital bed. Sometimes I wonder how my confrontation with Fang in that dreamworld would have ended had I not woken up.

My bedroom window overlooked the Johnson's backyard, as well as part of my own. From it I could see the exact location where I was attacked by Fang at the tender (and apparently delicious) age of five, and the place where my best friend Steven nearly died.

Fang looked old and miserable the next time I saw her. Her stomach revealed a starved ribcage, with skin pulled tightly over it. Splotches of fur were missing in places on her hindquarters.

It was early evening, the moon out and full but not in sight, the sky pockmarked with an overabundance of stars. I was finishing my math assignments and staring out the window at the orange dot of Mars. I was counting the stars just before Fang reeled me in.

She was near the sliding glass door leading to the Johnson's kitchen, whimpering noisily. I was surprised they couldn't hear her. Lights in the kitchen were on. Apparently Fang could see in, but the Johnson's couldn't see out. Fang drooled over whatever food was on their kitchen table. I watched her scurry and hide behind one of the maple trees at the sound of a voice. It was Mr. Johnson asking Steven to take out the trash. The sounds were muffled, but I could hear everything well enough.

I failed to understand the danger of the situation until

the door slid open and Steven stepped outside. The garbage can was by a stack of firewood far from the house. I wanted to yell out to my friend but I was petrified.

And a little intrigued.

Fang crouched behind the trunk of the maple tree as Steven got closer. She stood with her hind legs high in the air, preparing to pounce.

Back inside! Get back inside!

I only thought these warnings, my throat dry, my tongue unable to form the words. My palms left sweaty stripes on my shirttails as I tugged at them anxiously, fearful for Steven's life.

As he neared the garbage can, the back of Fang's body started to shake. Her hair stood on end, her head low to the ground. Her eyes gleamed. I could then make out the reflection of the moon in her eyes as it peeked between clouds: two white circles side-by-side. They seemed almost blue.

Run!

They both ran—Steven for the screen door, Fang for Steven. It all happened fast, yet blurrily slow. Steven carried the trash bag for the first few steps, and then threw it behind him. Fang leapt over it a second later.

"Not going to make it," I said after quick calculation.

Steven never had a chance. He was pinned a moment later, slammed hard against the side of the house. Fang stepped away wobbling. Steven shook his head, probably wondering if anyone had gotten the number of the truck that had just run him over. He sat up and found himself staring into the mesmerizing eyes of the beast.

I stood froze at my window.

Fang paced around him. She looked proud; it showed

in her eyes and in the way she strutted in half-circles. She howled an awful sound. The whole block must have heard.

Color draining from his face, Steven hugged his knees and rocked on his heels.

Fang tilted her head.

And then she pounced.

Blurry slow motion.

She bore claws, stretched wide to match the size of his face. Her enormous jaw gaped widely as it went for his neck. A dozen razor teeth sparkled. Her front feet stretched like a set of human arms. Fang's entire body flew through the air.

A shotgun blast shattered the silence. Fang's chest blossomed like the rose in my dream. Blood and flesh splattered the siding of the house and covered Steven's horrified face.

Fang flipped and landed in an awkward lump onto a sprinkler head, the top portion showing through the giant hole in her chest.

Dressed in Black

Sprawled out in front of Steven was the naked body of his mother. A bloody hole replaced much of her chest. Imbedded into her body and displayed around the yard were tiny pieces of silver from a homemade shell. Mr. Johnson clutched a shotgun a few paces away. Smoke swam out of the gun's twin barrels.

Her body had changed. Claws formed into manicured fingernails and paws into stubby toes. Her snout from elongated and grisly to a delicate mouth and button nose. The clumped and sweaty hair disassociated from its roots under the skin and floated off with the night's gentle breeze. Her arms and legs grew longer while an arched back straightened and lengthened, body curled into a fetal position.

Police surrounded the place later that night. They arrived on scene less than an hour after the incident. Shotgun blasts at eight in the evening in Brenden, Washington can cause quite a stir. Almost everyone on the block came out to decipher the noise, including my parents. They ran to the gate in the fence, where they found the Johnsons: Steven on the ground, Mr. Johnson still frozen over his dead wife with a shotgun in his hand. They ran back inside and called the police like everyone else that night. Screams came from all directions as one-by-one people discovered what had happened, or what they imagined had happened … the

fact that Mr. "overly-pleasant" Johnson had blown a hole through his wife in front of their only child.

I can still see the expression on Mr. Johnson's face. He glanced up at me through my bedroom window, tears streaming down his sad face. Weapons pointed at him from all angles. He surrendered peacefully, lowered the shotgun next to his dead wife, and sank to his knees with his hands on the back of his head. He then looked to the sky for his god, or perhaps to the moon, and prayed.

I looked up as well but could only see stars poking through the night. Maybe each star is home to a god, I remember thinking then.

Now I know better. Now I know that if there truly is a god, he wears black. Sometimes when my stomach churns for blood, those nights when my teeth hurt from those damn silver poison fillings, and I find myself under the blue moon, those nights my mind goes blank and I wake up full and sick and bloated and covered in gore, I know somewhere there is a god, and he is wearing black, and he is laughing at us all.

PART THREE
THE PHOENIX ROSE

The Earth Begins to Tremble

"The crackling fire does not disturb the murder of crows as they gather in the limbs of the dogwood. Always there are three: in this case, two in the tree and one on the shoulder of the elderly man hanging from the largest of the branches. They peck at his eyes, but there is no longer light behind them. His life has gathered like crimson petals below his feet. The black birds flutter as the fire climbs. The silver dangling around the dead man's neck glows orange before melting into his flesh. The earth begins to tremble."

– from *Crimson Petals*, by Cray Marrow

Eddie Hensen closed the book and reflected on his life. His gas station was usually dead at one in the morning, so he often filled his solitude by reading; imagination sometimes his only friend. At eighty plus years of age, he was close to death himself, so those final words touched him deeply. He pushed the book across the counter and looked outside to a black sky speckled with stars.

He preferred the graveyard shift. A six-shooter waited under the counter in case trouble surfaced. He had taken it out only once while he worked at the Chevron on Newman

Street, but only to scare away a man strung on crack who attempted holding him up with a yellow squirt gun. Eddie had never fired a gun before and didn't much care for them in general. He didn't even know if the one under the counter was loaded; it was just always there and had been for most of his life and he was too afraid to check, knowing he might blow his own head off in the process. For forty years he tried making sense of life as he worked random jobs, yet somehow ended up at the station, stuck in the town of Brenden, Washington, of all places, over a thousand miles away from the orphanage that ruined his childhood.

The clock over the door ticked past one when a white minivan pulled in, high beams (or so it seemed this late) blasting through the many windows of the small convenience store. The driver stayed behind the wheel as a young man on the passenger seat stepped out. He nodded to Eddie as he pushed through the doors. The OPEN / CLOSED sign swayed. The sleigh bells strung to the door jingled softly.

"Good morning," said Eddie with a smile.

"Mornin'," said the young man.

He looked no older than eighteen and reminded Eddie of his best friend growing up. He even had the same blond-brown mess of hair.

Eddie watched with caution as the young fellow went to the sodas in back, and then turned his attention to the driver in the minivan. Running vehicles and anxious wheelmen were red flags for your typical gas station robbery, but the driver simply closed his eyelids and leaned back in his seat, looking nothing but exhausted and nonthreatening.

A black Suburban pulled in next to the minivan and when it stopped its hubcaps kept spinning round and around.

The man that got out was much older and had a scruffy shadow of facial hair and a reversed ball cap that matched the rest of his black attire. He left the engine running idle as he stepped out, dropped the cigarette from his lips, and stubbed it out with the tip of his shoe. Smoke still leaked from the side of his mouth as he entered the station. His puffy black coat concealed his hands as he pushed through the door. The bells jingled.

"Good morning," Eddie said with the same smile he gave all his customers.

The man in the coat ignored him and wandered down an aisle of chips, jerky, and sunflower seeds. He moved around as if he had to pee and gave the young man a strange look as he squeezed past him to the counter.

"Two Red Bulls and a water."

The register beeped for each item as Eddie swiped them across the scanner. The receipt printed. He looked around him and waited for a bag of seeds or a Slim Jim to disappear into the older man's coat pockets, but he only seemed fascinated by the contents of each bag as he pulled them off the racks and tossed them to the floor. The young man in front of him held out a crumpled ten and rolled his eyes.

"Some people, huh?"

Eddie tried striking up as little conversation as possible with his customers. Who wanted to talk to old gas station fogies anyway? He rarely spoke anything other than pump numbers, aisles, and dollar amounts throughout his shift. Handing back a couple dollars and some change, he counted what he handed back to the young man and wished him goodnight. The bells on the door signified his parting and somehow Eddie knew something bad was going to happen.

The gun was under the counter waiting, loaded or not.

He twisted the band on his left ring finger a few times and thought of Annie and what she might say to him if she were still alive. They were only married a few years, but he could still hear her beautiful voice and that animated laugh that always made him smile. Her own smile was crooked and always curved up on the left side, leaving a dimple on the right. Every day the roses for sale on the counter reminded him of her perfume, and he always felt saddened when the last of them sold because it meant a memory of her was leaving and it left him feeling alone and guilty because every day he could still see the horrified look in her eyes as she fell …

Creamer packets fell to the floor. The man in the black coat had moved to the coffee and watched conspicuously as the two in the white minivan drove off. He seemed to take an interest in their leaving. He was definitely going to rob the place. He studied a collection of stale doughnuts.

"You got any fresh pastries?"

"Only what's out, sorry. New batch arrives tomorrow."

"It *is* morning," he said, poking his finger into a few of the doughnuts. "And these are hard as rocks. They got better pastries down the street." He licked his fingers before saying, "The coffee any good?"

Three silver cylinders: French Roast, Decaf, and Ethiopian Dark Roast. Eddie watched the man push down on each spout, spilling java over the counter and onto the floor.

"I can put on a fresh pot if you'd like," Eddie offered.

"I don't like coffee. Tastes like mud." He scoped the door and walked casually to the counter to join him. "You busy tonight?"

"As busy as any night."

A gun pointed to his face.

"Put your hands on the counter where I can see 'em, old man. I know you're carrying back there."

Eddie was tempted to reach for either gun, but decided not to risk it. The man in front of him seemed a little edgy. And edgy could be dangerous when mixed with firearms. He studied the man's face, hesitated, and put both hands on the counter.

"There's less than fifty in the register."

"Bag it." His beady eyes were restless, bouncing from Eddie to the register to the plastic bags to the counter where a gun was hidden somewhere below it. "Empty the safe, too." The gun barrel never left Eddie's face.

"I would if I knew the combination."

"Then give me the safe."

Laughing, Eddie explained that it weighed at least two hundred pounds, maybe more.

"I only keep enough in the register to make change. The rest goes in the safe. Only Brinks has the combination. You're robbing me for probably forty-three bucks and some change. And you're on camera."

Eddie pointed to the camera mounted on the wall behind him. A red light revealed it was at least powered on.

The hammer cocked back and the barrel pressed against Eddie's forehead.

"Bullshit. Open it or I blow your fuckin' head off."

"Look, son—"

"Open the register!" Perspiration formed at his brow, the gun a bit shaky. "Call me son again. I dare you."

Slowly, and in a way showing that he wouldn't go for his

own gun, Eddie swiveled to the register and pressed one of the many colorful buttons. Nothing happened.

"What's wrong now, old man?" He tottered the gun barrel. "We're not going to have any trouble are we? Don't make me cold cock your old wrinkly ass."

"No problems. I'll have to ring something up first. The drawer only opens during transactions." It was a lie, but could buy him some time. "Want to grab me one of those candy bars in front of you, or should I get it?"

The stranger reached blindly, snatched a Kit Kat, and tossed it on the counter.

Eddie scanned it and the register beeped. "Now we'll pretend you actually paid for this purchase." He mimed taking money from his faux customer, and followed through as he would any transaction. The printer choked out a receipt for one candy bar; the cash drawer popped open with a clang.

"Now put it in the bag, and give me your wallet, too."

"Son, I—"

"Now!" The gun smacked against Eddie's head hard enough to draw blood. "Slowly. If you even think about reaching for that gun I'll blow a hole through your eye and stump fuck you."

With one hand pressed against the counter, Eddie reached for his wallet and dropped it on the counter. He watched it quickly disappear into the man's back pocket.

The jingling of sleigh bells startled them both and for a second Eddie thought the man in front of him might fire and he winced and the gun jerked but the man hadn't fired and he was still alive and they were both looking to the door.

A naked man covered in mud and clumps of dirt staggered into the store with his hands outstretched toward them. His starved body showed transparent skin wrapped over bones. His eyes were sunk deep in their sockets, his mouth gaped open; he drooled a mucky black liquid that looked like oil. Each step he took seemed to take a year from his life. He was decomposing.

Eddie took a stealthy step to his right and grabbed the barrel of the gun previously pointed at his left eye and pushed the end away from his face. He heard the hammer strike down onto an empty chamber and silence thereafter. It wasn't even loaded. The lack of boom seemed to surprise the man holding it. Eddie could see through the other empty chambers. The man wrestled his gun free and stepped back.

Pulling his own gun from under the counter, Eddie reversed roles. He could see the chambers were loaded. "Get out the hell out of my station." He cocked the hammer. "And give me your gun. I'll trade you for this." He slid the Kit Kat across the counter.

"No way, old man," he said as he squeezed off three more empty rounds, the gun simply clicking.

Eddie lowered his own gun to the man's crotch and he reluctantly set the useless gun on the counter and turned to leave, but then stopped.

The naked monstrosity was closer and carried a smell of rot and decay. Jagged rips ran along his neck and over his ribcage, which leaked black and red sludge over the polished floor. His shoulders slumped as his arms and legs broke apart, his elbows and knees ending in sharp points.

"Point that thing at *him*," said the man in the black coat.

Red and black flowed freely from the various cracks that formed over the corpse's body. A large gash in his leg revealed a glimpse of femur and mushy muscle. His face slowly sank against the contours of his skull. Another step and his knee snapped in half. The skin was melting off him, leaving a bold smear trailing behind him as his slow zombie pace desperately quickened.

"Stop right there," said Eddie, trembling.

"Shoot him!"

Eddie fired and the gun recoiled. The bony shoulder arched at the impact, but the bullet simply passed through and failed to slow him down. The gun boomed again, hitting him in the chest. Thick blood oozed from the hole, but he still moved toward them, a crooked smile on his face. A third round jammed the gun.

The dead man pounced onto the black coat and the man who had just tried to rob him fell to the floor. Arterial spray arced onto the counter after an awful sound.

Eddie shrank back and found the floor, curled up, and hugged his knees. He thought of a horrible scene he once saw in an old horror movie—a field of blood, a crop stained by the red irrigation of man—and he had to quickly brush it away. He tried thinking of Annie again, but could only bring up the same image that haunted his dreams whenever he slept—her head hitting the rock after she fell, blood pooling around her as she looked up to him with empty eyes, the smile gone from her lips as he kissed her one last time and smelled the rose perfume on her neck as he held her in his lap.

The screaming stopped, but Eddie stayed behind the counter, too afraid to see what waited for him on the other side. He embraced the revolver as if he were protecting a child and looked down the barrel to see the gold tip of the bullet and thought of pulling the trigger once again so he could be forever with Annie and then he heard what sounded like an innocent voice.

"What is this maddening place?"

The headstone read: WILLIAM HILLCREST / BURN FOREVER
IN HELL / 1824 - 1862. Nearly a century and a half had passed
since Father William "Phoenix" Hillcrest had burned alive
while tied to a post in the middle of Towne Square Cemetery. His accusers placed straw beneath him and drenched
his body in alcohol as they pulled his arms wide and tied
him to what resembled the crucifix that once hung behind
his pulpit during services. His wrists bled from the ropes
that bound him. More straw filled his mouth as a gag and
poked from his collar and coat sleeves as if he were nothing
but a scarecrow. A silver crucifix necklace sagged around his
neck, somewhat foreshadowing his death before it glowed
red and melted into his chest. The roses around the lot had
burned with him, crimson petals curling black at their edges.
They were named after his grandfather, Phoenix, who had
first crossbred the variety; the name had passed down from
one generation to next like a curse. William Hillcrest had
been called Phoenix more times than he had been called
Father. But that was a long time ago.

A small fire in the distance created an eerily-orange
illumination in the mountains. Mars broke through an
otherwise black sky, as did the Perseid meteor shower and
its white brushstrokes. The moon was an evil red grin peeking through a large passing thundercloud. Lightning lit the

134

cemetery grounds in a flash of brilliance as a hand-shaped shadow from a nearby tree groped the weathered headstone. Another loud crack of light brought more ghostly hands to the grave; their elongated fingers dug at the loose dirt. The dark cloud above swirled violently as a third bolt touched down near one of the rosebushes. Dry leaves around it smoldered, blackened, and birthed a flame amongst the thorny branches and a moment later the entire plant was aflame, austerely mimicking the larger fire in the mountains.

The ground shook vehemently, cracking the thin layer of earth above the grave, the soft and wet dirt underneath eroding as bony hands clawed their way to the surface. The man who emerged was a collection of mummified skin patched over gray bones. His skull was cracked and leaking brown sludge. Worms rolled out of his gaping jaw and pushed through the mud filling his eye sockets as he crawled out. A spirally mop of shoulder-length hair dripped and draped over his shoulders, covering all but the crucifix necklace fused to his sternum.

He couldn't see his own headstone in front of him, nor the crow perched atop it, but he felt the bird calling him to feed as he rose on shaky legs. He reached for it and took the crow in his mouth and clamped down. As he took the bite his necklace dislodged and dangled. Hot blood flooded through what few teeth remained as it flowed down and through the rest of his body, coating him in the same red that surrounded the cemetery. Rosebushes lined the grounds and he could now see them as his eyes took shape within their once empty sockets. They were his roses, and they had survived without him for however long he had been gone.

After burying the bird next to his own grave, he plucked

one of the roses and placed it over the small mound, watching as flesh weaved together over his hands. Soon it covered his entire body. Muscles reformed under the bruised skin and around his bones. His heart began to pump again. It was all a temporary gift from the crow. For only a moment he was fully alive.

As he walked through the cemetery grounds only minutes after his resurrection, he could already feel his body re-decomposing. His face had all but disintegrated by the time he made it to the gate—still the same metal gate after all these years. His legs moved him forward in an industrial, mechanical way. Each step became strenuous. Dried flakes of flesh fell to the ground like ash. Skin shriveled around his skinny arms and legs and sank below outlines of bones. He was dying once again.

William Hillcrest stumbled out of the cemetery and looked back to the collection of headstones. In doing so, he had ripped a hole in his neck.

So many have died, he would say through his rotted teeth if he were capable of speech. No words came out as he realized his predicament. *Dead but still dying.*

A single crow cawed in the distance, fluttering from a tree hidden by the fog. The undead priest held his loosely flesh-covered skeletal hands in front of his loosely flesh-covered skull and saw with a pair of eyes turning from plum to prune that he was dead, yet somehow not dead. Again he heard the caw of a crow and felt it calling him to feast. Closing his eyes with a set of sunken lids, he listened.

First there was nothing but the eerie stillness in the night and a humming breeze, but then came the *click-clack* of feet as the eager bird approached. It was ten feet away,

and then five. The tiniest of drums beat in the quietness: *bum-bump* ... *bum-bump* ... the heartbeat of the crow. With his eyes closed, Father William Hillcrest could see only

(crimson)

the crow's heart as it beat gently within its black-feathered chest cavity; the blood within pumped through its veins and he could see with his mind the spider web of red that filled its small body, blood flowing freely. The red beating heart; it thumped in his ears until they melted away and fell to his feet. And then the crow was only in his mind after losing most of his other senses. Wings fluttered around him before sharp claws dug into the crusty cracking meat left on his slender shoulders. It perched onto his exposed clavicle. His eyes now gone, Father Hillcrest turned his head to see the blood-pumping scarlet organ beating rhythmically within the bird. Glowing white surrounded the heart and traced each ventricle and artery and vein as blood pumped through the small creature. If the priest had eyes to open, he would see two blue spheres of light staring back at him.

Hillcrest fell to his knees. The bird somehow stayed perched. It cawed once more, and was then forever silenced as he bit into it to drain its warm life-giving blood. He sucked the bird dry and then dug another grave for the second generous bird and gave the sign of the cross over his chest. As with the first, he plucked another burnt-edge crimson rose—a Phoenix Rose—with his bare hands. A few thorns sliced into his fingers, but the wounds quickly healed. He placed it over the small mound of dirt. Already he could feel himself reanimating as he rose from the ground and walked naked down the path leading out of the cemetery.

Reaching for the heavy burden hanging around his neck,

he remembered his death. He had clutched the crucifix in his hand just before passing to the other side, the image of Christ on a cross branded forever into his palm. It was still there in his resurrected state and it was probably there for a reason he had yet to uncover. A second cross had burned onto his chest. He felt for it and the scar was still there.

Relieved that it no longer burned, he grasped the silver crucifix tightly as he walked on, his body slowly slumping and degrading in form. He was quickly going now and could feel his skin shrivel, his appendages growing weak and wobbly. He knew he needed to find new blood to stay alive, or stay dead, or stay whatever he was until he figured out why he was even wherever he was in the first place.

The town had changed since he last remembered it. Lights of various sizes and colors and shapes glowed from every direction, blinking, blinding, flameless. Metal rods with lights shot upward from the sidewalks, covering black stone roads in an orange glow. Monstrous noises filled the normal silence. The air smelled dank and was difficult to breath. The moon seemed dimmer as it smiled over him. Fewer stars filled the sky. Red lights flashed by speedily in one direction of the road while white lights traveled the opposite direction—the source for most of the noise. Horseless carriages zoomed by at unexplainable speeds, stopping and starting to the colorful lights hanging above the roads. It was wondrous to watch as he approached some kind of station up ahead made of glass.

A lengthy white carriage moved away from the building while another as black as pitch rolled to a stop. Two red lights glowed softly behind it like two eyes filled with wrath. His body yearned for blood, his stomach snarling like a wolf, lips dry, throat parched; he hoped the people inside would offer to help him find some sort of nourishment, or at least to loan him some clothing, but as he got closer it appeared that one of the two inside was robbing the place. A younger man dressed in a puffy coat pointed a revolver to the older gentleman behind the counter. A red aura floated around him. Blue swirled around the other. Hillcrest could hear the evil one's heart pounding in his chest; closing his eyes, he could see it pumping life throughout him as he could with the crow.

With strained effort, he entered the station.

Unknown Where

Still embracing the revolver, although he knew it would prove useless as protection, Eddie somehow made it to his feet. He didn't dare look over the counter to the mess of the dead man on the floor. *What is this maddening place?* It was such a strange question, but apparently the answer was a place where the dead rise and feast on the living.

"I don't know who or what you are, but please don't hurt me. There's not much meat left on my scrawny bones."

Humor was Eddie's only sanity.

"When *is* this?" said the voice behind the counter.

After a long pause, Eddie said, "This is now, buddy. Sunday morning. Early." He hoped it was what he wanted.

"The nineteenth century?" The voice calm and sincere, of all things.

"Who exactly are you?" asked Eddie.

"William Hillcrest. I am a servant of God."

"Well, I'm sorry to have to bring this to you, but you're in the computer age. Century twenty-one. You must be a long way from home." Eddie leaned over the counter far enough to see the top of the dead man's head. Blood covered everything under him. He leaned back again to hide the sight and waited for a full minute in silence, attempting to control his breathing. His pulse raced.

"This is my home," William Hillcrest said and hesitated,

140

"but not my *when*."

Eddie looked up to see him peering over the counter at him. Black muddy hair dripped onto his face as an upside-down man offered a bloody smile. Although completely nude and covered in a mess of red and brown, he could pass as any ordinary middle-aged bloke. He was no longer decayed and semi-decomposed as before; the man just needed a long shower and to brush his teeth.

"Will you help me?"

"Help? You look like you just crawled out of the ground. Of course you need help. You just killed a man; hell, you sucked the life right out of him. What do you expect me to do, offer you my neck? I'd rather take my own life than let you take it."

"I only took his blood." Wiping his mouth, he smeared the mess, looking embarrassed more than anything.

Eddie was somewhat relieved not to see fangs protruding from his mouth. "How can a servant of God do such a thing?"

"Are you a religious man?"

"Of sorts." Eddie returned the gun and rose behind the counter. There was nothing the gun could do, or any gun for that matter. The shots he fired had only passed through the dead guy anyway. And deep down he knew he'd never be able to use it on himself. "I haven't gone to church in years."

"Apparently, neither have I," said William Hillcrest. He took a silver crucifix necklace around his neck with one hand, closed his eyes, and gave the sign of the cross with the other. "Did you ever take communion, Eddie?"

"How do you know my name?"

"It is stitched onto your clothing."

"Right," Eddie sighed and out came trembled breath.

"There's no need to be scared," he said and glanced uneasily to the floor. After a shared uneasiness he continued, "You've taken communion, I gather?"

"Sure, the bread and water deal. Sometimes wine."

"It doesn't matter what is used as long as it's symbolic. Do you know why you take this sacrament?"

As if his afterlife depended on a response, Eddie said, "For the promise of everlasting life."

"The wine—or the water—represents what?"

A chill ran through Eddie Hensen's old, crooked spine. *Blood.*

"Will you help me?"

"You won't do to me what you did to him?"

The man on the floor was torn open at the throat.

"No."

Eddie grew deeply concerned as he thought it over. "This guy on the floor … he isn't going to get up and start walking around, is he?" Vampire, werewolf and zombie stories he had read as a child ran through his mind, undead creatures drinking blood or eating flesh to stay alive as they ruled the earth forever dead. The gun was suddenly looking like the lesser of two evils. If it came down to it, Eddie would rather eat a bullet and test his luck at the gates of Hell than walk the earth in such a recursive, endless life.

The priest smiled.

"It's complicated, but I assure you he will not get back up. I could start with clothing if you have any to spare."

The dead priest wasn't modest by any means, but the naked, filthy man looked cold as he hugged his chest and shivered, his knees coupled together.

"And you won't eat me, or drink me, or even look at me like you're going to—"

"No."

"Why?"

"You seem like a nice fellow and your heart is pure."

"And I should trust you?"

"You must have faith."

"What about him?"

"He was going to kill you."

"His gun wasn't even loaded."

"But his heart was black. He was going to kill you, one way or another."

Annie was probably in heaven laughing at him. Each day without her was torture, as if it were his penance to suffer alone in this personal, secluded Hell. Perhaps this Hillcrest fellow was here to lead him out. He looked the part.

"Do I have a choice?"

"Life is full of choices."

The livelier body of William Hillcrest moved closer to the counter. His eyes went wide at a vase display of flowers. "These are nice." He passed the backs of his fingers across the petals of three remaining long-stem red roses. "Coincidence did not bring us together this morning. There are three roses, and three of us." He pulled one from the vase, smelled it—looking somewhat displeased with their lack of aroma—and tossed it over the dead body on the floor.

It was then he saw Eddie's book on the counter: *Crimson Petals*, by Cray Marrow.

He flipped through it, his index finger running along the pages. "Is it any good?" He opened to a random page, his red lips tracing the words.

"I just finished reading it," said Eddie. "I'm not sure what I think yet."

He flipped to the opening page and read:

"With life there must come death, and with death, life. That is the balance in this world. The pure shall not leave in death, but be guided to other worlds. If one must be guided, another must be protected to live, and if one must live, there must surely be balance with death."

"What is it about?"

"Well, it's like any other novel, I guess. Life. Death. The journey and everything in-between. There's a part in there about two brothers running through wheat fields I don't quite understand, and another about a man who may or may not be a werewolf. A little horror. A little literary. The novel jumps all over the place. I'm not sure about the ending, though … not sure I even like it. The guy hangs himself on a dogwood tree as the world around him burns. I think it would make more sense if he lived. I don't know."

"Sometimes a forest needs to burn before it can fully live again."

"A chance to start over."

The man who called himself William Hillcrest then said something that chilled the blood running through Eddie's veins as he closed the book and handed it to him.

"Perhaps it's time to start over again."

Together they burned down the station.

LINEAGE / 1862

Prior to William Hillcrest's death, he studied the hidden, darker side of his religion. The deacons Francis Dormant and Allen Edgar willfully offered assistance, as both were interested in his research. Desire for such knowledge was frowned upon by the church in general, but that hadn't stopped them.

"What do we know of Judas of Iscariot?" he asked to no boy in particular. On the table in front of Father Hillcrest lay an open Bible, a stack of weathered leather-bound books older than the three of them combined, and various scraps of foolscap with notes scribbled by fountain pen. Hundreds of pages were marked for reference with names and numbers sporadically jotted; bookmarks of twine lay between most pages of the books currently under observation. Open next to them was Hillcrest's money pouch containing last Sunday's offerings from the congregation; a paltry collection of coins.

"He betrayed Christ," said Allen, "for thirty pieces of silver." A silence followed, so the deacon added, "He felt horrible after Christ was condemned, and ..."

Francis took over, reading from the Bible after flipping to a bookmark, "'Then Judas, which had betrayed him, when he saw that he was condemned, repented himself, and brought again the thirty pieces of silver to the chief priests and elders / Saying, I have sinned in that I have betrayed the innocent blood. And they said, What is *that* to us? See thou *to that* / And he cast down the pieces of silver in the temple, and departed, and went—'"

"'And hanged himself,'" Father Hillcrest added. "Before his suicide, he went through much suffering, and partook in numerous evil deeds. Some say the man became mad. Please, read on."

"'And the chief priests took the silver pieces, and said, It is not lawful for us to put them into the treasury, because it is the price of blood,'" said Francis. "That was from the twenty-seventh chapter of Mathew."

Father Hillcrest took a large silver ring from what seemed like thin air. He flipped it end-over-end along the backs of his knuckles. On the face was a crucified dragon. "After Christ was condemned, what color was the robe the soldiers dressed him in?" He knew the answer. He was simply testing his deacons.

"Red," said Allen.

"Verse twenty-eight: 'And they stripped him, and put on him a scarlet robe,'" read Francis. "Why red?"

Father Hillcrest smiled. "Red is a very powerful color. But it is Judas we are concerned with for this study."

"Blood is red," said Francis, an outspoken thought.

"Good," said Father Hillcrest. "And …"

"And Judas took sacrament for the first time with Christ and the other apostles. He drank a symbol of Christ's blood, and ate of his flesh."

"For eternal life," said Allen.

"But not for Judas," said Father Hillcrest, "'After the sop Satan entered into him.'"

Francis looked dumbfounded, flipping pages. "Where is that?"

"John, thirteen-something,"

"What's *sop?*" asked Francis.

"It's unimportant. Let's move on to one named Vlad Tepes of the fifteenth century, also known as Vlad the Impaler. What have you learned from your studies?"

Allen spoke first. "He was known to punish his victims by impaling them on stakes, to publicly display them to frighten away his enemies."

"He killed tens of thousands of people in this fashion," said Francis, "and lined them around the city."

"Yes," said Father Hillcrest. "He had quite the thirst for blood. What do we know about his father?"

"His father was also named Vlad. Vlad the second, I think," said Francis.

Allen added, "Vlad Dracul."

"Which brings us to the Order of the Dragon, a secret fraternal organization of knights founded by King Sigismund of Hungary in the early fourteen-hundreds; what have you discovered in your readings?"

"The Order was aimed to uphold Christianity and to defend the Empire against the Turks," said Allen, pointing to a sketch he had made in his notes-taking. "They wore emblems. A dragon hanging on a cross, wings extended like the arms of Christ."

"You have taken to your assignments with much enthusiasm. Vlad's father gained the Dracul name much later in life. *Drac* in Romanian translates to *dragon*. Hence, *Vlad Dracul* translates to *Vlad the dragon*. *Ulea* or in this case '*u-l*' means *son of*."

Father Hillcrest made both young men jump as he slammed the old silver ring onto the table. When he uncovered it, the reptile stared up at them.

"Son of the dragon," said Francis.

"Doesn't *drac* also translate to *devil?*" asked Allen.

Father Hillcrest smiled. "Yes. *Drac* has a double meaning in this case. So we have Judas of Iscariot, and Vlad Dracul, but there was a third I had you study."

"Elizabeth Bathory," said Francis.

"Over a hundred years later. Also known as Erzsébet Báthory. What have you learned of this foul creature?"

"She was searching for eternal life?" asked Allen.

"One could say that."

After much hesitation, Francis said, "By bathing in the blood of children from noble birth. She associated herself with self-proclaimed witches, sorcerers, alchemists, and soon took up their arts. She was fascinated with beauty and felt that without vanity she was nothing."

"I read," said Allen, "that it started when she struck a servant girl. Some blood got onto her skin and she later thought she looked younger because of it."

"Her alchemist acquaintances agreed," added Father Hillcrest. "Mostly to maintain their hospitality with her, for she was very powerful. This "brilliant discovery" of hers led her to believe that if a little blood could help her complexion, a lot of blood would do even better. She began seeking out beautiful virgins, killing them—hundreds—and drinking and bathing in their blood."

"She even *drank* their blood?" asked Francis, looking ill.

"She had a thirst for blood; in this case, literal. All three subjects in our study had a thirst for blood. All three—"

"What about Judas?" interrupted Allen. "Judas didn't kill anyone, or bathe in blood, or drink blood, or impale anyone—"

Understanding swept over the deacons. Judas *had* figuratively bathed in another's blood. And, in the same manner, Judas *had* tasted blood—a symbol of blood anyway—and he *had* placed another on a stake, so to speak.

"I believe these three are connected. You may think I'm insane, and may not want to continue with these studies after tonight, but I believe these three are connected by some kind of disease, something similar to vampirism."

Both had heard the term vampire before, and until this night, they thought of it as only folklore. Allen Edgar grabbed the crucifix around his neck with a white knuckle grip. Francis Dormant, not owning such jewelry, gave the sign of the cross over his chest.

"Judas may have been the first, damned for all eternity after betraying the Christ." He removed his own silver crucifix necklace and held it out to Francis. "Here, take it … even if you think I am crazy, I want you each to take precautions."

"What about you?" asked Francis, who took it anyway and placed it around his neck.

"Hopefully I am wrong about all this, and medicine holds the true answer to their condition. Another subject for another day: a disease known as *porphyria cutanea tarda*, a blood disorder in which the over-production of phorphyines in the body begins to make the blood too "dirty" for the liver to cleanse. Some have even started the practice of bleeding out those who suffer this so called disease at regular intervals, forcing the body to produce new "clean" blood. The practice is still in the experimental stages, but I am hoping that the folklore regarding vampirism is nothing more than this ugly disease represented in a terribly wrongful fashion."

"What about the other two you had us study," asked Francis, "Vlad and Elizabeth?"

"They may have been part of this lineage. Judas, according to the Bible, was damned for his betrayal, and was cursed to roam for all eternity, undead to the world. Maybe he crossed paths with them sometime in their lives."

"It all makes sense," said Allen.

"Not to me," said Francis, holding Father Hillcrest's crucifix flat against his chest.

"According to folklore, vampires have an aversion to crosses, to silver, and can only be put to death by wooden stakes ... Judas was responsible for putting Christ on a cross. He betrayed him with thirty pieces of silver. He symbolically drank his blood for eternal life."

"Why can they not see their own reflections?" Francis wondered aloud, referring to his own understanding of the subject. "Is it guilt? Can they not look at themselves because of the guilt they carry?"

Allen said, "Maybe Vlad the Impaler was not cursed at all, but merely working on destroying the vampire legend?"

They were all valid questions, but Father Hillcrest sent them home for the night. It was growing late and he had yet to prepare for next Sunday's services. Before getting ready for bed, he took a deep breath, sighed, and blew out the candles. His dragon ring and the bag of donations were gone from the table.

THE CRUCIFIX

A crow greeted Eddie and his new friend as they pulled into the driveway of an old apartment complex. The sign in front of the building read BRENDEN ESTATES; atop perched the black bird. The apartments along Heritage Way were run down and poorly lit, like a ghost town hotel. Eddie lived in Apartment #5 on the first floor.

He had lived alone for most of his life, and never dated after his first love, Annie, a woman he had barely discovered before she died. Aside from those passing through his gas station, Eddie rarely had the opportunity to get to know anyone. Annie was fifty years gone, yet he still wore her ring on the chain around his neck.

They sat in the truck a while, the engine idling. The only light in the cab was from the soft yellow glow of a light post a few parking spaces away, and the red illumination of the truck's brakes. Eddie sighed deeply. "I'm not sure what to say. I keep expecting to wake up in my bed, you know? A dream perhaps."

Maybe that's all life is—one lucid dream from which you hope to wake.

"It's all gone," Eddie said. "The station's gone. Burned down. And I can't wake up from any of this. Here I sit, in the middle of the night with the living dead—who poses, by the way, no threat of eating me, or drinking my blood."

"I do not wish to eat you, nor do I wish to drink your blood," said the naked, blood-covered corpse sitting next to him. "They called me Phoenix," he said.

It came out of the blue.

The same crow from the sign fluttered down and landed on the hood of the truck.

"They were a breed of roses passed down the generations of my lineage from son to son. Ever since I can remember, the townsfolk called my grandfather Phoenix, and likewise my father. Later, after both passed on, I took over the gardening and inherited the name."

"And here you are," said Eddie, "risen from your ashes after you were burned at the stake a century and a half ago. Like the legendary bird."

A second crow landed on the hood and called out.

"Perhaps that's my purpose," said the priest. He grabbed the silver crucifix around his neck and met the stare of one of the crows. "To rise up from my ashes. To make things right. Sometimes we must fall in order to get back up again; sometimes we must lose everything to gain something new."

The sparkle of Annie's ring caught the dead man's eye.

"I hate gas stations," Eddie said, mostly to think of something other than his lost love. "Putting on a fake smile in the oddest of hours, dealing with loitering druggies and alcoholics, checking the tank levels, cleaning the restrooms … But it's what I've always done since my days at Westbury—worked my knuckles to the bones. Now the station's burned to the ground, maybe it's my time to rise and start anew. Maybe it's *me* you're here to save."

The apartment smelled of expired milk; a carton lay on the counter with its cap lost amongst the pile of dishes in the sink. Empty boxes from frozen dinners were piled on the garbage lid, scantily covering the contents beneath and balanced with perfection. Every nook of the place was layered in fine dust. Besides dirty laundry hanging over furniture, the rest of the apartment was rather clean for a man living alone.

"This house of yours is remarkable." William Hillcrest stared at the light fixture on the ceiling fan and gave one of the four blades a whirl, amazed as it cycled around. He unscrewed one of the bulbs until it went out, and then screwed it back in. He did this to the remaining three bulbs before examining the carpet. "Never had I imagined the future to hold such marvels." His hand brushed across the carpet and up the side of Eddie's worn couch. He rose from the floor, inspected a coffee stain on the center cushion and took a seat.

"I don't own the building, just the flat," Eddie said, returning from his bedroom with a change of clothes, "but it's a place to call home." He sat across from him on the leather La-Z-Boy and set the clothes onto the ottoman. "Father Hillcrest?"

"Please, call me William."

"William, then. I would feel more comfortable knowing *you* felt more comfortable …" Eddie eyed the blue jeans, sweater, and socks between them. "Sorry, I couldn't find clean underwear, but the outfit should fit you nicely. You're about my size."

"I am sure they will be fine," he said, slipping into the jeans.

"Would you like something to drink?" asked Eddie, already on his way to the kitchen. "I've got beer, soda …" he smelled the milk on the counter and grimaced, "water—"

"Water will be fine."

"Good, because I'm out of beer and soda. Looks like I need to do a little shopping. I'm not used to company." Eddie returned with two waters, handing one to his guest.

"All this is so interesting." He held the water bottle up to the light and squeezed the plastic a few times before figuring out the cap.

"Tell me about it." Eddie downed half his bottle.

"Tell you about what?"

"It's just an expression, like how's it hanging?"

Another confused expression crossed his face.

"Tell me about the chain you carry around your neck. "It was the only thing on you when you entered the station."

William Hillcrest reached beneath his collar and pulled out the silver crucifix.

"I cannot imagine how frightened you must have been—how frightened you must be now, as we speak—having seen a cadaver like myself, naked, no less, and covered in earth, staggering into your presence—"

"I'm still trying to forget." Eddie finished the rest of his water. The sweat on his brow was finally drying. "That, and burning down my station after sucking the life out of one of my customers … well, an armed robber anyway. Take my mind out of this lucid nightmare and tell me about that good ol' wholesome symbol around your neck. Please."

"When I turned eight, my mother gave it to me as a gift. We were never a wealthy family, so her giving it to me was quite extraordinary." He held the charm up for Eddie to see.

It resembled pewter more than silver. The shape matched the burn mark on his palm.

"It was given to her by *her* father—my grandfather, caretaker for the church. How he got the crucifix is a mystery. Some in the family say he found it, some say he molded it from old silver coins, and there are even some who claim he stole it from a body in the morgue—another place where he tended gardens. Knowing my grandfather, and his later insanity, I am inclined to believe the third of these stories.

"My mother wanted me to have it for protection. She had worn it around her neck the majority of her life, and had fallen ill only once or twice during that time, never severe."

"What was your mother's name?" asked Eddie.

"Emma Lillian Hillcrest, by marriage to my father. She was a beautiful woman. James, my father—Phoenix— always said it was a work of God that brought he and my mother together ... that, or blindness; her face was made of silk and his from leather. She said that as long as I wore it close to my heart, nothing could hurt me; it would protect me from the evils in and of the world.

"The following winter she began coughing and became bedridden. The doctor said her lungs were filling with fluid. But by then it was too late. I sat by her side for two weeks, holding this crucifix in one hand, holding my mother's hand in the other. I kept insisting she take it back, at least until she was feeling better, but she always turned it down. She made me promise to never remove it from my neck."

"Did you ever take it off?"

"I gave it to one of my deacons."

THE FIRST TAKEN / 1862

Francis Dormant held the silver crucifix within a fist of white, the chain hanging around his wrist. He took it with him as he ventured outside to see who had called his name. With the heavy rain beating down on the roof, it sounded more like the wind than a man or a woman, but he checked just in case. A tree tickled the wall closest to his bedroom. A crow perched on one of the sills. It was the bird that woke him, its feathers pattering against the glass as it ruffled them dry. A flash of lightning lit the darkness around him with a thunderous roar.

Within that flash, he noticed there was not just one bird by his room, but half a dozen, all fat and huddled underneath his window. A few crows pecked the earth, for worms perhaps. A second flash revealed another six of the birds gathered in the oak's branches, the rumble more distant. Francis was about to step back indoors when the sparkle of metal caught his eye.

He held the candlestick, but it didn't offer much light. Wind rushed melted wax down the sides as he tried to hide it from the rain. The necklace dangled just above the flame. He looked past it to the crows. A hint of silver as one of them ripped at the ground. A sphere of yellow surrounded Francis as he walked toward the object in the mud.

A crow cawed as he passed the tree. None seemed

bothered by his presence. Those on the ground didn't stir; they weren't feasting on worms, but maggots turning in the carcass of one of their peers. A dead crow lay before the others, torn at the gut, picked hollow. Red beaks fed eagerly at the white larvae. The silver object was in the middle of the mess.

Francis shooed the birds away with his foot, and one attacked his ankle before flying to the tree. The others followed and stared down at the boy. A soft flash of lightning showed him a frightening image—two dozen or more black beady eyes bearing down on him from above, all their beaks red.

With help from the yellow light around him, he found a ring resting in the flesh; a maggot squirmed within it. As he reached for it, the crucifix burned against the soft skin at his wrist. While protecting the wick of the candle from the rain, he had scorched the little cross until it was hot and black with carbon. He rubbed the burn and reached again.

Most of the large ring was buried in the bird, the band upright. As he pulled it free, he turned the face of it toward him, which was round and flat like a coin, its creases filled flush with blood and insides from the crow. He used a patch of wet grass to clean it out and revealed a crucifix, much like the one in his hand. Instead of Christ, a dragon hung in His place, with wings outstretched as if nailed to it. It was identical to the emblems worn by those in the Order of the Dragon. Sigismund of Hungary might have worn a similar ring, perhaps even Vlad Dracul.

A second crow cawed.

Father Hillcrest's crucifix felt heavy in his hand; he regretted ever having to give it back, but was only borrowing it for as long as he would let him. It still felt warm from the candle. The thought of it burning him ran chills down his spine as he imagined a scar of the cross forever marked on his skin.

The crow before him must have found the ring and swallowed it and for whatever reason it had died outside his bedroom window. The other birds had torn their friend apart to get to it. And now Francis Dormant, young deacon in the church, happened upon it. It could all be coincidence; however, he felt he had to get the ring to Father Hillcrest.

Wind flickered the candle out, leaving Francis in darkness. A half moon hid behind the trees. The rain had started again, first soft, and then in downpour. He sat there a while, the rain washing the ring clean. A dragon on a cross. A band of silver. The flesh and blood of a crow washing away at his feet. A sick sacrament for the other black birds watching from the tree. *'I have sinned in that I have betrayed the innocent blood'* he had read earlier of Judas, *'and he cast down the pieces of silver in the temple, and departed, and went and hanged himself.'* Francis imagined a man hanging from the tree in front of him with his eyes pecked open by the crows like two pitted olives.

Water pelted him as he stared at the ring and speculated what brought him outdoors, and then he remembered. Someone outside had called his name ever so softly. At first he thought it was the wind playing tricks, but somehow the sound had drawn him outside, where he found himself kneeling over the body of a dead crow, digging within its opened stomach like the carnivorous birds, and finding the old silver ring.

Fran-cis …

He turned on his heels, heart in his throat. It came from behind him, but no one was there. He placed the ring on his index finger—two fingers might have fit within the band— as he rose from the ground. The crows in the oak mocked him; he half-expected one to call his name.

Francis turned to his window. Waiting for him was a reflection of bright blue eyes. They bore down on him from a black shadowy essence twice his size, directly behind him. He closed his eyes and, with the crucifix, reached back—for what, he was unsure. He felt nothing and turned around despite any subconscious warning and opened his eyes, but nothing was there. Another trick of the night. His heart pounded. The crows cackled again, all dozen cawing madly. Rain continued to pour. His clothes were soaked through and he couldn't help but shiver, both scared and cold. As he turned back around, the blue eyes were waiting for him again in the window. They glowed brilliant and blinding as the black spirit changed shape. Wing-like appendages stretched outward as if to embrace him, twice as wide as the creature was tall, a mouth opening in the black to swallow him whole. It loomed over his reflection, his own eyes glimmering in the glass.

Francis Dormant did the only thing he could think of besides wet himself. He ran.

The moon peeked again from between two gray clouds like an unfocussed eye watching over him.

Francis threw the candelabra over his shoulder, but there was nothing there, yet he could feel that nothing preying upon him. He waited for black appendages to wrap around his body and choke the air from his lungs. The cross tips of the crucifix buried hard into his hand—the passion comforting—while his other hand held the growing cramp at his side as he ran as fast as he could muster.

It didn't dawn on him that he was distancing himself from the safety of his home until something grabbed his foot and he fell to the ground, face first. Not the hand of his pursuer, but the branch of a rosebush. Francis felt a sprain climb to his calf and thorns stabbing his leg like the crown of thorns placed onto Christ.

He watched puffs of air leave his mouth, his chest rising and falling and trying to keep up with his heart. He waited for blue eyes, but he was alone. Fog filled the emptiness around him. At any moment he knew he'd be taken by the black form. It was out there waiting.

Francis worked his leg free and noticed the single wilting flower, a red rose trimmed in black. It was pressed flush against the ground. His body had smashed it flat. It was the only rose on the plant; the rest of it was as barren as the dry and twisted fingers holding his foot. For the moment, he wasn't at all concerned about untangling himself, nor were his thoughts on the shadowy essence that had chased him to this point; he was instead instantly infatuated by the rose. He picked it from the ground and let the thorns sink in. A trail of blood ran down his fingers—nearly to his elbow—as dark as the petals. Francis brought it to his nose and inhaled.

It was then he felt the sting of thorns. Francis threw the rose to the ground as if it had bit him. Back in the mud, it no longer held vibrant color, but was dead and wilted, the once red petals now gray and shriveled flakes of ash, the hollow stem as brittle as a bone in a bird wing, like the crows back at the house where he had found the ring.

Francis looked at his palm, but the ring was gone. Three

lacerations leaked his oil. As he wiped the blood onto his legs, a heavy cloud darkened the sky and covered what was left of the moon. Mud danced to life as heavy drops from above crashed down around him. He was already wet, but the downpour soaked him through in seconds. Francis clawed at the earth around him. The ring had to be there somewhere. His foot pulled loose from the rosebush as if it were tumbleweed. He got to his knees and brought rock after rock to his face in hopes of finding it somewhere in the muck; he used the crucifix to pick at the wet ground around him. He listened for the cling of metal striking metal, or the luck of it simply slipping back onto his finger. But luck wanted nothing to do with Francis Dormant. The ring and the dragon were gone; no one would ever believe he had found it, not even Edgar. A ring from the Order of the Dragon, found right outside his bedroom window, in the belly of a rotting crow, and he had lost it whilst chased by black fog with blue eyes. Who would believe such a story? It sounded as contrived as any fib from a young boy's vivid imagination.

Francis slapped a cold wet hand against his face, but found he wasn't dreaming. He stood up and looked around, still a bit dazed still from the fall. Maybe he had been dreaming. Perhaps lucidly. Perhaps he had sleepwalked, sleepran, sleepfell into the mud and woke up thinking he had lost what was never really there. Perhaps his studies with Allen and Father Hillcrest had burrowed deep into his mind and simply wanted out.

Feeling absurd, Francis shook some of the mud from his body. The rain caused brown to run down his arms and legs. Natural brown hair stuck to his face. He let the sky wash over him, the moon just a ghost behind the cloud cover. A crack of thunder bounced against the mountains from afar, and from not so far away the sad cry of a wolf called out to the night. Francis stood like a cross, arms outstretched, his head tilted back with his face to the sky. He couldn't get any wetter, and he felt more awake than when he had first left the house, as if he *had* been asleep. The crows. The ring. The field. The red rose. Was it all a dream? Blood running the length of his wrist was real enough; the rain smudged translucent red over his skin. He looked to the rose, which only held the colors of decomposition. The rosebush it once connected to was only a twisted stump of weather-hardened wood, no larger than a forearm and hand with elongated and thorny fingers sticking out from the ground.

Rain fell hard as he made his way home.

Francis had run farther out than he first thought, but soon he was at the oak tree sheltering the crows, then the house, and then his bedroom window where a black moving shape on the ground filled him instantly with panic. It was a black crow pecking at the dead one beneath his window. The oak tree came to life as five cawing crows fluttered down from the branches and joined in on the feast. Another half dozen called out from within the tree. An even dozen. Thirteen if you counted the dead one ravaged at his feet. A glint of silver drew him closer.

Francis watched his hot breath pillow from his parted lips like a steam engine.

He shooed the birds away with his feet as he stepped closer. Most flew back to the tree, but not the one tearing apart the carcass. It pulled at black entrails, not feasting, simply tearing the bird apart. Francis kicked it away, but it fluttered back, not the least bit intimidated by his presence, nor his boot. Not until he brushed its feathers with his hand did the bird give up and join the others. It pecked him and let out a caw and flew away. For what seemed the second time that night, Francis reached in to pull out the ring. He let the rain wash it clean, revealing a dragon crucified on a cross.

Another crack of lightning lit the night.

Francis stood and was met by his reflection. A drenched young man stared back at him, hair plastered to his head. It wasn't his reflection to which his eyes were drawn, but to the glowing blue eyes from the shadowy figure next to him.

THREE

Eddie grabbed a couple more bottles of water from the kitchen and handed one to William Hillcrest, who was starting to look a little pale on the couch. "I found some pita bread by the microwave. I can't remember ever buying it, but it still looks good. Sorry I don't have much to offer in terms of food." He untied the bag and handed him a piece. "Appropriate, don't you think. Unleavened bread and water. It's like our own private communion. If you don't mind my asking, why did they burn you at the stake? The town priest, of all people."

"Because of the manner in which they found my two deacons, Francis Dormant and Allen Edgar," he said, and paused to smell the bread. "I don't mind you asking. If you are willing to help me, you at least deserve to know why I died, whether or not it explains why I am even here in the first place.

"They found Francis first. One-by-one I noticed those in my congregation gathering around the gate leading to the chapel. And then I saw the horror hanging on the fence through the window in my rectory. His body—what was left of it—was held in place by the post stabbing through his neck. One of his arms was hunched around another post like he was trying to hold onto it for dear life, but it was only part of him—a combination of his head, torso and right arm. Blood was still dripping from his waist to an ungodly puddle where his feet should have been.

"His mother was the only one that did anything. "Francis," she said. Just his name. Tears fell from her eyes like rain. I offered to help, but she slapped me in the face and pushed me away saying it was my fault this had happened. The crowd just stared, not one of them able to find the courage to help lift her son from the gridiron.

"It looked like his body had been ripped—or pulled— in two. His torso perched on the fence like a scarecrow. Everything below his waist was gone. Intestine dangled out, some of it reaching the ground. His mouth was cut open in an elongated scream. She ran to him and tried to force his eyes closed, but they were gone; two black holes stared back and dripped down his face with a color far unlike blood. She tried to close his mouth, but his lower jaw was flaccid. "I'm here for you now, Francis," she told him. Without his legs, he was light enough for her to lift him off the fence on her own. No one but me offered to help.

"Laying Francis on the ground, she noticed the small bag tied around his neck, the initials W and H stitched onto it. *My* initials. Loosening the tie, she poured its contents and counted out a handful of silver coins. She took two and placed them over his empty eye sockets, pulled him close.

"A second piece of Francis was found by a portly farmer named Frederick Henessey. He volunteered each Sunday with yard upkeep at the church. He hadn't heard the commotion at the front of the building until he ran around the corner screaming for help, but no one seemed to notice his outcries. Most were busy watching Mrs. Dormant on the ground near the fence. "Legs!" he yelled to the crowd. He shook a stranger on the arm and said, "There's just legs back there," and then shook the shoulders of a woman as lifeless as everyone else. Frederick wanted to slap her; I could see it in his eyes. He wanted to slap all of them. He walked over to Mrs. Dormant and saw the head, torso and arms of Francis in her lap.

"Frederick kneeled next to her and said, "The rest of your son is around back. I can take you to him." She glared at me as if it were my fault and said, "All this silver is yours if you carry him for me." She handed him the bag of coins—tithing from the week prior—and had to force him to take it. He carried the boy as if he were holding a bag of mulch, and walked with Mrs. Dormant to the back of the church grounds, and I was the only one to follow. We cut across the lawn and past my garden of roses and I prayed along the way. It was all I could do.

"The lower half of Francis was in one of the rose flower beds, nothing more than a waist and stomach protruding from a pair of britches, legs sprawled in a V-shape. One foot pointed skyward, the other was missing completely. Besides the blood pooling from his waistline and where the missing foot was ripped away at the shin, his britches were spotless. Three red roses with blackened edges—my Phoenix Roses—rested on his crotch, bound together by a silver ring with a crucified dragon on its face.

"Frederick placed the top half of Francis down next to the legs so that he was again almost a whole boy. The only thing missing was his foot and, as if on cue, the town Sheriff joined the three of us. He held the third and final piece of Francis Dormant in one hand, and in the other, my crucifix necklace. He said he found the boot—with the foot still inside—on the mat in front of his house, as if it were a cat begging for a bowl of milk. He said he found my silver necklace clasped around the bootstrap."

A siren from a fire truck blasting by the apartment interrupted the story and startled them both. Another one sounded like it was on the way. Eddie moved to the window and parted the curtains in time to see the red and white flashes of the second fire truck as it passed the complex. The wailing siren startled his guest out of his seat to join him at the window. They both watched as a few police cruisers sped by. They were headed to Eddie's station.

Unknown When

"This is a strange time in which you live," said William Hill-crest. His long, dark hair seemed to have grayed since they arrived at the apartment.

"It's the end of the world as we know it," said Eddie, "and I feel fine."

"The end of days?"

"It's a song, but I don't feel fine. We can't stay long. They will be looking for me soon with questions I can't answer."

"Those in the red chariots?"

"No, the red chariots are off to try to undo what we just did at my station. It'll be the black and white chariots coming for me, or perhaps the sheriff's white paddy wagon. Either way, they'll haul me off, ask me questions, and lock me up in a rubber room for the rest of my life for killing that guy at the station and then setting the station ablaze."

"You didn't take that man's life. He was robbing you with a firearm. It was me who took his life, and—"

"You don't exist." As the words left his mouth, Eddie realized it could be true. Maybe he conjured up the whole thing in his subconscious, creating his undead friend here just to cope with what had happened back at the station, shock perhaps; maybe he killed the robber and set the station on fire to cover it up—a conspiracy between Eddie, Eddie's mind, and the dead imaginary priest who now

stood next to him in his apartment as he spied through the curtains. It all made sense. "I killed that guy, at least that's how authorities will see it, and they'll have questions, questions I can't answer to their satisfaction because it's all ludicrous nonsense—you being dead and all—such as what happened to the man on the floor before he turned all crisp like, and why they found two bullet casings in the store that don't match his gun—because *I* shot you—and who owned the charred black Suburban out front with the spinners, and why the register was found open and empty … Why I fled the scene and torched the place." Eddie was rambling, but it was all he could do to keep himself from losing it. He was talking to an undead priest in his apartment, watching fire chariots race by. "They'll come looking for me, so we can't stay here long. I don't know where we can go, but we can't stay here tonight."

William Hillcrest placed a cold hand onto Eddie's shoulder. He looked as though he had aged ten years since they first met back at the station, nearly middle-aged. He looked sincerely into Eddie's eyes and said, "Forgive me for all I have wrought upon you. I have made it so you must sacrifice everything for my benefit, including your life if these men of authority find you. I don't know how to repay you."

Eddie looked around his apartment: to the couch in the living room with the stains and holes in the fabric, to the kitchen and its ever-growing pile of dishes, to the littered carpet and mildewed bathroom. He had given up trying to impress anyone years ago. He had the apartment because it was the only place he could afford while working nights at the station. He had been alone his entire life. As an orphan, he had no immediate family. As a young adult, he had chosen not to make a family. Annie was in his twenties and seemed lifetimes ago. As a man of thirty to forty, he had lived in isolation, and from forty to twice that number, he had also chosen solitude, a life of survivalism, making ends meet and nothing more.

"In a weird way," said Eddie, "I think you have already repaid me. Whether or not you are in my mind or somehow in my world, you have given me life again. I know that sounds strange, maybe a bit hokey, but it's true. You've given me purpose."

"What purpose is that?"

"*My* purpose is to help you find *your* purpose. You died. You died a horrible, painful death I can't even begin to imagine. But, for some reason, you came back. You were burned at the stake and now you have risen from your ashes in my time—my *when*, as you say—and have stumbled into my miserable little life. Ever since Annie died, I've been alone in the world, tortured somehow in my own personal hell. I feel like I've been waiting for this kind of adventure. We need to find out why you are here. We know what keeps you alive—or walking upright, anyhow—because I can see it in your face. You're growing old before my eyes. You need blood or soon you'll start looking *my* age. Back at the station you were nothing but a rotting corpse. You were falling apart before you … well, before you took that poor fellow."

"He was going to kill you."

"He would have shot me just for the Kit Kat." Eddie laughed uncomfortably. "I saw it in his eyes."

"I could see it in his heart," said William Hillcrest. "His heartbeat was red, though black deep down; his corruption glowed around him in an aura the color of blood."

"Does it hurt?"

"What, dying?"

Eddie thought of Annie falling against the rock.

"*Decaying* might be a better word. When I first saw you, before you ... well, you were basically broken bones held together by flaps of skin. And you got worse as you moved through the store. Does that part of it hurt? I guess that's what I'm asking."

"After death there is no pain. What I feel is the workings of a body that has surpassed death. I feel nothing but the burden of my scars." He held out his hand to show the cross burned into his palm, and then felt for the identical mark on his chest as he stared out the window to the busy night lights.

Eddie stood with him a while, and then asked what he was really wanting to ask.

"Does death hurt?"

It was a question he'd been asking himself ever since he had applied for his Social Security, before he realized it wouldn't be enough to get him by, which was the reason he started working the night shift in the first place. Eddie feared passing over into the great unknown, the great above or below or wherever death would send him. It wasn't that he feared the existence of Heaven and Hell, or the possibility of going to either of those places, to meet a god or whatnot, but the possibility that there would be *nothing* waiting for him on the other side. Simply switching off life like a light switch, or cutting the strings of a marionette—*that* is what scared him most. Maybe Annie was waiting for him on the other side. Maybe she wasn't. If there was nothing but a blackness or a whiteness beyond life, he wanted to know if pain would be the last thing he felt—not love, not compassion, or an understanding, not even forgiveness, but pain. Eddie feared that death would hurt.

William Hillcrest looked to his feet. "I thought you might ask me if there's really is a god." He smiled, adding, "To which I would have said, 'that's something you will need to remember' or something clever. Does death hurt? In my case, everything leading up to my death involved pain, but death itself, the passing over … it hurts no more than opening a window for air. Death is just another stage in life."

"We really should be going." Eddie took a deep breath, as if preparing for his next stage in life.

"How long do you suppose we have?"

"Until they come knocking." Eddie glanced at the clock hanging in the living room. The hour hand was between the one and the two. "If the criminalists sent to the scene are anything like they are on television, then they could be banging on the door by sunrise. Probably late morning, though, but we shouldn't chance it." He could tell his new friend had no idea what he was talking about.

Eddie gave his apartment a once-over. This would be the last time he'd set foot in a place he could call home. Until his last breath, he'd be on the run. His old life was gone forever. They could take his truck north, he guessed, and could make it across the border to Canada before the authorities ever ran his plates. CSI would process the gas station, determine who was working the shift; they'd run the plates on the Suburban out front and link it to the corpse next to the register—the money burned to ash but presumed stolen—and they'd come looking for Eddie once they put it together he was on the clock that night and that his truck was missing. Eddie had no known living relatives they could interview, so they'd look for him at the apartment after pulling his employment history, look for him there, find him and his truck AWOL, and Eddie would quickly become key suspect in a homicide and arson. He didn't know if his prints were on file—unless they inked him at the orphanage—but either way, they'd use a search warrant or bust his front door to match his fingerprints with those at the crime scene if there were any to process. They'd be looking for the missing gun Eddie had stashed behind the seat of his truck. He would have to ditch the truck.

So many scenarios went through Eddie's mind that he had to sit down. He sat next to his dead friend.

"Vancouver?" he said.

"Sounds haunting."

And then it struck him. They couldn't flee to Canada. Crossing the border nowadays required two forms of identification. He had read that in the paper somewhere. His dead friend was at a loss, and so was Eddie, who only had a Washington State driver's license and a single credit card to his name. Out of habit, he checked for his wallet. An empty pocket reminded him that the robber at the station had taken it and slid it into his own back pocket. It was pointless to fret over it now. Credit cards would leave trails.

"We'll have to shack up at a motel for the night. At least until we figure out our options. We should get out of Brenden for sure. There's a dive just past Seattle called … oh, I can't remember. It's on Freemont Street. None of this makes sense to you, I know, but bear with me. I need to think this through."

"I don't mind—"

"We'll need cash. Eddie rose from the couch and headed to the kitchen. He pulled a coffee tin from one of the cabinets and reached inside and pulled out a wad of bills—his emergency stash. He organized the bills, laying one on top of the other, amazed to find there was over four hundred dollars' worth of twenties, about a hundred in tens, and an inch-thick wad of fives and ones. About seven or eight hundred dollars. Eddie wrapped a band around the wad of green and turned back to his dead friend.

"This stuff makes the world go around. There's an ice chest down the hall if you want to grab it for me. We should take whatever's edible, whatever's good in the fridge."

William Hillcrest looked confused.

"Ice chest. Right," said Eddie. "It's plastic … it's the big red box down the hall with a white top. You can't miss it. If there's stuff still in it, just dump it on the floor."

There was more in the apartment than he first thought. He filled a grocery bag with a few boxes of crackers, canned goods—almost forgetting the can-opener, Ramen soup, and any nonperishable he could find.

Plastic ground on plastic as William returned with the cooler.

"Why is it red if it's meant for ice?"

Eddie laughed and grabbed a jar of peanut butter and half a loaf of bread. "I'm not sure why. There are usually only two options: red or blue. I liked the red, I guess." He opened the fridge and pulled out a bottle of rum and a half-empty two-liter of Coke, a package of bologna that still looked edible, and some cheese. He tossed it all into the chest. Everything else in the fridge was spoiled.

FALLING APART

They were on the road no longer than ten minutes when he asked Eddie if they could pull over. He had eaten two pieces of the round cut meat slices and a few pieces of pita bread and they wanted out of him. His stomach lurched as he reached for the door handle. The truck not quite to a stop, he fell out and rolled onto his side. Bottled water and chunks of red and white purged from his mouth and onto the gravel along the road. A sign above him read: SOFT SHOULDER. He didn't know what it meant, but guessed it dealt with the gravel beneath him. It wasn't soft by any means, but it wasn't the black hardened surface the truck drove on either.

"You okay down there?" Eddie leaned toward him. The safety harness bound him inside what he had called *the cabin*.

William thought he might have to vomit, but nothing came up. He spit bile.

"We may have a problem," he said to Eddie.

Eddie's face looked concerned. "I had a feeling we just might. You're dying on me, aren't you? Here we are with all this food, and it wants nothing to do with you."

William joined him inside the truck, wiping his mouth. He took the bottle of water Eddie held out to him, hesitated, and drank half of it. His stomach instantly lurched again, and the water coughed out of him.

"Don't worry," said Eddie. "It's just water and this truck is far from pristine."

Lights on the front of the truck illuminated the road. Vehicles ahead left demon trails of red. In the opposite lane, pairs of white light rushed toward them. In *his* time, William could see the stars, millions of them. Now he counted only five above the skyline, and a sixth he knew was not a star at all, nor a comet, but something anomalous because of its slow travel across the sky.

"How old were you when you died?"

William held his hand up to his face so he could see the backs of his knuckles. He knew what Eddie implied. He felt the change taking over him; not pain, but a weakening. His hand was much different than the hand he had used to place the rose on his fallen victim back at the station. His hand had changed with the rest of his body. It was middle-aged, slightly wrinkled and weathered, like the hand he had used so long ago to keep his place in his bible as he read to his congregation.

"I was not much older than I must appear to you now."

"That's what I was afraid of. Buckle in. We should hurry before you start falling apart on me. You look pale, and I don't think it's because you just yacked up your supper."

Eddie's fingers met William's brow.

"You're getting cold. I think you're decomposing."

William scratched his wrist. Lines of skin peeled away. Blood rushed to the wound, but the color wasn't quite right.

"I need blood."

"We'll work on that," said Eddie. "We've got a while 'til the motel. Tell me what happened to your other deacon."

THE SECOND TAKING / 1862

Dew was settling for the night as gray clouds of winter fog swept into the valley. Allen Edgar was at the woodpile just outside his disappearing home. Despite the chill, Allen rubbed a sweaty forearm across a sweaty forehead. He had been splitting wood for nearly an hour and was close to being finished with the chore. The two piles lay in awkward humps around him. Wind wheezed through a nearby oak and blew its dead leaves to his feet. Another gust of wind brought a sighing much like a drawn-out pronunciation of his name: *aaahhh-len.*

He lifted the oil lamp at his feet toward the noise.

"Is anyone there?"

The only response was another wind-exhaled sigh.

Allen buried the axe into the large stump he used to split the logs and took the oil lamp with him to follow the sounds. It only took a few steps to make the house behind him fade away, and a few more for the stump and piles of split wood to vanish within the fog. He stopped at the base of the tree and listened.

Silence and nothing more.

He was about to turn back when he heard a fluttering within the tree branches above him. A large black crow with beady eyes and a curved black beak cawed before taking flight with its satin wings. It landed ten paces away on a wooden fence post. He could only distinguish a silhouette of the bird through the dense fog, but could see its wings flapping, struggling for balance. Another crow landed on the post next to it. Another, one he hadn't noticed in the tree, flew from a higher branch and joined the others.

A gust of wind caused more leaves to rain over him. Shivering, Allen turned and started walking back to the house, holding the oil lamp close for warmth. The crows at his back bode him farewell.

And then he heard his name.

It's only my imagination, he thought, and then heard it again.

Allen spun on his heels. A group of ten or more crows had gathered while his back was turned. Some were on fenceposts; most were pecking the ground like chickens. He walked toward the gathering near the fence, the oil lamp raised in front of him. The two-dimensional silhouettes slowly became three-dimensional as those perched on the fence joined the mass feeding on the ground. They tore at an indistinguishable mound near the thorny dead remains of an old rosebush. Not even when he set the lamp on the closest post did they flee. He picked a small stone from the dirt at his boots and tossed it to the ring of crows. They fluttered, and one cawed, but most stayed. One tore away a chunk of lax matter and took flight.

After a long hesitation, Allen climbed over the short wooden fence and landed on the frozen-mush ground. The birds scattered, but only after Allen stepped on one's wing by accident; after a mad cry, the entire band flew off, as if they worked from a single mind. He watched their flapping bodies bob up and down as if strung from imaginary

puppeteers. They flew back to the oak tree, which had been swallowed by the fog.

Left behind were the skinless remnants of something large; the meat on its pockmarked body had a grayish tint like the air around him. Maggots squirmed within the carcass. As he wondered what even brought him out here in the first place, he couldn't help but feel watched. The fog was all around him and he was alone in his soft sphere of orange light.

The sound came from behind him.

Allen swiveled in time to see a dark form with gangly appendages before it faded into the night, like a black sheet carried by the wind. He knelt to the ground, wondering if it—whatever *it* may have been—had seen him, and he found himself resting in the remains of not a wild animal, but a human body. Allen vomited as he backed away, his knees covered in gore. He smeared his fingers on the field grass, wiping away the gelatinous decomposition. A single yellow maggot crawled over the back of his hand. He shook it off and nearly screamed.

The orange light around him dimmed as the wick in the lamp burned the last of the oil. Through the sparse light loomed a dark shadow at least two feet taller than a man. Its glowing blue eyes glared down at him.

Edgar ran until his chest burned and his sides ached and he was hundreds of yards farther into the field, completely lost in the heavy fog. He ran until his legs gave out and he fell to his knees, scraping them raw. Holding his side, he rose and walked for close to ten minutes, thinking hope was lost and that he would walk forever in a purgatory of mist and be taken by that strange blackness, and then he stumbled upon the rose. Thorns snagged the cuff of his pant leg. It was strange to see a flower blooming so marvelously at such a late hour; he wondered how anything could be so

(blood)

red. Everything around him was a mixture of gray, yet the rose bled with color; just the sight of it filled his heart with warmth and took the fear away. He wanted to rip the plant from its roots and hold it like a shield for protection, but he couldn't destroy such a beautiful thing.

Without it, he found the fence and crossed over, knowing he was close; he just had to follow the wooden posts until he saw the old oak. And then he found it, the birds gone from its naked branches. The fog began to dissipate, as if showing the way home.

He could see the house now—he was so close, if only had had taken the rose—and the mounds of split oak, the stump on which he had used to chop the wood, and the hole in the round where the axe used to …

Behind him, the creature called his name.

Allen felt cold breath down the nape of his neck and imagined a towering shape as dark as the night, eyes that would turn his hair white as their blue light sucked the life out of him, an abysmal smile revealing a blood-filled mouth opening ever so slowly, outstretched arms like the wings of a bat wrapping around his body and squeezing until nothing remained. The eyes casting twin reflections of Allen losing his mind in a silent scream.

THREE

"Whatever took Allen Edgar that night split the young boy into three sections, as it had with Francis Dormant." William Hillcrest felt the hunger calling him as Eddie drove them to a place called a *motel*. His throat thirsting for blood, he continued telling the tale.

"Allen's foot was found by Geoff Dormant, Francis' father, of all people. Geoff Dormant was on his way to buy fruit at the market when he saw the foot nestled in a bush. At first he thought it was nothing but a boot, and then he found a young boy's foot inside, much like his own son's foot found only days prior. He brought the appendage with him to the market, smiling and waving it around to those around him as they looked to him with crazed eyes. He was no longer George Dormant; he was displaced from the world, lost in insanity. He set the boot in a bin of cantaloupe and smashed his head against the brick exterior of the market until he joined his son in death.

"A larger piece of Allen—his head, upper torso and arms—was found on the fence posts around the church grounds by his mother—an all too familiar scene. I remember the look on her face as she ran to him. She tried to get him down herself—no one else offered their assistance— but the post buried into his neck kept ripping the skin, and what was left of his body just slid further down the iron. He held onto the fence involuntarily, like Christ to the cross. His head drooped against his chest. It was all so terrible. She knelt before him in a pool of his blood. No one offered to help, except yours truly, but she wanted nothing more than to push me away from her son. She pulled again, pulled him closer to the ground, and the upper half of Allen tore free with a horrible sound and he fell onto her in an evil embrace. She kissed his neck, his awful drained skin. She lifted his face and tried to wake him from his sleep, but his eyes simply looked back with their emptiness. His eyes were gone. Black ran from their empty sockets and down his cheeks as he smiled at her with a mouth sheared from ear to ear."

"Dear God," said Eddie, "like a jack-o'-lantern." He shifted in his seat uncomfortably.

"Very much like one, yes."

"I presume they found the last third of your deacon?"

"Allen's lower half—minus a foot—was found on the Sheriff's doorstep in one mammoth lump, soaking his porch red."

A long silence filled the truck cabin.

"Both my deacons: torn to three and left for us to find."

"And they suspected *you?*"

"Not at first. The townsfolk gathered for their funerals. We buried them the same day. I even ran the services. I remember it was raining, as if God were crying. I remember everyone throwing dirt onto the coffins as we lowered them into the plots. All eyes on me. All but those I helped bury. We never found their eyes. I could not help but think that inside each of their coffins my deacons were forced to smile.

"It wasn't until weeks later that I was apprehended; they pulled me from the chapel during Mass. They marched in, six dressed in black, the Sheriff shouting, "Murderer! We have found the murderer!" Two of his deputies were behind him and holding rifles pointed to the pulpit in case I tried something rash or made a run for it. Three others were there, but I don't remember their faces, although one held rope and tailed the group. I knew half of them personally, knew their secrets from confession. As they walked up the rows of pews, I remember seeing dark auras floating ahead of them all. A black mist, like that which I saw around the man at the station. Red filled their eyes.

"I remember apologizing to the congregation for the intrusion as they tied my hands behind my back, everyone craning their necks as they led me out of the chapel and onto the courtyard.

"Once there, a crowd of people I didn't know spit in my face, punched me in the gut, bloodied my lip with the stock of a rifle. The rope was yanked hard behind me, strange hands holding me upright as the two with rifles—once my friends—held a barrel to my chin to prop it up and another to my heart. The Sheriff dangled my silver crucifix necklace—the one I loaned to Francis—from his finger-tips, swaying it back and forth with pendulous conviction. I watched tiny reflections of the cross sway back and forth in the black of his eyes."

BLOOD

By the time they pulled up to the motel on Freemont Street, Eddie was panicked. He wasn't scared for his own life, but for the life—if it could be called such—for his new friend. The red neon glow of the vacancy sign in the truck didn't help. William Hillcrest had stopped aging, but his body hadn't stopped deteriorating. A vile smell of human decomposition worked the glands in his throat. William's eyes had sunken deep into their sockets. Where he had scratched his wrist, a black gash remained. *How can the undead die?*

Aloud, he asked, "How does this work?"

William turned to him. He face was maddening. If he laughed, it would be pure lunacy. His face was melting.

"… after the sop Satan entered him."

Even his mind is going, thought Eddie. *Will he forget who I am and come after me like he did with the man at the station?* Eddie had shot William twice, yet the dead priest had taken the other. Sucked him dry. "Your heart is pure," he had said, or something similar.

"It's three in the morning. Where are we going to find blood at this hour? There's a market down the street, but it doesn't open until seven or eight. I think it has a butcher."

An ambulance sped down the highway.

"A sacrifice," said William. He was rambling.

"Hold on, Father."

Eddie put the truck in reverse, grinded into Drive, and spun the tires as he sped past the motel and back onto the highway. Lodging could wait. And the hospital would have blood. He figured it would work, that blood from the living, whether in person or in a bag, would do the trick. It was a hospital after all. "Where do you keep your blood for transfusions?" he imagined asking the reception desk, but he was all out of options. It had to work. Eddie guessed he had three hours before his friend turned back to what had first walked through the door at the station—a walking corpse thirsting for blood.

"Judas may have been the first, damned for eternity." William's prune-like fingers brought the silver cross around his neck to his lips. He kissed the top of it with purple lips. "Burdened to walk the earth… feasting like a wolf." His voice was becoming hoarse as his throat decayed.

There wasn't much traffic. Eddie took the truck up to a steady eighty miles per hour. The speed limit was fifty-five. A blue sign with a white H blew by and before he knew it they were turning down the road to Brenden Memorial. Large white letters of EMERGENCY ROOM greeted them. Eddie turned down a section marked VISITOR PARKING and stopped in the closest handicap stall. If anyone was handicapped, it was his dead friend riding with him. Eddie's clothes, once snuggly fitting the man, were now baggy. The button-up shirt draped over his shoulders as if on a hanger. He had lost half his mass. Gray teeth showed though the widening holes in his cheeks. Most of his left arm was gone, now just a holey sock of skin pulled over bones.

Eddie had to act fast.

He spotted the ambulance by the Emergency Room

entrance doors. The same one that had sped by them at the motel. He figured paramedics carried supplies of blood somewhere in the van. Rush in. Rush out. There was plenty of commotion happening within the hospital walls, but there was no one near the ambulance and its rear doors were propped open like the wings of some giant bird.

"I'll be right back. Don't go anywhere."

It felt strange leaving him alone in the truck, but it would be easier without him. Eddie slid out and the cold morning air ate away his tiredness. With his hands in his pockets, and chin down, he walked from VISITORS PARKING to the van. Next to the sidewalk the sprinklers hissed water onto the sod.

Eddie tried to walk as inconspicuously as possible, perhaps a guest waiting to see a friend, or just some old guy with insomnia out for a stroll. He wondered about the hours of visitation. Three in the morning was pushing it.

Just some old fart out for a stroll, he told himself. *No need to pay attention to Eddie.*

A small cramp pinched his side as he passed the ambulance. He slyly peeked through the open rear doors. Blood covered the floor, but it was otherwise empty. Stopping about ten feet past the van, he turned to the front of the medical van and, as he had hoped, the driver was gone. The ambulance abandoned.

No longer caring for sleuth, Eddie scurried to the back of the van and pulled himself into it, his side burning, air billowing from his lungs in white puffs. Spent gauze and blood covered the floor. Stainless steel. Oxygen tanks. Spider webs of plastic tubing. Eddie didn't know where to start. Any moment they'd be back. There had to be some sort of refrigeration unit somewhere in the mix and he had to find it or scram or he'd have to return to the old chalkboard to design a new plan to keep his dead friend alive.

His eyes searched frantically, bouncing from drawer to drawer and handle to handle. He imagined a pair of paramedics spotting him from inside the hospital—the glass double-doors nearly faced the back of the van—and running toward him, telling the woman at the reception desk to call the police. And then he found it: a small fridge. A fine cloud of cold wisped as he opened it. Inside were a few bottles of clear liquid, a few bottles of brown, and two bags of blood: B and AB. Eddie tucked them both underneath his shirt. They felt like ice-packs. He closed the small door, expecting to be caught red handed as he turned around, but he was still alone. One of the bags nearly dropped down his pants as he leaned down to let himself out of the van.

He looked up in time to see two paramedics walking toward him, one covered in gore. The other held a hand radio to his mouth and said something into it. Eddie's heart somehow left his chest and worked its way into his throat. He stopped breathing and looked directly at the blood-soaked paramedic with guilty eyes as he clutched the bags under his shirt, trying not to drop them down his pant legs like some kind of misplaced colostomy bag.

"Good morning," said the clean one, and they walked right past him.

LINEAGE / 1862

Father Hillcrest studied in his chambers for his next sermon. He would start with The Kiss of Judas, the single act signifying who in the gathering of apostles proclaimed to be the son of God. A kiss on the cheek from Judas to Christ, a signal to the Romans whom to arrest. A foretold betrayal. *'Friend, do what you are here to do,'* said Christ according to John. *'With a kiss do you betray the son of man?'* according to Luke. All for thirty pieces of silver. He would then move to Akeldama: the field of blood. According to the Acts of the Apostles, Judas later used his bribe to buy a field in which he *'burst asunder in the midst.'* Matthew stated that Judas attempted to return the silver and then hanged himself. In other books he was stoned to death, and in others he was crushed under the wheels of a chariot. The differences in Judas Iscariot's death intrigued him most, and he hoped it would intrigue his congregation as well as it had with his two deacons. Perhaps the differences were scripted in so many different ways because no one really knew what eventually became of Judas. Perhaps he had been cursed to roam the earth forever for his sins, the penultimate punishment for betraying the man who promised eternal life to all mankind. Did Christ simply allow the betrayal? Surely he had the power to prevent such a thing from happening, so did that mean he actively *caused* the betrayal? If that were true, then all accounts of Judas being cast to Hell for this sin was misconstrued. If it was such a necessary step for Judas to betray Christ in order to bring salvation to humanity, then was Judas punished for the very bringing of salvation to humanity? And if Judas had no choice but to follow this predestined path, would he not have had free will, thus no moral responsibility for his actions—as innocent as a child, yet cast to Hell for it? This would lead Father Hillcrest into his third piece: The Harrowing of Hell: Christ's descent into the depths of Hell directly following his crucifixion. *Descendit ad inferos.* After Christ's death on the cross, the earth shook as the veil in the temple was torn between worlds and those that were dead rose from their graves to testify to the living throughout Jerusalem. During this time, it is written that Christ descended to the great inferno to visit the spirits of man imprisoned there. Some chose to stay while others chose rebirth into the world, redeemed from God's judgment as Christ endured the penalty of their sins for that short while. Perhaps he found Judas there ... to lead him out from a place he hadn't deserved. Perhaps he was one of the dead raised again to walk the earth. It would be an interesting, thought-provoking sermon.

sᴀ̃ᴄʀᴀᴍᴇɴᴊ

He was nothing more than burnt skin wrapped over a skeletal figure by the time Eddie returned to him with the bags of blood. His face had all but sunken in, the eyes shriveled, jaw pronounced and somewhat elongated, as if life had been drained from the man and his body left to bake in the sun.

But there was no sun. It was still two or three hours before sunrise and undead William Hillcrest sitting hunched in the front seat as Eddie approached the truck wasn't the most pleasant of sights. The moonlight had nothing to offer but horrid shadows in the truck cabin. He was greeted with a black-rotten smile.

Eddie opened the door and tossed the bags onto the seat. Hesitating, he climbed in and sat behind the wheel.

Father Hillcrest, or William, as he liked being called, looked from the bag of blood to Eddie, and Eddie wondered whether or not he would rather have *Eddie's* blood, but a skeletal hand brought one of the bags to his face. The smile widened. Using the silver crucifix hanging around his neck, his dead friend stabbed into the bag. A finger slipped through to widen the hole and it came out crimson. Eddie couldn't help but stare as William brought the offering to his lips and drank.

With the blood came life and the life returned color to his lips and cheeks as the red coated him from within and

filled his face with flesh and his nearly empty sockets with eyes, the tears in his skin meshing back together. He was aging in reverse and when he reached Eddie's age, Eddie felt a little saddened because he quickly grew younger and soon could pass as Eddie's son. The blood acted as a fountain of youth for William Hillcrest, as if he were drinking not from a medicinal bag, but from the chalice of Christ. His arms and legs filled in until he fit into Eddie's clothing as he had before. He turned ten years younger before Eddie's eyes, and then ten more until he was the same William Hillcrest he had helped dress back at his hole-in-the-wall apartment complex.

Lyrics from *Crimson Petals* ran through his mind as he watched the man rejuvenating next to him. One of the main characters in the novel was in a rock band and often broke out into song:

> *"Scratching the itch / The skin peels away / And deep inside, bugs crawl / You feel the sting / Beginning to burn / And in this black, you're dying to learn"*

"It feels worse than it looks," he said to Eddie, "Burning in reverse is the only way I can describe it."

This is exactly what he looked like when he died, Eddie surmised, *the day he burned alive at the stake*. Eddie looked to the silver crucifix around his neck and then to the second bag of blood on the seat.

Eddie reached for the bag, but William stopped him.

"There is a difference between an offering and a taking," he said. "What I have is not a gift; it is a curse."

The strong hand let go and Eddie brought the cold bag

of blood to his face, flipped it end over end as he inspected the red syrup within. He wanted to poke a hole and drink the nectar, to turn back time—a chance to be young again—and to erase the bad from his past. But time was a constant. If drinking the blood worked as it had for William, it would only prolong the inevitable: the end of his own miserable life. There would be no turning back time. Annie was gone. Dead. There was nothing he could do to bring her back, unless he visited her grave and offered *her* the blood.

"It turns your piss black."

"What?" For a moment Eddie had forgotten all about the man sitting next to him.

"Piss. Urine. Drinking blood turns it black. Imagine urinating beef gravy. Trust me, stick to your bottled water."

"When did you—"

"While you were gone."

Eddie tossed the bag to the seat and grimaced. He had passed kidney stones before and would never forget seeing blood in his urine. "Black?"

"Black like night. Are you familiar with the sacramental practices?"

Eddie nodded. He had attended Mass with Annie on occasion, and soon after she died he had gone to a mixture of religions. His guilt had him searching for answers, but organized religion didn't offer the answers he was looking for, so he eventually gave up the search. He had eaten the flesh—wafers, crackers, pinched-off sections of bread—and drank the blood—water, wine, even grape juice at one place—of Christ nearly every Sunday for close to two years.

"Some sects have ventured beyond symbolism, sacrificing others to *drink* their blood, to *bathe* in their blood."

"What was her name?" asked Eddie. "Elizabeth Something … She was that psycho who drained kids into bathtubs and splashed around in their blood because it made her skin look younger."

"One of many examples. Blood-drinking is yet another practice, or vampirism."

"Bela Lugosi was always the best."

"I am not familiar with that name in my studies."

"He wasn't a vampire in real life. He played one on television."

William Hillcrest raised an eyebrow.

"Right, no television in your time. He'd bite someone on the neck—usually dashing young women—to *turn* them. He'd transform into mist or a bat and fly around scaring people. *Dracula* spawned a bunch of movies."

"As in Vlad Dracul?"

"I guess. The stories have been around for hundreds of years. If we were in the movies, you'd fit in somewhere between a vampire and a zombie."

The eyebrow rose again.

"Never mind."

KISS OF JUDAS

The drive back to the motel wasn't easy. While half-listening to William Hillcrest talking about the betrayal of Christ, Eddie's mind wandered back fifty years to when he and Annie were still together, and the night he found the shirt.

Their first house was a single-story, two bedrooms and one bathroom, a model already twenty years old when they bought it. They couldn't pass on the price. Brown shag carpet covered the bedroom floors and hardwood everywhere else. The exterior needed work—the light-blue paint unkempt and peeling in places—but most of the trim was decent. The front lawn was like any other lawn in the neighborhood, mostly mowed green weeds with yellow dandelions poking through and spotted in places where dogs had peed. Near the walkway to the front door was a large rock with their address, 8448. It was perfect for the two of them.

He had met Annie at the mill about five years after he left the orphanage at Westbury. They worked together for a few months. Eddie was in packaging, Annie in receiving. They dated for close to a year before she asked him to marry her. It was unheard of back then for a woman to propose to a man, but Eddie accepted and they married a week later in a Catholic church. Eddie was never big into religion, but he attended Mass with Annie nearly every Sunday.

Things were looking up until Annie's shift changed at

the mill. Eddie moved jobs soon after. For a while, Sunday was their only time together as they tried to make ends meet. Their love held them together. It had to. And then something changed. Eddie would start to cuddle and she'd push him away. *We have too much to do*, she'd say. Sometimes her brother would stay over while on break from school and their one-day weekend would be shot to pieces. Sometimes she didn't come home until close to ten. *I'm going out with some friends after work*, she'd say or, *I might have to work some overtime*. It nagged at Eddie for months.

The white button-up shirt with the lipstick on the collar drove it all home. It looked like a shade Annie would wear, but the shirt wasn't Eddie's; it wasn't even his size. He found it on the couch one morning, as if she had left it there for him to find. He saw Annie through the front window kneeling over the flower garden with a spade in one hand and an uprooted Marigold in the other. She looked up and their eyes met. Eddie held up the shirt. Annie smiled and continued transplanting flowers. Rage ran through him as he stormed out. The screen door banged loudly against the front of the house. He still held the shirt.

Annie dropped everything and asked in a shaky voice, *What?*

This, said Eddie.

It's a shirt.

I know it's a damn shirt! Is this your lipstick?

Annie took a step forward and examined it.

It looks like my shade.

It is your shade. And this isn't my shirt.

Eddie threw it at her. She caught it in a crumpled mess as he took a threatening step forward.

It looks like one of your—

This would choke *me. And your lips are all over it! Working late, huh?*

Eddie took another step, forcing her back.

I don't know—

He didn't let her finish.

You don't know how your lips ended up on someone else's neck, is that what you're trying to tell me? Maybe you just tripped and fell against someone and you accidentally started necking, is that it?

Eddie pushed her.

Hard.

Maybe you just tripped, he started to say, but the words caught in the back of his throat as he saw it happen before it happened, the rock with their address etched into it—8448—as the edge of it met Annie's skull, the *crack* as her head split open, the expression on her face, a mixture of confusion, terror and love, her eyes like blue orbs, tears welling around them, the white button-up shirt falling to her side and absorbing her blood as it pooled beneath her in a nearly perfect circle, the life draining, her eyes rolling back and connecting for a brief moment to his. In a matter of moments, she was gone.

Eddie put the truck in park and stopped the engine. He was in tears. The Super 8 motel sign hung above the complex and filled the cabin with yellow light.

$\cup$NKNOWN WHY

The room was a typical motel getup: mismatched furniture, white paint-blasted walls, paisley wine-colored wallpaper trim, burgundy / teal / white flower-patterned curtains, stained beige carpet, an air conditioning unit slapped against the window, the smell of thirty-year-old cigarette smoke forever in the walls, twin beds with military-tight sheets and comforter sets matching nothing else in the room, the bathroom / toilet / kitchen area littered with water damage and plaster patches, bleach lingering on the towels. William Hillcrest was amazed at the small room, as he was with Eddie's apartment, but nothing impressed him more than the fuzzy television screen. The look on his face when the thirty-two inch Sanyo hummed to life was priceless, as if a door to another world had opened. His knees buckled against the edge of the bed.

He inched closer to the image, which showed an evangelist and a nine-hundred number: $3.99 for the first minute, $1.99 for each additional minute. He reached out to the screen and static electricity sent his fingers flying back, and then he reached out again, palm out, the hair on the back of his hand standing as he moved it across the front of the tube with a crackle of more static.

"This is amazing," he said. "How does it work?"

"You wouldn't believe me if I told you," said Eddie.

"You must."

Eddie took a deep breath as his friend tapped the small man on the screen as if he were trapped inside.

"Somewhere far away," said Eddie, "some church in Michigan, according to the address on the screen, they're filming with video cameras and broadcasting it through radio waves. That's how they used to do it. It could be different now. Anyway, through antennas or cable connections, or even the internet nowadays, television sets like this one can pick up those waves and display it on the screen, like this guy here in the blue suit."

The man on screen yelled for donations as William played with the volume buttons.

"Good god, he can get even louder."

For a while they fought with the volume, William pressing the buttons on the set, Eddie with the remote.

"And how does this box display this man?"

Eddie took a deep breath. "Inside this box is an electron gun."

"A gun?"

"Well," said Eddie, "it's not really a gun. It's just called that. It doesn't shoot electrons; they're pulled from it to the screen, within what is called a cathode ray tube."

Eddie pressed the power button on the remote. The set clicked off.

"When the set is turned on, like *this*," said Eddie, pressing the power button again, "a positive charge is sent to the screen. Electrons, which hold a negative charge as well as the image, are then pulled to the screen. In this case, a portly fellow with gray hair and bushy eyebrows. Television 101. Everything's changed now with flat screens."

"Can others see this man of God?"

"Millions upon millions if they want to watch, but he's no man of God. He just wants money. Look, there are other channels."

Click.

"Here is a pack of lions hunting water buffalo."

Click.

"A game show."

Click.

"A Spanish channel."

Click.

"Yan Can Cook."

Click.

"Looks like … some kind of mall with people trapped in it. Ah! Romero's *Dawn of the Dead*. Look, there's you!"

A blood-drenched zombie missing part of his arm and most of his face lurched across the screen. Even though he moved at a snail pace, those he chased were not far ahead.

"This is what I was talking about earlier. See, this guy's dead—probably bit by one of the other zombies—and he'll eat those other people to stay alive. You don't want to watch this, though."

Click.

"News."

Text scrolled by a burning building. The time and temperature were displayed at the top right of the screen.

"That's your station," said William. "Those are the red chariots we saw earlier."

Eddie turned up the volume.

ARMED ROBBERY AND ARSON lit up the screen in bold white lettering, a picture of Eddie in his early sixties below it. Most of the building was charred and still smoking. Fire crews concentrated on the burning pumps.

> *"… local resident Eddie Hensen, eighty-seven, was on duty. Brenden Fire Department pulled his remains from a gas station moments ago in what authorities are declaring armed robbery and arson. One witness claims to have heard multiple gunshots prior to the fire and explosions, and saw two men leaving in a light-colored truck. Officer Milton of the Brenden Police Department had this to say …"*

> *"I feel sorry for the guy. Eddie's run this station for years. Always a pleasant fellow with a smile on his face. Our only lead is the Ford Bronco parked out front.*

The scene cut to a blackened vehicle taken by the fire.

> *"I know Eddie well enough. It's his truck we're searching for. The two who did this probably shot him, took the cash, torched the place, and took off with his truck."*

The scene changed to that of a female reporter with blonde cropped hair and a face full of makeup.

> *"The eye witness was unavailable for comment. We'll keep you posted as this story progresses. In other …"*

He turned off the television and felt an immense weight against his chest. To the city of Brenden, Washington, Eddie Hensen was dead. He suddenly felt sick to his stomach.

"We have to leave. They will be looking for the truck."

"We just got here; where else can we can go?" asked William. "Everyone thinks you're dead."

"I don't know, but we can't stay here."

Eddie replayed the hotel check-in. The man at the counter had asked for his ID, but had never really looked up from his book to check properly. He was engrossed in *Rapture*, by Thomas Tessier. He remembered the cover—a young woman covering herself from someone peering into her window, a staircase just to the right of her. He and the hotel clerk had never made eye contact.

"Maybe we can. We just need to ditch the truck. As long as the man at the counter doesn't recognize my name, or doesn't watch the news, I think we're fine for now. We can park it anywhere but here. Maybe behind the Vons across the street. You have to do one thing for me, though."

"Anything," said William.

"I need you to sit in the front seat of the truck. Pretend you're driving. Touch everything: steering wheel, steering column, dashboard, radio knobs, seatbelts. Everything. Even the keys. The door handle, too, inside and out. We have to make it look like you were driving. I need your fingerprints to be all over the place."

"What are *finger* prints?"

"I'll explain it all later. It's imperative that it looks like you drove the truck."

"Why?"

"Because you don't exist. They'll expect to find traces of me in the truck, because it's *my* truck, but having your prints in there will send them on a wild goose chase. I hope. They'll be looking for a man who doesn't exist! You died over a hundred and fifty years ago; to them you don't exist, and now, because they think that dead guy you drank at the station was *me*, I don't exist. *Eddie Hensen is dead.*"

Even as he said it aloud, it all seemed to make sense. Eddie Hensen needed to die to make everything right in the world. To start over again.

Like the lead character in his book.

THE BETRAYAL

In the heat of the moment—as cliché as it sounds—Eddie had wanted Annie to fall, wanted her to suffer; he wanted for something terrible to happen to her for cheating. Eddie had pushed her. She fell. She died. Her dying had been an accident, but the rage behind the push all those years back was no accident, and if anyone deserved to die, it was Eddie. According to the Bible, Hell was a fiery place where the damned burned forever in agony, layers upon layers of fiery death, a place much like the modern world, or so Eddie surmised, and it only suited him to forever dwell there for his actions. To the public, Eddie *was* dead—a burnt corpse found at his station, the single place where he had wasted most of his life. For the last fifty years he was nothing more than a demon wearing a mask with a fake smile.

He parked the truck across from Vons. Leaving the keys in the ignition, he kept on the lights, and propped open both the driver's and passenger side doors. The truck sat idle and cockeyed within the lines, the front-left tire slightly rolled over the cement stopper; with luck it would look ditched.

William Hillcrest's fingerprints were scattered around the ins and outs of the cabin. Eddie had wiped his own sets of prints from the gun he'd taken with him from the station. He threw the revolver in the bushes after removing the remaining cartridges. The last thing he wanted was for some kid to find it in the morning. He didn't need another death over his head. Annie's was plenty enough. He only had to take *one* life—his own—to balance things out in the world.

"What are you doing out here?" he asked himself.

Eddie wiped the oil from the gun onto his pant legs. He could still see the look in her eyes, pleading *why, Eddie, why* and the empty gaze thereafter. Dilated, dead … a reflection of miniature Eddies looking down to her, one of his hands slightly outstretched in a last-second failed effort to save her from the fall after it was already too late. He would never forget that image. It was reported by police as an accidental death—her head making contact with the address marker in the front grass after falling in the yard, a skull fracture—*Disseminated Intravascular Coagulopathy*, doctors had called it. Blunt force trauma to the back of the head. He had tried to tell police what really happened, but the words never came out. He just couldn't look away from her body and all the blood spilling out of her and that last, almost pleading expression frozen on her beautiful face … the slightest of smiles; every time he closed his eyes he could see the single dimple in her cheek. Whenever he dreamt of Annie she'd wear that same sad smile as if she were wearing a mask—a plastic face to forever haunt him. Autopsy later revealed Annie had bled to death over the few minutes Eddie stood in shock over her fallen body. She wasn't dead, but merely unconscious. If he could have stopped the bleeding, he could have saved her life, but instead, Eddie had taken it away from her.

I deserve death. He thought it fifty years ago; he thought it now. *Not Annie, not the stranger at the station, not even William*

Hillcrest all those years ago. I deserve to bear the cross around my neck. I deserve to be tied to a post and burned alive for what I've done. I need to burn so I can start over again. "Sometimes a forest needs to burn before it can live again," Father Hillcrest had said. *A chance to start over again.*

After ditching the truck, Eddie started the long walk back to the motel.

"Please forgive me, Annie," he said aloud.

He pulled a small piece of glass from his pocket. It was the only keepsake he had taken with him from the orphanage in Westbury where he grew up. A strange keepsake with an interesting story, one of those odd things in life you keep stashed away for years and years for some unknown reason, not knowing when you will need it, *if* you will need it, or why you even carried it all those years to begin with, until it calls for you.

Eddie used the sharpest point to cut a jagged line from his elbow to his wrist and continued his walk to the motel.

THE CROSS

With this around your neck you will live forever. William Hillcrest's mother said those words the year he became a deacon. *It will keep you safe and will lead you through eternal life.* He remembered how she had said *through* eternal life, not *to* eternal life, as he often heard the phrase. The day she gave him the necklace he had promised never to take it off, and in keeping that promise it had always kept him safe. It was the same with the roses; around them he felt warmth and comfort, always. But he had broken his promise the night he loaned the necklace to Francis Dormant, whom he suspected had taken his ring, and then Allen Edgar, who had stolen the tithes from his chambers. Perhaps the necklace wasn't a sacred talisman after all, but a cursed piece of silver.

The coins were silver, he thought as he heard a *click,* the door, and Eddie Hensen entered the room holding his wrist. Blood leaked between his fingers and dripped steadily onto the motel room floor as he staggered, a saddened expression on his face. Dry tears lined his cheeks. He looked scared.

"What have you done?"

William rushed to his side and peeled away Eddie's fingers. The wound welled with black and red. His arm was cut lengthwise up to his elbow.

"My gift to you." Eddie half-smiled, half-cringed. "With life there must come death, and with death, life."

William covered some of the exposed laceration with his own hands as he walked him to the kitchen area. Blood ticked into the sink, mimicking the clock hanging crookedly on the wall.

"Yours is not mine to take. Why have you done this?"

"I'm already dead. Didn't you catch the news?"

"You have cut your own wrist."

Water from the faucet trickled over the mess as he tried to wash it clean. Eddie pulled away and pried open the wound. It bled steadily into the sink.

"I've read the Bible," said Eddie. "Most of it. Christ knew he was going to die. He sacrificed his blood to save the souls of others. They drank his blood for eternal life and I want you to drink mine for the same purpose. I don't deserve to live for the things I've done. You deserve life over death, not me. I deserve to suffer, Father."

"Do not call me Father."

"Then you are Christ! You have died and resurrected—"

William Hillcrest slapped him hard across the face. A pink handprint quickly surfaced from underneath his old and wrinkled face. Eddie stared at him, stunned, as if he had just woken from a dream and realized he was awake. Losing some of the color in his face, he looked to his bleeding wrist and grabbed tightly, ashamed. In one smooth gesture, William slipped the silver crucifix necklace from his own neck and placed it around Eddie's.

"Forgive me, Father," whispered Eddie, as if in silent prayer. He twirled the cross within his fingertips. "I cannot take this. It means so much to you."

William set a hand onto Eddie's shoulders and prayed.

THE HARROWING OF HELL

Already Eddie could see the blood pulling back from the priest's graying skin, his eyes frosted and glazing over, the muscles in his legs and arms weakening, his joints starting to buckle … *aging* might be an easier description. Eddie's own flesh felt hot as blood dripped from the sting of his self-inflicted wound. William Hillcrest was done drinking blood, he could tell, and wanted nothing to do with the blood Eddie had offered—the blood dripping all over the floor; not even the spare bag on the motel dresser held his interest any longer.

Eddie couldn't help but think of the Last Supper as depicted in DaVinci's painting, with Christ on one side of the table offering his flesh and blood to the apostles, a symbolic gesture of obtaining life eternal. Christ knew then of his death, that one of his followers—one of his friends—would betray him, a man named Judas Iscariot. He and Eddie were one in the same, and Eddie couldn't help but think of William Hillcrest as a Christ-like figure in his own predicament. When he had first risen from his ashes back at the cemetery, did William know why he was here? Was his purpose to save Eddie, like Christ descending to Hell to save souls of the damned following his death at the cross? Did Father William Hillcrest descend to this earth, this hell—Eddie's hell—to pull him out of it following his own savior-like death? He had definitely managed to pull Eddie from a lonesome and pitiful life into something odd and fantastic, something almost otherworldly. For over fifty plus years Eddie had let his life slowly pass over him as his guilt for Annie's death slowly ate at him until there was nothing left. For fifty plus years Eddie had fallen into the depths of a spirit prison of sorts to be dealt his torture, his damnation, his punishment for killing the only person he had truly loved. Eddie had taken Annie's life prematurely and this man of God—this Father William Hillcrest—had harrowed Eddie's hell. And Eddie betrayed him.

He looked to William's sad, forgiving eyes.

The cross felt heavy around his neck.

"*Thank you,*" he said to those sad eyes.

The dead priest smiled, his lips cracking and darkening to blue. A bony hand wrapped around Eddie's neck; the other still held his shoulder as he looked to the cross he'd given him.

"I wish our travels could have ventured longer. I was beginning to appreciate the strangeness of your world and everything within."

"I wish I could have had the chance to introduce you to Dr. Pepper." Eddie couldn't come up with anything better.

"I wish I could have had the chance to meet him."

They both shared a laugh, but only Eddie knew why.

Eddie stepped back and glanced around the motel room and inhaled the lemon stench. The cut on his arm swelled and continued to bleed, his pulse beating hard and painfully against the tight grip he held around it. He laughed despite his condition, water welling in his eyes, and when the laugh ceased it left behind a half-smile / half-frown, for they no longer needed the blood, they no longer needed the motel, because they were both dying. Eddie barely knew what was real anymore, but he knew he was losing a friend.

William Hillcrest's hand fell to his side as if he could no longer support the weight. He had aged another ten or twenty years just standing there. He still gave no indication of wanting Eddie's blood, nor a drop from the stolen bag of blood on the dresser. Maybe he was tired of pissing black.

Eddie smiled again. "I figure I have about an hour," he said as he held up his bleeding arm. "I could drive you back to …" He had no idea where he could take him.

"Back to the cemetery would be fine. The one with the roses."

"That would be Brenden. Where will you—"

"I rose from the ground, so I guess that is where I must fall."

"I'm sure you could use some sleep. You look terrible." The poor guy looked like he was pushing a hundred, his thin skin taut around his shrinking body, the hair on his head dirty gray. Part of his neck had started to open like a zipper.

"Does it hurt?"

"What?" asked William. "Death? Not this time. You?"

"Stings like … like I'm bleeding to death because I cut myself."

"After death, there is no pain."

Ashes Fall

William Hillcrest was nothing more than the morbid creature that had first visited Eddie back at the station by the
time they reached the cemetery. He couldn't speak, because
his vocal cords had decomposed. Messed hair covered most
of his face like a dirty mop draped over a rotten cantaloupe.
Eddie had helped him out of the truck but he didn't stay
long enough to watch him rest in peace, as the saying goes.
He had only looked back once before driving off into the
night and toward the orange-glowing mountains.

A thin layer of gray covered Brenden as ash from the
not-so-distant fire fell over Towne Square Cemetery. The
stars were all but hidden within the flurry. Soon he was looking over a headstone reading: WILLIAM HILLCREST / BURN
FOREVER IN HELL in barely legible letters. A crow with elec-
tric blue eyes waited on top of his headstone and opened its
black beak. William couldn't hear its plea for sacrifice. His
ears had disintegrated like the ash at his feet. He couldn't
even see the bird because his eyes had rotted away, yet he
sensed the creature as he first had when climbing out of his
grave not long ago. It was an offering to live again; he only
had to drink. He sensed the blood, a crimson aura etched in
black—like his roses—pulsing within the bird, each heartbeat rooting red light throughout its body. A skeletal hand
reached outward and the bird fluttered anxiously, as if eager

to shed its life, and cawed silent frustrations when he pulled his hand back. The red pulse within it dimmed, as well as the blue glow behind its stare.

Over fifteen decades old, William Hillcrest looked without eyes to the sky and without words he said *it is finished* as ash from the fire in the mountains fell onto his face. The ground shook vehemently as he collapsed, his own grave swallowing him as the rosebushes around the cemetery engulfed in flame.

THE THIRD TAKEN

The dashboard clock read a blurry 5:45 as the truck slid to a stop on gravel somewhere along Route 19. Red pooled next to Eddie on the seat. For the last few minutes he had driven in search of a break in the fence leading out of the forest, and for a while he thought he'd never find one. His uncut right hand put the truck in park and fell, splattering onto the warm mess. He leaned over and grabbed the rope on the passenger side, which had soaked up his blood like a wick. Eddie barely had the energy to sit up straight, but the thought of returning to Annie kept him going. He managed the door handle and stepped out to a warm easterly wind. He walked through the gap in the fence and let the smoke enter his lungs. With Hillcrest's silver crucifix in one hand, rope in the other, Eddie walked against the wind and toward the fire.

PART FOUR

RUNNING IN CIRCLES

SOUNDS IN THE FIELD

The sound was similar to footsteps crushing white-frozen grass the morning after a cold front, like hardened spears of frosted green crackling under boots. Crisp wind rolled over the field, howling through the wheat. The stalks glimmered and swayed. *Crunch* … soft and distant, *crunch*.

Crouching to the ground, Joel Brady whispered to his younger brother, Mitchell, "What do we do?"

"Bolt?"

"I dunno …" whispered Joel.

Joel imagined a prowling beast, its back legs shaking, tail raised, and jaw snarling and dripping with a thirst for blood. He grabbed at his chest and felt his heart *boom! boom! boom!* like the bass drum in a marching band.

Through the dark haze he could barely see the mud caked to the soles of his boots. The wheat flattened below him was wet with dew, not snapped flat, but bent, for it was a month away from harvesting and still alfalfa green. A few months from now summer would dry the field a golden brown. The stalks closest to the fence were already turning a dried-out shade of yellow. It was there the crunching originated.

Acres of blackness surrounded Joel and his brother as they searched for something they couldn't see. On the other side of the fence—a hundred yards away—was a silhouette of Joel's minivan. If they wanted to leave, they had to cross paths with whatever was in the field.

A smile formed on the corner of his mouth as he thought of something horrible. If there *was* something out there, he only had to outrun his brother.

Mitchell tapped him on the shoulder, making him jump, and motioned to the flashlight. He pointed the bulb end to the noise.

Are you crazy? He took the flashlight away from him, contemplated using it himself, but decided against it.

Crunch.

It had moved forty feet to the right. Both of their heads turned in unison to the noise. To their disappointment, the creature had not left them, but a small path had opened to the minivan.

Joel held the flashlight like a club.

Crunch.

Mitchell dug inside the backpack on his shoulder. He produced a pocketknife and flipped open a three-inch-long blade. Its gleam attracted Joel's attention.

Joel whispered, "We'll wait a few more minutes and then I'm using the flashlight. It might only be an opossum or something."

"Or a mountain lion," Mitchell added. "Is it *opossum* or *possum?*"

"Shh." Joel wondered a moment if there were mountain lions in Washington. He hoped not. "There aren't any up here."

"How do you know?"

"I don't."

"What if it's a bear?"

What would a bear be doing in a wheat field? It could be anything: a skunk, a raccoon, or some other nocturnal animal, a field rat perhaps. *Definitely not a bear. Crap, it could be a wolf.* Joel thought of every possibility, even another person, and his imagination took over. He remembered a movie they'd seen years back in which a group of campers, one by one, disappeared as each was mutilated by a nine-foot-tall grizzly bear. "I'm gonna go look for Amanda," one of the campers would say, and then they would disappear for good—head ripped off by a bear paw the size of a catcher's mitt. Then another would head off to look for the one looking for Amanda, and then they'd be taken and gutted like a trout.

Mitchell, who was more into horror, probably imagined a man in a hockey mask sporting a machete or a chainsaw, a leather-faced man wearing the skin of his victims, or a young towheaded kid with glowing blue eyes.

Crunch.

"Does it sound like it's getting closer to you?"

A softer *crunch.*

"I can't tell," said Mitchell. "My depth perception is messed up out here. Sounds close. We should use the flashlight. I'd rather know what's chasing us if we decide to run."

Another rustling came from the same location.

"It might charge us," said Joel, no longer whispering. "Then again, if it does, we run."

"Where?"

"To the van … but not *that* way," said Joel, pointing the unlit flashlight to the outline of the vehicle. "Feel like running?"

"I will if a freaking mountain lion's chasing me!"

Crunch.

Joel knelt lower and picked up a rock.

Mitchell did the same.

"When I shine the flashlight, if it's something big, a wolf or something, throw the rock close to it—away from where we'd run—so it has to hesitate. We'll start walking slowly closer to the van. Walk slowly and quietly until we absolutely have to run. Got it?"

He could tell his brother never once thought it could be a wolf and was realizing just that.

"Sure," said Mitchell after a breath.

They both stood. The crop in front of them was as high as their chests.

Mitchell put his pocketknife in his pocket and grabbed the strap of his backpack; the other held a rock the size of a baseball.

Joel held the flashlight ready, as well as his own rock.

"What about these?" whispered Mitchell, signaling to the equipment at their feet, easily gatherable with a free hand.

"I'll be able to take them both after I get rid of this thing." He tossed his rock into the air and caught it. "Ready?"

Crunch.

"No …" said his brother, barely a word at all. "Sure."

Joel pointed the flashlight to the noise and clicked it on. His heart missed a beat when no light shined from the end of it.

Without saying a word, Mitchell removed the backpack once again and unzipped the largest pouch, peering inside with what little moonlight revealed. He pulled out a handful of D-cells.

Joel unscrewed the bottom of the Maglite, removed the four dead batteries, and traded them with his brother. *Always a Boy Scout.* At least they would get to see what was chasing them in the dark, as Mitchell had so eloquently yet horrifically put it.

For a second time, they readied themselves for the worst. Joel pointed the functional flashlight to the darkness and waited for the

(crunch)

and then clicked on the flashlight and a bright yellow beam—almost white—broke the night. It rested on a pair of red eyes.

Warm blood rushed to his face, or maybe rushed *from* his face. It all happened in less than a second before he turned off the flashlight.

Almost hysterically, Mitchell asked, "W-what the hell was that?"

Joel managed a reply, "I have no clue."

Crunch.

The sound coming toward them.

"Is it a wolf?" asked Mitchell.

The glowing red eyes had appeared dog-like.

I don't know *what* it is, but it's looking right at us."

The flashlight clicked on and they again returned their bright reflective color.

"What are you doing?" asked Mitchell, then he seemed to realize that as long as they had the flashlight on the creature, they knew its whereabouts.

They stared at the hypnotic eyes for close to a minute.

"Let's just start walking slowly," said Joel, clenching his rock. He then traded it for the gear at his feet—two wooden boards with lengths of rope joining their ends. One was broken in half.

Another *crunch* from the direction they were heading.

Joel moved the beam to the noise and found a second set of red eyes.

"Wait, move it back," said Mitchell. "Move the light back to the other eyes."

"But this one's right in front of us."

Mitchell grabbed the handle and part of his Joel's hand as he forced it back to the previous target. As the yellow-white beam progressed from left to right, dozens of red eyes shined back.

$\mathcal{P}$re-$\mathcal{P}$roduction / $\mathcal{E}$arlier

The sun was a few hours from setting between the brown humps of mountain. Wispy clouds promised a beautiful sunset of purple and blue. A Boeing 737 lifted from the Brenden Airport runway and filled the silent pre-evening with a thunderous roar before leaving behind trails of fluffy white. Joel and Mitchell watched from a fence made of wooden poles and sagging barbed wire. It outlined a crop of greenish-golden grain of either wheat or barley. They chose the outskirts of the airport for one reason: exposure.

After a moment of speculation, they returned to the minivan. Mitchell took a sheet of paper from the floorboard—a printed map to the airport—and crumpled it. "I'll be right back," he said and walked back to the fence. He stuffed the wad into a hole in one of the posts.

Smiling, Mitchell joined him in the van, closed the door.

"What was that for?" Joel asked.

"When we come back tonight, the headlights will pick up the paper like a reflector and we'll know where to stop."

"If we don't find it, we'll keep driving and find another place tomorrow."

"It's only a piece of paper."

"Yeah, with driving directions from *my* house, with *your* fingerprints all over it. You watch CSI? They can pull fingerprints off a bologna sandwich."

"No one's pulling fingerprints," said Mitchell, "because we won't get caught. Who's gonna be looking for two guys down unregulated privately-owned—no trespassing—Alder Road at one in the morning?"

"True," said Joel.

They scoped out the field a final time using the video camera. Joel made sure the internal clock was set, and then panned left to right over the field. Mitchell smiled and waved to the camera as it passed him. Joel spoke into the camera, "We're now on the outskirts of town. As you can see, Brenden Airport is in the distance a couple acres away. And here's Mitchell, looking like a moron … and behind him, just beyond that fence line"—zooming in—"is the field we've chosen. About six or seven hours from now, we'll be in the middle of it. We'll try to get some footage, but I don't know if it'll turn out. It might be too dark."

"You should've bought a light for it," said Mitchell.

"Wouldn't it look funny, don't you think, if someone from the airport—or whoever owns this field—happens to see a bright light moving around in it late at night?"

Joel finished the video log by saying into the camera, "Now me and Mitch are going shopping for supplies"— panning right to left again—"so, next time you hear from us, it'll be dark outside … and we'll be out there."

The camera recorded the back of Mitchell's head and Joel's hand pointing to the field.

Dowels were almost ten bucks apiece for eight-foot sections an inch and a half in diameter. Two-by-fours were cheap, but they would be too heavy to lug around. They settled on an eight-foot slab of fir, three inches wide, three-quarters of an inch thick; they had it cut it in half.

Mitchell found a fifty-foot bundle of clothesline rope and held it up to show his brother.

"Anything else you can think of?" Joel asked as they walked down an aisle of mirrors.

They walked past a gangly man gazing into a bathroom mirror and stayed silent until he was out of earshot.

"You have a protractor at the house?" Mitchell asked.

"Yeah. It's old—high school math class—but it works."

"Batteries!"

"Batteries?"

"In case the ones in the flashlight go out. Or are out," said Mitchell. The last bit sounded like one giant over-voweled word: *ourout*. "Or. Are. Out," he reiterated. "D-cell."

"Are you sure?"

"They'll be by the registers."

"*Thayal-B*, huh? Sounds like cramp medicine."

"Yep. They come in little *Joel* caplets."

Both laughed as they approached the teller—a blonde girl in an orange smock.

"Nice tat," Mitchell said to her.

"Do you carry protractors?" Joel asked.

"I thought you had one at home?"

"I think it's broken and taped back together."

Julie—according to her name badge—said, "That will be eight-oh-eight. Try Staples next door."

Joel gave Julie a ten and gave the change to his pocket. "Thanks."

"Have fun with whatever you guys are doing," she said and began ringing up the guy they saw by the mirrors.

Joel drilled holes into the ends of the two four-foot sections of fir. Through these holes, he looped and tied off cut lengths of rope, so that when pulled taut, the peak of the triangle was waist high with the board planted on the ground. Mitchell made a different tool: a hat, a paperclip, and the twisty-tie from the plastic bag from a loaf of bread. He straightened out the twisty-tie and made a loop at one end like a hangman's knot and affixed it to the bill using the paperclip—a hat with a sight. He wore it while he sketched geometric designs on a notepad. They looked good, like Aztec symbols or something. They waited until midnight before going out. Dressed in black, nervous, and a little anxious to get started, they drove to the outskirts of town, to the field that separated Alder Road from the lone runway of Brenden Airport.

WALKING THROUGH MUD

They almost passed the marker when Mitchell blurted out, "There it is," and pointed to the white wad of paper in the fence.

Joel killed the headlights after pulling off the side of the road. They both sat in the darkness of the cab, looking to the black field.

"We should let our eyes adjust before going out," said Mitchell. "Wait until we can see some stars, at least." He tapped the twisty-tie on his hat.

Joel looked out a foggy window and realized his brother was right. Mitch was a geek when it came to astronomy, mathematics, physics, and just about anything else scientific, such as knowing a wad of paper would shine like a bulb when reflecting a headlight beam at one in the morning. A few stars were poking through the black canopy and he could make out the wheat stalks and the outlines of wooden fencepost.

"What's that bright star?" asked Joel, pointing to the brightest object in the sky.

Without looking, his brother said, "Sirius."

"Yeah."

Mitchell laughed and looked at the star. "That's its name. S-I-R-I-U-S. Seriously, it's Sirius."

"Like the Satellite Radio company?"

"Yeah, they ripped off the name. Their logo's a cartoon dog with a star for an eye."

"Makes sense. Didn't they go bankrupt or something?"

"Probably. Don't stare at it too long, or you'll start seeing it everywhere."

Joel looked past the field to the airport tower. It flashed white and blue each time the light rotated. Next to the moon was a red pockmark. It didn't twinkle like the other stars, so he assumed it was a planet.

"Is that Mars?"

Mitchell stared into the field as if expecting the stalks to part. Without looking away, he asked, "Next to the moon, to the right?"

"Yeah," Joel said, wondering how he knew such things.

Mitchell mind was an oddity. He probably knew the proper way to set a broken leg, how long a person could live feasting on his own flesh, the number of primes between one and a thousand, why the sky was blue, how much he'd weigh on Jupiter. He could solve most situational problems using mathematical equations and logic others would rarely consider, but was a klutz when it came to hand / eye coordination. Joel was the opposite. They were messing with yoyos a few years back and Joel had quickly learned some of the advanced tricks. Mitchell would say, "Look, it's asleep," with his Duncan resting on the kitchen linoleum, the string slack. "It's not asleep," Joel would tell him, "it's dead."

"We have a game plan?" Mitchell asked.

They drew sketches earlier, but hadn't finished a design. The guys on *Scientific Universe* made it look easy—Mike and Joe from Iowa or Ohio or someplace.

"We should wing it," said Mitchell, as if reading his mind.

"Yeah, we should wing it. Ready?"

"Sure."

Doors clicked open as each exited the van. Mitchell grabbed the backpack and put it on as Joel opened the hatch to get the rest of their gear. They met at the fence. Joel handed him one of the stick-rope tools so they each had one, and put the flashlight in Mitchell's pack with the protractor and rope.

"Remember to step high over the stalks if you can, and try to settle your feet between the rows of wheat." According to the show there would be plenty of room to nestle their shoes between rows without trampling the crop. If they high-stepped and concentrated on their foot placement, they could walk through the field without leaving a trail. "Remember to brush your stick after us like they did on the show."

"Got it," said Mitchell.

In turn, they climbed over the barbed-wire fence and entered the field. The other side was nothing but muck sucking their boots. Looking behind for a trail, Joel was pleased not to see one. They ventured further out and the ground became firmer, and crunched slightly under their feet. After ten minutes of high-stepping, they were a hundred yards into the field. The white minivan seemed a mile away.

"My feet are about to freeze off. How about you?"

"Yeah," said Mitchell.

The field appeared to glow. Countless stars speckled the sky, the Milky Way like a river through the middle of it. Mars was twice as bold as it had appeared from the van. The entire field felt alive, flowing and glowing like the ocean at night.

"Should we start here?"

Mitchell looked around the field. "This place is as good as any. What do you wanna do?"

"I guess we just make a small circle and go from there."

"Sounds good to me."

"You want to start it?"

"Go for it."

After a hesitation, Joel unwound the rope from the board and unraveled it until the board was at his feet. He put his foot on top and pulled the rope taut in the center, making a triangle shape out of the strange tool. Keeping his left foot stationary, Joel worked his right foot up and down in a stamping manner, counter-clockwise around his planted left foot. Since the crop was somewhat green, the stalks didn't break, but bent nicely under the wood. After six or seven compressions, a circle eight feet in diameter formed.

"Well, that was easy."

Both stood in awe at their very first crop circle. The geometric pattern only had a radius as long as the board, but the spiral pattern was impressive.

"How big should we make it?"

"As big as we want," said Mitchell. A wide grin filled his face.

"Want to try it out?"

Mitch was already at his side, his own crop circle tool in hand.

"Yeah, move over."

Mitchell dropped the wooden part to the ground, his fingers clutching the middle of the rope. As it unraveled, he put his right foot in the center of the board and pulled at the rope. He kept his left foot on the ground behind him so he was able to mash the crop with his right and stay balanced as he worked his way around. He lined the left edge of the board to the outer perimeter of the circle Joel had made and stomped his way counter-clockwise, flattening the wheat formation into an even larger circle, now sixteen feet in diameter.

"How big is it?" Joel asked, knowing his brother would be calculating already.

"Well," said Mitchell, "Pi-r-squared gives us area. Our radius would be eight since we've each gone around. Squared would be sixty-four, times pi, or about three, we'll say … A hundred ninety-two square feet give or take."

"Wow."

"Yeah," said Mitchell. "Took less than a minute."

Joel knew equations were running through his brother's head: *times four, times four, times four, times four*, which would give him the new area each time one of them made it around.

Joel went next, following the same counter-clockwise pattern. His brother watched him go around from the center. Joel met him back in the middle when he was finished, the circle now twenty-four feet wide.

"Seven hundred seventy-eight square feet," Mitchell informed him. "Plus or minus a few feet, of course."

"Of course," said Joel in awe. "Our first crop circle. Cool!"

"Way cool."

"Want to go around again?" Joel waited for an answer.

"I've got a better idea. I'll start, but when I'm a good distance away, you start behind me."

"Behind you?"

"Not *right* behind me … from where you would start next after I work my way around."

"Gotcha."

With both going around they could work twice as fast.

Each time they made a round, it took exponentially longer to finish. After two additional treks apiece, they were exhausted, legs sore, shoes soaked. Stalks poked through Joel's socks in a hundred different places like the foxtails back in California, and pricked his ankles like fleabites. His toes had turned numb, his lungs burning despite the cold. They met once more in the center of the circle. Only twenty minutes had passed since they started.

"How big?" Joel asked through a sigh.

Mitchell counted on his fingers and exclaimed, "Seven!"

"Seven what?"

"We've gone around seven times." His breath choppy. "Four foot boards—radius of twenty-eight feet—diameter of fifty-two." He looked to the sky as he calculated.

With the crop flattened, the formation looked pressed into the field, as if some gigantic cylinder had fallen onto the land.

"Twenty-three hundred fifty-two feet."

"Huh?"

"Surface area," said Mitchell. "Give or take a hundred feet. Freaking huge, that's how big."

For the amount of time it took them to create the formation, they spent as much admiring their work.

"Looks like it's glowing," said Mitchell.

For a moment longer, they sat in the field and looked around the four-foot high wall of wheat outlining the flattened stalks. The spiral effect was more obvious with the circle much larger, as if a tornado had touched down. It didn't look like the labor of two guys with sticks and rope, but the work of aliens or some other unexplainable phenomenon, like ball lightning, a vortex, a spaceship landing site, hungry gophers, maybe even the resting place of a fifty-foot cat who had curled up to rest its fifty ton mass. Anything but twenty minutes of creative spare time. It was laughably easy.

"Now what?" asked Mitchell.

"Let's make some lines."

Mitchell nodded and straightened the hat on his head. He readjusted the twisty-tie and searched the sky for his favorite planet. "Mars," he said.

Joel attempted to look for it but gave up. They all looked the same to him now; just twinkling celestial objects.

"Just over the airport tower. The brightest one, that direction." Mitchell extended his board and pointed with it. "Why don't we go that way for a while? And then we can make a smaller circle off the end of it or something."

"Sounds good."

They walked the perimeter of the circle, toward the airport.

Mitchell, still sporting the backpack, dropped his crop circle tool to the ground, the rope clutched in his hand. He aligned his makeshift sight and placed the red planet within the ring of plastic-coated wire. For fifty paces he crunched a line of flat crop while keeping Mars as his focal point.

It was one of the tricks they learned from the documentary. As long as one's eye never strayed from the target, a straight line could be produced. That is exactly what his brother did as Joel watched from inside the circle.

He heard a cracking sound before Mitchell said, "Guess this is far enough."

From fifty or so feet away, Joel could barely see his brother, and didn't realize why he had stopped until Mitchell joined him in the circle.

Raised in Mitchell's hands were the remains of his stomping board, broken in half, its rope dangling to the ground.

"I guess we never considered the field being wet."

"Well," said Joel. There was silence for close to a minute as each looked at their surroundings. "Let's just make another small circle where you left off and see how long we can last with mine."

Mitchell followed him through the newly flattened trail.

Joel high-stepped twenty feet further from where Mitchell had left off, his board raised over his head like a soldier stowing his rifle over water; the rest of Joel was hidden behind wheat as high as his chest.

"Does it look like I'm in line with the path you made?"

Mitchell took a few steps back and composed a line— using his arm—from the path to the top of Joel's head.

"Perfect."

Joel performed a slow sombrero-like dance as the shape of another eight-foot circle took shape. He went around again, making the diameter sixteen feet. He was about to go around again but stopped to call Mitchell over.

"Come check this out."

Joel pointed to the much larger circle once Mitchell joined him.

From the center of the smaller circle, the enormity of the larger formation had revealed itself. The outer lines of the fifty-six-foot-wide circle stood out, as well as the tunnel leading to it. Moonlight shimmered off the flattened surface. It was beautiful and eerie, and sent chills both good and bad down Joel's spine.

A sound startled them: like wheat stalks being smashed under feet.

Crunch.

The second sound sent them to their knees, both looking to the curved wall of wheat separating them from what had made the noise.

After silence, Joel whispered, "*What the heck was that?*"

"Hopefully nothing with fangs."

In a slightly louder voice Joel said, "It's probably a rodent. I bet we scared it away."

Crunch.

They jumped.

"Pretty big freakin' rodent," said Mitchell.

"*Shh* ..." Crouching low to the ground, Joel Brady whispered, "It sounds like it's getting closer."

CONCEPTION / EARLIER

Joel picked up his brother at Seattle Airport Wednesday afternoon after a quick flight in from Sacramento International. Mitchell was on summer break from school and had a month to kill; Joel had to work during the week, but had weekends free. During the days, Mitch lounged around the house reading, or went for walks touring the town. When Joel got home they'd play basketball, see a movie, or do some moderate landscaping around the house. This was how most summers went for Joel, and it was starting to get old.

Nothing was on the tube except infomercials for juicers, rotisseries, and exercising equipment. Joel flipped through channels until he found a show with fuzzy black and only a timestamp at the bottom right that read *Strange Universe*.

The outline of a man—the top half—slowly came into focus. He wore a hat with something dangling from the bill. The camera zoomed in to an indistinguishable face. The man holding the camera spoke in an altered voice. Captions ran along the bottom of the screen to translate.

"As you can see—or maybe you can't—my friend here is working on the initial circle, which is the first step to consider when making your design."

❧

Joel and his younger brother were instantly entranced by the television. They watched as a more-focused shot of a man circled around in a field. The camera changed to his perspective and the shot showed a pair of feet standing on a plank with rope coming up from both ends. The frame rotated as he circled around and repeated a process of lifting the rope while smashing whatever crop was underneath. Crunching noises filled the speakers. The camera zoomed back to reveal a perfect circle of smashed wheat around him. The point of view changed once more, revealing the same man surrounded by a black round pit.

"Notice how I enter the field. The wheat is about waist high, so I'll step over it as best as I can. I'm able to plant my feet within the rows of wheat. They're usually between four and six inches apart for most crops."

Feet rose into view, up and over the stalks, and then vanished. The camera turned to the board he was holding. He waved it back and forth behind him as he walked.

"Brushing behind prevents trails in or out of the field."

A faint, wavy trail vanished after it was brushed by the board. Another camera shot, much closer and clearer, revealed both men in the center of their first miniature circle; the shot panned to the man with the strange hat. His face was blurred. The other stepped out from the smashed wheat, enough so that the left edge of his board overlapped the downed stalks. As if goose-stepping with a strange sling, he began to press flat an outer ring.

Joel and his brother watched unblinkingly as a rather large circle unfolded on the screen.

They revealed how to use stars in conjunction with slightly modified hats to make straight lines, and provided instructions on crafting crop-smashing tools using inexpensive materials one could purchase from any home repair store. More footage showed just how simple it was to make a crop circle. The two mysterious men explained how to make rings with un-flattened centers using one person as a stationary anchor, the other holding a length of rope. They showed how to make semicircles and other elaborate geometric designs using a protractor. It all looked so easy.

"We have to do this," said Joel.

"And we have to film it," said Mitchell.

Post-Production

Panting, Joel made it to the white minivan with Mitchell right behind him. His heart racing, he and his brother simultaneously busted into laughter.

"Freaking cows," said Mitchell.

The crunching noises in the field were nothing more than local livestock. Not mountain lions, bear, nor any other threatening carnivorous animal. Cows.

The glowing red eyes had given them a start, but the clanging of a cowbell broke the tension. Apparently, the dirt road near the airport was free range, and neighboring cattle had gathered near the fence to investigate the noises in the field.

Joel hopped in the driver's seat after putting the equipment in the back of the van.

"That was freakin' hilarious," said Mitchell as he opened a Red Bull. "We gotta have more cowbell." It was a bad impersonation of Christopher Walken. He took a swig and said, "This stuff is nasty, but it works. Kinda gets you here," he said, using his thumb and middle finger to clamp around his neck, "just below the ears."

"What are *cows* doing out here at one in the morning?" said Joel.

"What are *we* doing out here at one in the morning?"

"Good point. Cows. Never been so scared in my life."

"I know. That was awesome."

Joel grabbed the video camera from the front seat, turned it to Record, and pointed it at his brother, who was putting on a second sweater.

"Cold out there," Mitchell said, and smiled into the camera. "From here it doesn't look like we did anything." He turned and looked into the black field.

Joel zoomed in and captured black fuzziness.

"Somewhere out there is our very first crop circle. You probably can't see much, but out in that darkness is a circle over fifty-something feet wide with a straight line just as long that connects to a smaller circle, about sixteen or so feet wide. We were, uh …" a hint of laughter behind his voice "not quite done, I think, because we were cut short by something that plain creeped us out."

"Cows," Mitchell said in the background, and then, "*Creeped* is not a word."

"Anyway, we'll explain everything back to the house. We're not going back out there anytime soon. As you can see …" Joel zoomed out and focused on the broken tool at Mitchell's feet. "We had us a casualty. The ground was a little wetter than we thought—well, we didn't think there'd be *any* water out there."

Joel laughed again before asking, "What are you doing?"

The camera captured Mitchell standing like a flamingo. He had the toe from one of his socks pulled past his head.

"Taking off my socks. They're soaked through. We should get rubber boots next time."

"And some new wood for our tools. Maybe the dowels."

"I was thinking pipe," said Mitchell. "You know, like plumbing pipe or whatever it's called. That heavy-duty but light stuff. Maybe an inch round or something."

"That would work."

"You know what they're going to call this one?"

"What?" Joel zoomed in to his brother's contorted face.

"They'll call it the Brenden Airport Crop Circle. Those crop circle enthusiasts always give them generic names like that. A city and a location. Real basic." He finally managed to pull off the first sock and started on the second. "Man, my shoes are *caked* in mud. There's got to be an inch stuck on the treads. It felt like I was walking on platforms out there. There's even an imprint from the board on my right one."

Joel spoke back into the camera as he moved off his brother's dance and back to the field. "We just kind of winged it. Not bad, in my opinion. According to the clock on this camera, we were out there for a little over an hour, and most of that time was figuring out what to do and checking out the crop circle. It's kind of cool out there. Almost glows. After flattening out the larger circle, it kind of seemed like a spotlight was over us and that anyone passing by on the road would be able to see us. Now that we're back at the van, everything looks black. You can't even see what we did."

"We could probably take the camera with us for the next one," said Mitchell. He was putting on fresh socks.

"Where'd you get extra socks?"

"From the van. I brought 'em."

"You bring *two?*"

"One for each foot, yeah. The camera doesn't have a light, but there might be enough natural light once we're out there for us to film some of it."

REPRODUCTION

The following morning, they were planning their next proj-ect. Two projects, in fact. The plan was to head out an hour earlier than the night prior—both figured it would still be dark enough not to draw suspicion—and to not produce one crop circle, but two, one right after the other.

"I figure we'll only need an hour or two tops for each," said Mitchell. "Unless we get spooked again. And we can't do it near the airport this time. I was thinking just east of Brenden—Shelton. I did a Google satellite map before you got up from your beauty sleep and the place is surrounded by wheat fields. Well, at least it looks like wheat. Most of the town looks like little yellow rectangles on the map.

"Yellow?" said Joel.

"Not quite yellow. More of light-sand-tan than yellow. Crayola would have called it *Saudi Yellow.*"

"Like Indian Red?"

"Didn't they get sued for political correctness?"

"Maybe," said Joel. "I don't think Saudi Yellow would fly, either."

"See, right here," said Mitchell, pointing out the fields alongside Route 19. "And it's within the flight path—or whatever they call it—of Brenden Airport, close enough that the planes would be low so passengers could see from their windows."

"Cool. We'll check it out after Home Depot."

"I checked online. They have these eight-foot sections of one-and-a-quarter-inch pipe for sale for four bucks. They're threaded at the ends, but they'll work for what we want. PVC was cheaper, but it would probably break easier than the wood."

"Anything you haven't figured out this morning?"

"Yeah, your design. How far have you gotten?"

"Done," said Joel. "I worked on it last night."

Joel pulled out the lined paper and showed him a sketch.

"What is it? Looks like Pac-Man impaled on a cocktail toothpick or something; got him just before he reached a power pellet. Or a bird pecking at a seed."

"A bird? You don't see it?" Joel turned the image around.

"Ah. Clever … your name." He admired it. "Cool."

"What do you have so far? Looks like you've been busy."

Papers with geometric designs littered the coffee table, as well as pictures of crop circles from around the world.

"Nothing *now*." He crumpled a recent sketch. "If we're going to make *your* name, we have to make *mine*."

Joel smiled. "The trick is to make it symmetrical."

"There's no symmetry in your name. The 'O' the 'E' and the 'L' yeah, if you draw them like *that* …"

"You know what I mean."

"Man. 'M' is really going to suck, but I think we can pull it off. The rest of my name is easy. We'll definitely need the protractor. Especially with your bird's beak and my native guy's double-chin."

Joel watched him sketch the formation. It took only moments and then he turned the page for him to see. It was mirrored, for the most part

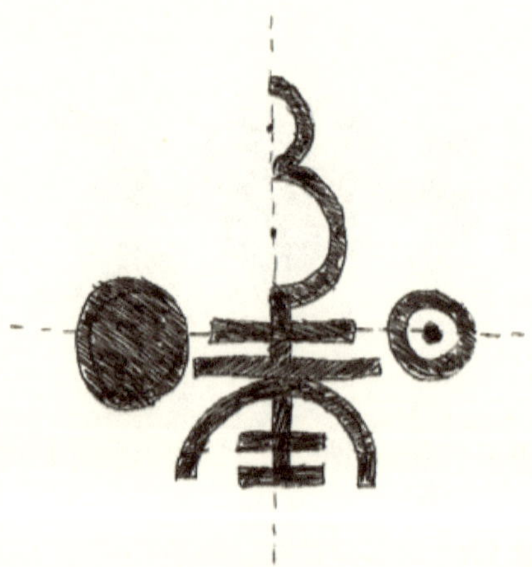

Laughing, Joel said, "That's awesome. It looked like you were drawing some kind of angry face with a black eye." He put it next to his own. "They both look hieroglyphic."

"That should throw people off."

Later that afternoon, they walked the aisles once again at Home Depot. They found the piping from the ad and bought a hacksaw because Joel couldn't remember if he had one back at the house. Mitchell found rubber boots, which seemed oddly placed in a home improvement store.

The same girl was at the checkout stand. She caught Mitchell staring at her tattoo before saying, "I remember you." Her voice was cute, a little raspy. She rang up the section of pipe, the two sets of rubber boots, and then the hacksaw.

"Weren't you here yesterday buying rope?"

"That would be us," said Joel.

"And batteries," said Mitchell. "D-cell."

"*Right*," she said. "Quite the project, huh?"

"Yeah," said Mitchell. "Tomorrow we'll be back for a shovel and some lime."

"I bet," she said as she bagged the hacksaw."

"Do you have a drill at home?" asked Mitchell.

"Who, me?" she said.

"No, sorry." Mitchell had been staring again and quickly turned to his brother.

"Yeah," said Joel.

"Cool."

Joel handed the girl exact change for the purchase.

"See you boys tomorrow," she said. "Both shovels and lime can be found at the far end of the store. We don't carry headstones, though." She smiled and rang up the next customer.

"She looks familiar," said Mitchell as they walked out the glass double doors.

"She rang us up yesterday."

"I know. I just mean she looks *familiar*. Like I went to school with her."

"Back in California? I doubt it."

"She looks like Natalie Portman from that movie where she played the stripper."

"*Closer?*"

"Yeah, but without the pink hair, when she wasn't wearing the wig. She has the same pouty face. Or maybe Kiera Knightley, just without the accent. Sometimes those two could pass as twins. The teller looked like a mix of the two."

"I don't see it."

"No? Maybe it's just me."

"It's just you."

When they turned onto Route 19 toward Shelton, it was a matter of picking which field looked easiest to trespass. For a few miles, wheat fields lined both sides of the two-lane highway. A stretch of Saudi Yellow split by paved road. They drove for five minutes down 19 before turning back.

"Does it matter to you which field we use?" asked Joel. "They all look the same to me. We could basically drive out here tonight and pull over anywhere. There's not even any barbed wire, only cheap fencing stretched over fencepost."

"There's a gravel road up ahead," said Mitchell. "Slow down a second. It's not on the map. We could park the van a little ways down there so no one would see it from the highway. The last thing we want is for highway patrol to see the van parked on the shoulder and think it's abandoned, only later to find crop circles in the fields not far from where they found it. *That* wouldn't be good."

A Boeing flew overhead with a roar.

"Perfect," said Joel.

Mitchell waved at it and said, "What time is it?" He looked at the sun. "Twelve forty-five-ish?"

Joel looked at his watch, knowing Mitch was close. "It's about ten 'til one"

While Mitchell held each section of pipe tightly against the workbench, Joel drilled quarter-inch holes through the ends. The clothesline fit easily through and they tied sections of the rope to the pipes in similar fashion as they had with the wooden planks.

"This'll work great," Mitchell said, entering the house.

"*Thistle*, huh?" Joel closed the door behind him.

Mitchell tested the first of two tools on the brown shag carpet in the living room. He mocked smashing down an initial round. He went around the carpet once more wearing the boots. Rubber boots, khaki shorts, a T-shirt boasting JESUS WAS A HOLEY MAN; that was his brother in a nutshell.

Joel tied off the rope on the second tool and tried it himself, minus the boots and wacky T-shirt. "Nice." He leaned it against the couch and grabbed the camera. "Go around a few more times on the carpet, Mitch. I have to get this on film."

The red camera light turned on and through the viewfinder Joel focused on the tan interior of the minivan, Mitchell sporting his strange hat, and finally past him and through the passenger window to another field of darkness. The camera kept auto-focusing on the window until his brother lowered it.

"Here we are," said Joel, "the future home of the Mitch Crop Circle in Shelton, Washington."

Joel recorded fuzzy black.

They had parked off the gravel road about four miles down Route 19 as they had previously determined. So far, not a single vehicle passed them on the adjacent highway. It was a quiet night.

Still holding the camera, Joel exited the cabin. Gravel crunched under boots. He panned around to record their surroundings. The moon was bright, but the sinister sky overpowered everything else. Directly behind the van were blinking lights from a landing plane. He wasn't sure if the camera was picking up anything, but as he circled in place, the center of the screen followed the horizon: dark blue on top; black on the bottom. He recognized Sirius this time and smiled. Farther away was the Brenden Airport, and even farther away a soft yellow-orange glow against the mountain range. As Joel completed the turn, Mitchell was outside the minivan and checking the contents of the backpack one final time to verify they had everything they would need.

"Ready to do this?"

"Waiting on you," said Mitchell.

Joel turned off the camera and handed it to his brother, who put it in the bag with the rope and other supplies.

They decided to start with Mitch's design first since it would be the larger of the two and by far the most time-consuming. "Yours will be easy," Mitch had said earlier that day. Each wore extra clothing: two pairs of socks under their boots, thermals under their jeans, long-sleeve shirts, and sweaters, and Joel a beanie this time. It was warmer than their last outing, but still below fifty and would only get colder as the night progressed, possibly in the low forties. They were professionals now and had everything planned in advance.

Each grabbed a pole from the back of the van. It was the only thing Joel carried with him into the field this time. Mitchell carried everything else on his back.

Joel entered first with Mitchell following. The wooden fence was easily hurdled and the wheat was five feet in and started waist high. It was a few inches taller than the last crop and seemed drier. It was difficult to tell the color at night, but had appeared earlier as more yellow. The wheat had a smell similar to wet hay and cooked cauliflower. Because of its height, it was more difficult to step over, but within minutes they were far into the field. A car passed, which made Joel turn, but it kept on going. They were too far into the field to be seen from the road.

Concerned with nothing but the road, Joel mused. *No one ever looks into fields when they drive. Passengers maybe, but never the driver. This late, the only thing interesting to a driver would be what was on the radio, or the dashed lines painted on the asphalt.*

Mitchell had stopped to watch the car as well. When it was out of sight / out of mind, he continued high-stepping and brushing the tops of the stalks behind him.

The ground mushed under their feet.

"I I like the wooden planks better," Joel said.

"Why?"

"These aren't that heavy, but after holding them chest-level long enough, they quickly *become* heavy."

After ten minutes they were hundreds of feet into the

field, the minivan just a Matchbox toy car in the distance. With the moon above, they stood within a moving silver sea of wheat, only their torsos visible.

"I'm already working up a sweat," said Mitchell, "but my face is about to freeze off."

The wind was soft, but chilling. The field softly hummed.

"This is probably a good starting point," said Joel.

Both admired the field, mostly to catch their breaths.

"It's amazing how much you can see out here," said Joel. "The moon works like a giant spotlight."

"The stars are incredible," said Mitchell. "You can't see this stuff in the city."

"What's that upside-down double-u?"

"Cassiopeia." He wasn't looking at Cassiopeia, but at all the constellations.

"There's the Big Dipper," said Joel. "I know that one, at least. And there's the Little Dipper next to it. The one at the end of the handle's the North Star, right?"

"No." For a moment, Mitchell was silent. "See the bright two stars that make up the right side pan on the Big Dipper?"

"Yeah."

"Follow the line they make until you see the next bright star that aligns with them. That's the North Star."

"It's not very bright."

"No." Mitchell held up a splayed set of fingers. "Imagine that star is the center of a flat, rotating disc, with all these other stars printed on it." He rotated his hand. "Everything in the sky rotates around that star. Well, sort of. It just looks that way. That's why you can always seem to find either the Big or Little Dipper somewhere in the sky. Because they're so close to it."

"I always thought *that* one was the North Star." Joel pointed to one of the brighter stars in the sky.

"Most do. That's actually Arcturus. It's a couple hundred times larger than our sun. It arcs off the handle of the Big Dipper, hence the name."

"What?"

"Arcturus means bear. Ursa Major and Ursa Minor? Anyway, are we going to study astronomy or do this thing?"

"I say we start here and go *that* way." Joel pointed the direction opposite of the van.

"We can use that yellow house light—or whatever it is—way over there for reference."

They started with the trickiest letter first, the 'M', by following the basic steps for smashing a circular shape, but halving it from the get-go and starting from the outer edge first. It was Mitchell's formation, so he made the first arc. As planned, he gave the backpack—as well as the protractor—to Joel, and tied one half of a forty foot section of rope to one of the straps on the pack and the other around his waist. He high-stepped toward their target until the rope pulled tight. Joel stood there motionless and watched the counter-clockwise progress as his end of the rope traveled from zero degrees onward. Mitchell went around and kept the rope tight the entire time, which produced one of the humps of the 'M.' His brother and the rope, in other words, had become an extended arm to the protractor. Joel told him to stop once they hit 180 degrees. From end to end, the arc was eighty feet across, and four feet wide. The next hump was smaller—opposite of Mitch's drawn design—but still sixty feet across.

Instead of forming the 'I,' Joel traded hats with his brother and headed toward the yellow light of the distant house. He counted a hundred steps while keeping it within the loop of the tie—quite a distance, his aching thighs told him—before walking back to his brother.

"Your turn."

Mitchell made the main section of the 'I' by starting at the end of the second hump and cross-sectioning the long straight line Joel had created. They took turns high-stepping from each end. Mitchell went farther out and smashed six rotations in the field—a circle forty-eight feet in diameter. On the opposite end, Joel made only a starting round, and then called his brother over. Tying himself to the backpack, Joel high-stepped a little less than twenty feet out from the small circle, and had Mitchell pull the rope.

"Rotate around with me. I'll keep the rope tight as I go around like you did." Joel went around an entire rotation, had his brother release about three to four feet of rope, and had him pull it tight before going around a second time. This gave the second circle a bull's-eye appearance with an outer ring eight feet wide and forty feet across.

They made it look easy, as if it weren't their second crop circle, but their hundredth. The rest was a cakewalk compared to the first two characters. The 'T' was another long cross-section, the 'C' a semicircular arc a hundred-something feet in diameter, and the 'H' just two parallel smaller cross-sections at the end of the long path Joel had made. The entire formation was completed in two hours. A majority of that was them soaking up the moonlight.

"This thing is colossal," said Joel.

They stood at the end of the second hump. Even with

the two of them inside the formation, the individual characters in Mitch's name were easily recognizable.

"It really is," said Mitchell. "No cows this time to scare us away, either. Let me see the backpack."

Joel took it off and handed it to him.

"I bet this looks cool from the sky," said Joel, "just like those Peruvian things, you know, those carvings in the ground you can only see from a plane or helicopter."

"The Nazca Lines?"

"Yeah. *Geoglyphs.* That's what they're called."

"I saw a show on that once," said Mitchell as he dug through the bag. "Discovery Channel." He pulled out the video camera and set the backpack on the ground next to their tools. "Everything looks fine through the camera. I hope this turns out, because it looks awesome." He panned and recorded in silence, and then broke it by saying, "Well, my name is Mitch, and this is my formation." It sounded like an Alcoholics Anonymous introduction. "I don't know about Joel, here, but I could use a break for a while, maybe a Red Bull, and then we're off to one of these other fields out here. Someplace close to this one, so they're found around the same time. The Shelton Hieroglyph Crop Circles, they'll call 'em, or something lame. If we're lucky, these will track all sorts of crowds: crop circle enthusiasts, camouflage-wearing scientists, Fox Mulder, Dana Scully, maybe a stupid little girl who hears angels clapping whenever she's in them. Should be fun."

The red light clicked off and they soon carefully high-stepped their way out of the field and made it safely to the minivan.

SHAPES IN THE FIELD

Joel drove them back into Brenden for a breather. They stopped at a Chevron a little after one in the morning. Both were thirsty. Joel let the van idle while Mitchell ran into the gas station convenience store for drinks.

"You sure you don't want a pick-me-up?" asked Mitchell. "Red Bull, Monster, Amp, some No-Doze, Go Girl?"

"Just water."

"Any preference?"

"No, just get me a Dasani or something."

Joel rolled down the front windows to let in the night air. He couldn't help but look to the car at his left. The man in the SUV tapped his fingers against the steering wheel while he looked to the glass entry of the station. The man saw Joel looking and flipped his head back—the current greeting between two men who didn't know one another. Joel turned his attention to the radio. He cycled through the channels but the only thing worth listening to was "Fake Plastic Trees" by Radiohead, Thom Yorke careening *'it wears me out'* over and over again. The lyrics were confusing, but the music was good.

Mitchell returned with two Red Bulls and a brand of water Joel didn't recognize. He joined him in the van and threw everything on the seat.

"I got you one just in case you need it later."

"Eh, why not," said Joel. He grabbed one of the small blue and silver cans, popped the lid, and drank a third of it. It tasted like liquid Pixy Stix.

Mitchell was done with his own by the time they pulled onto the highway. They drove a few minutes in silence. The fields were not far away.

"Put the water in the backpack," said Joel. "We might want it later while we're out there." The dashed white lines held him for a moment. "I was thinking that since my name will be so much easier to do than yours, we should make the main circle huge."

"Sure," said Mitchell. "How big were you thinking?"

"I don't know. Maybe a hundred feet across."

"If we went around thirteen times, that would be a hundred and four feet. We could go bigger …"

"Nah. A hundred plus is fine. If we still have energy, we can go around more. We could always make the other letters bigger."

"True."

Once they turned onto Route 19, both kept staring to the fields. From the cabin there was nothing to see but blurry black and the reflectors flashing on the road ahead. The crops and the sky appeared one and the same.

"Man," said Mitchell, "even if someone driving by *were* looking for something in the fields, there's no way they'd ever see anything. I can't see more than ten feet out."

Every time a car passed in the opposite lane, it took a while for Joel's eyes to adjust and for the fields at either side to reappear. It was like driving down a dark tunnel. He hated driving at night and his eyes were letting him know it.

Squinting, Joel said, "I think that's the gravel road."

"I think so, too."

No one was behind them, so Joel slowed down to about ten miles per hour and rolled down his windows.

"Yeah. That's it. Can you see anything?"

"No … wait—no." Mitchell flashed the Maglite but could not find their crop circle.

"Help me find another side road," said Joel.

A dirt road greeted them not far ahead.

"How about here?" It wasn't really a question and his brother didn't answer. "I think this is the next field over."

"It is," said Mitchell. "The fence was continuous until this road, so it must be."

Joel turned left onto the unmarked road and parked. He killed the engine and killed the lights and they both sat there in the cabin looking into the adjacent field.

"Ready for round two?"

"Let's do it."

They waited for a lone set of headlights to pass them on the highway before opening the doors and stepping out.

Joel opened the hatch. "Where's the other stick?"

"What?"

"The other pole. There's only *one* back here."

"Maybe it slid under the seats."

"No. There's just the metal one and wooden one. Joel's voice grew panicked as he searched. "I know I put mine here. Where'd you put yours?"

"I thought I put it back here."

"You *think*, or you *know*?"

Mitchell slapped his forehead and peered onto the roof.

"You put it on top of the van?"

This also wasn't a question.

"I put it on the roof while I was taking off my shoes and socks. I remember putting the backpack on the front seat and grabbing a sweater from the back, but I don't remember taking it off the roof."

"You didn't leave it on the ground somewhere?"

"No. I'm a moron. I left it on top of the van. It must have rolled off somewhere close, though. It couldn't have stayed on top of the van long."

"Don't you think we would've heard it roll off, or some kind of clank when it hit the ground?"

"If it fell off while we were on the gravel road, yeah. On the highway, no. I had you crank up the radio when that Tool song came on."

Joel sighed loudly.

"Let's just drive down the road and see if we can find it," said Mitchell. "It's got to be close. Drive slow. I'll use the flashlight."

Joel backed onto the highway. He drove up and down Route 19, as well down the first gravel road.

"We're never going to find it. We've already wasted half an hour."

"It has to be here somewhere. It didn't just disappear."

"Do you *see* it anywhere? Because *I* sure don't. I can't believe you left it on top of the van."

"*Sorry*. Mistake happens."

"Wait, what was that?"

"What?"

"Shine the light back on the right side of the road." Joel slowed significantly. "I saw something shiny."

"Where?"

"Far to the right. Past the ditch."

"That?" Mitchell pointed the beam to a section of fencing. There was something shimmering in the loose wire.

"Is that it?" asked Joel. He pulled to the shoulder and looked past his brother.

"What is that, a tire iron? What's a tire iron doing hanging on the fence?"

"I don't know, but I'm getting tired of looking for our pole. Let's just forget it. We can come back tomorrow when it's not so dark. You can use the wooden one since you lost your good one."

"Sounds good." Mitchell rolled up his window and turned up the heater.

Joel drove them back to the second field. The dashboard clock read 2:02 before they exited the vehicle.

"You want to lead us out this time?"

"Sure." Mitchell climbed over the fence.

Joel followed and brushed the wheat behind them.

"Is this far enough?"

They were about the same distance into the field as they had started with the last formation.

"It's *your* formation," said Mitchell. "You start it."

Using his pole, Joel worked his way around. And then again. And again. They didn't speak much as they smashed the large circle; they didn't need to. Mitchell joined him on the fourth round. Joel made the fifth, Mitchell the sixth, and so on. Two water breaks and an hour later, they had completed their largest formation yet, an 'O' over a hundred feet in diameter. Mitchell's wooden plank broke on his last time around; Joel finished it for him.

They made the 'J' next, a quarter-circle outline. Since Joel made most of the largest circle, Mitchell sported the backpack for the curves and dotted the 'J' with a smaller circle only twenty-four feet across. They traded the back-pack and metal tool back and forth as they finished his name. Joel made the semi-circle outline for the 'E' and finished the design by smashing a perpendicular 'L' at the end.

By the time they were finished, both were fatigued, sweaty, and sore. The larger circle seemed mammoth. As the crow files, their entire first crop circle could have easily fit within it. Mitchell set the backpack down in the middle of this circle and they high-stepped back to the smaller circle of the 'J'. It was the best place to film the larger circle, and from it Joel could pan the camera from side to side to capture the entire cylindrical impression. The counter-clockwise swirl in the wheat was impressive, a large downward spiral.

"This thing is freakin' huge," said Mitchell.

"I know, I can't help but keep staring at it."

They admired the formation a while, discussing stupid things such as which animals sucked blood, such as ticks and leeches. It was an odd subject; not the best thing to discuss before sun-up, but Joel had started the conversation by telling his brother about the garlic he sprayed around his yard to keep mosquito population down during the summer.

Joel drank what was left in the water bottle and handed it to his brother.

"Where'd you leave the backpack?"

"I put it in the middle so we could find it." Mitchell turned on the Maglite and pointed it to the center.

"Jesus!" Joel fell to his knees, his heart racing. He grabbed the flashlight from his brother.

"What?" Mitchell joined him on the ground.

Next to the bag, something large had moved.

Running Through the Mud

Oh God something took him Joel deliberated as he looked over his shoulder to his younger brother as he ran and he … he stopped for a breath and watched Mitch disappear into a mist of swirling black … dropped his pole and ran without him and ran and he ran … the flashlight bounced from side to side, casting triangles of yellow ahead while something black ate his brother … the flattened stalks glowing as he ran and the eyes behind him glowing as he ran … *I only have to outrun my brother* he first thought when they saw the eyes in the field that were simply cows *and this is not a cow or a mountain lion or a wolf or an animal of any kind* he thought as he tripped over something thorny in the field and fell flat onto his face and cracked his head and for a second he admired the red flower of a rose and wondered if the red on its petals was blood and he got up and ran and he ran and … he ran with gasping breaths … for air as the black swirl finished his brother because he screamed, and Joel turned back to see if he was still there but he wasn't and a marvelous free-flowing shape of black turned in his direction … *chasing me chasing me, oh God it's chasing me now* and the van shrank away as he ran in the wrong direction to the road as warmth dripped down his face from where a sharp rock had cut him when fell hard next to the rosebush and he ran to the road and the van was … it was too far away to turn back … his brother was gone and he dropped the flashlight somewhere and ran to the road leaving lightning-like trails through wheat that couldn't be brushed away and he ran to the white light of a truck barreling down the highway with only one bulb … and *maybe he could help* he wondered as he ran … and he ran to the fence and over the low barbed wire that cut his shins and his ankles and his palms and he waved his arms frantically into the air to the man in the truck … and he … and he ran into the road and looked back one last time and saw nothing was following him and then turned back to the light.

Part Five

Death of 'Odd

TWELVE

… have a taste, Dad?" Charlie had turned fifteen two months ago; there wasn't a party.

Emotionless, his father finished the bottle of beer and held it out to him. From the grimace on his face, the last gulp must have tasted terrible. He held a book in his other hand—something with *Son* in the title. "Maybe in a few years I'll let you taste how awful this crap really is. You wouldn't like it anyway."

"How would you know if you never let me have a sip?" Charlie knew his dad was drunk again; he could tell by the bloodshot eyes and flushed face. His head bobbed like a bobble-head doll, only less dramatic. He carried an odor around with him—a mix of *piss-belch-fart* was the only way Charlie could describe it.

"Your grandpa, *my* dad … once told me that there's no sense in drinking if you don't plan on gettin' drunk, otherwise it's a waste of good booze," his father said, surprisingly without slur for how sloshed he had become. "Know what that means, son?" he set his book aside. It fell in the dirt. *Crimson Petals* by Cray Marrow.

"No."

"Well, when you find out, I'll let you in on a sip. Deal? Deal. Wanna recycle this one for me?" He held the bottle out to Charlie a second time and Charlie took it. "Don't tell your mom how many I've had. She'd kill me."

Charlie had no clue how many beers his father had over the course of the day. Ten? Twelve? He stopped counting years ago. The record was two-dozen once on a Saturday. He drank more on warm summer days it seemed. The accident with Todd happened during summer.

Leaving his father alone in the barn, Charlie took the bottle out back and put it with the others. If one good thing came out of his father's alcoholism, it was that Charlie and Cindy got to split the recycling money. It was usually about ten bucks apiece every two to three months, a nice little bonus to have come allowance time.

Charlie lifted the lid to the aluminum trashcan and threw in the brown bottle. He had contemplated taking a swig from the remains of the bottle first, but decided not to after smelling it. *Piss-belch-fart.* It clanked loudly, but didn't break. He grabbed for it and was about to try again but saw Todd at the screen door at the back of the house.

Todd squinted at the moon as if in pain. Sometimes in certain lights, it would look as if Todd had drawn all over himself with red marker; sometimes the scars looked purplish, or gray. His head was ill-proportioned to the rest of his body and unsymmetrical. His eyes turned from the moon to Charlie. He brought his hand to his mouth, the tips of each finger meeting at a point, and patted his lips. It was the sign for *eat.*

After the accident, Charlie and Cindy took up sign language as an after school program. In a full school year, both he and Cindy had learned enough signs to talk to one another. After another two years, they were signing somewhat fluently. It was easier to communicate with Todd that way, with no worries of him sounding strange, or making too much noise. Sometimes it was kind of like using a secret code only they knew. His mother also knew sign language; she had taken classes long ago in college and could remember some of it. His father couldn't care less about the language. He thought it was a waste of money and a waste of time, except for the inappropriate signs Charlie taught him, like *dumb*, and *ugly*. He knew the sign for *drink*: to mock swigging back on a bottle.

Dinner, signed Todd, followed by *Charlie*, a sign Todd had given Charlie, which was similar to *dumb*, except Todd bounced a C-shaped hand against his brow instead of a balled fist.

Charlie shook his head and signed his own word he had given Todd, the letters o, d, and another d. Odd. If Charlie could be Dumb Charlie, Todd could be Odd Todd.

What's for dinner? signed Charlie.

Stew, signed Todd, and *beans*.

Seeing his brother sign *beans* made him sad. He couldn't help but think of Joey Bean.

"Mom, what's for dinner tonight?" asked Cindy.

She's was almost as tall as Charlie, depending on her shoes. At the table she and her brother were level. Charlie sat next to her.

Stew, signed Todd from the other side of the table.

"Aww ..." said Cindy. "Todd said we're having stew. We had it two nights ago. Are we having anything else? Todd doesn't like stew."

Stew love, signed Todd.

A *clang* stopped the complaining. Mom had dropped the pot, too hot to hold. Steaming broth splashed in a tunneled wave out from the pot and onto her hand. A spatter of meat and potato covered the tile countertop. Some fell to the linoleum in splotches.

Bread, signed Todd. *Smell?*

Sure enough, the smell of burning garlic bread followed. Mom turned back to the oven, pulled open the door, and fanned at the billows of smoke. Her mind must have been elsewhere because she grabbed the tray and burned her fingers. She swore to herself, and then repeated the curse loud enough for neighbors to hear, over and over again. Her face flushed, tears welling in her eyes.

Both Cindy and Charlie watched in disbelief as she swatted the stewpot onto its side, spilling the contents everywhere. Without oven mitts, she opened the oven door, grabbed the hot tray with both hands, and heaved it across the room. Bread bounced off the far dining room wall. A blackened piece of garlic bread nearly hit Cindy in the head. The tray banged against the hutch, cracking glass in one of the small doors. Mom crouched to the floor, her hands held upward, red and shaky.

Todd rose from his seat. He stood in front of her and signed, *I love you.*

Mom looked right through him. She simply cried and stared at the kitchen window to a reflection of her sad face staring back.

After a long silence she said, "I'm going outside for fresh air."

"Hand me a beer, would'ya, Todd," Roy said. His words sloshed as freely as the remaining sip in the longneck he threw to the recycle can. The bottle missed and fell against the lid on the ground. Roy sat in damp grass behind the barn, wet from the leaky faucet valve he had yet to replace. Susan had asked him weeks ago to fix it. The hose was on, but without a purpose. Water pooled from the green snake farther away and fed some overtaking weeds. "Hand me that beer and come sit with me. I'll tell you about *my* dad."

There wasn't much light around the barn, only a single bulb stuck out from the socket near the main entrance. It cast yellow over Roy. The six-pack by his feet was five short.

Todd looked to the beer. *Dumb*, he signed. His scars looked black under the light.

"Fine, I'll get it myself. Yes, dumb. I don't know very many signs, but I've seen Charlie and Cindy use that one well enough on each other." Roy reached for the last of the longnecks. "What's the sign for father?"

Father.

"Right," said Roy. He twisted off the top, took a swig. "What about grandfather?"

Grandfather.

"Like father, but twice. Makes sense. I'll tell you about my dad, your," *grandfather*, Roy finished by signing. "Your grandfather was almost as horrible a father as me. He used to beat the living shit outta your dad. How'd you like it if you forgot to take the garbage out and I backhanded you across the jaw? That was my dad. He died the year Charlie was born."

Todd turned back to the house, and then to Roy.

"One time me and Dennis—your uncle Dennis—we

were at the dinner table and couldn't stop giggling. I don't remember what it was about, but we used to always get each other laughing over something. Maybe he made a face. Anyway, we hadn't even taken a bite and he caught us smirking. Slammed his fist on the table. Made your grandmother jump. We all jumped."

Roy chugged half the beer and continued, "Usually, he sent us to bed without dinner. Not that night. That night, for some reason or another, he decided he needed us to dig a trench in back for irrigation. The sun had already gone down, but he made us dig that trench with only a light like this one shining over the yard."

He pointed to the single bulb. "We were out there two hours, way past ten, before he called us in for the night. Our food was still on the table, cold. We ate and went straight to bed. Slept in our dirty clothes 'cause we were so tired. All night we listened to him and your grandmother argue."

Another swig from the beer.

Todd looked over his shoulder to the house.

Late, he signed.

"Watch?"

Late.

"Would you stop signing? You know I can't understand what you're saying. You telling me the time?"

Todd developed a painful expression on his face as he tried to compose the word, "'ate!"

Roy, bemused, lifted the bottle again to his lips.

"'ate."

"Eight?" Roy simply stared at his disfigured son.

Todd looked back to the house.

"Time to eat," asked Roy, "or you already ate?"

Father, Todd began to sign, but Roy ignored him and continued his storytelling.

"Your grandfather could be a horrible person sometimes, but he wasn't as bad a father as yours truly. He got us through life. Taught us things. How to fish, how to run a farm, how to make an honest dollar by working hard for it. The only thing he failed to teach me was how to put down a horse." Roy swirled the last of his beer, following the liquid around as he spied through the opening. He drank it down and cringed and threw the bottle off to the side. He couldn't even look at Todd.

"You're a good kid, Charlie."

Todd corrected him, taking much effort at his own name. It came out like a cough: "'odd!"

"Todd, right. Sorry, it's late."

Silence entrapped them: Todd focused on his father; Roy unable to focus on anything at all. He started to drift and felt a soft pain at his side.

"Dad," he heard from somewhere far away.

His side hurt.

"Dad."

Roy woke up to Charlie standing over him, kicking him in the side, holding one of his beers.

Charlie had offered to get Dad—he was out at the barn, drunk. He knew he'd be passed out against the barn door, snoring, half a cold beer still in his hand. The scruff on his face and neck seemed to have grown in that short time, a five o'clock shadow a little after eight in the evening. His oily hair was a matted mess, his shirt wrinkly and buttoned incorrectly. The hand not holding his beer held his crotch, as if he had fallen asleep adjusting himself. Perhaps he had.

"Dad."

Nothing.

"Dad."

Charlie kicked him in side and called even louder. It was like speaking to someone hard of hearing.

"Wake up, Dad."

His father only groaned.

Charlie picked up some dirt and threw it at his face.

"Dad."

He only swatted at the imaginary fly at his nose and grumbled.

"Time to get up, Dad."

"Okay, Scharley," his father slurred. Again he swatted the fly.

"Dad."

Still nothing.

Charlie bent down and pried the bottle from his hand. At first the fingers refused to let go, but then slid down and plopped on the ground. Charlie hesitated, and took a drink. It was nothing like soda, like he expected, but was bitter and grainy. It tasted awful. He held the bottle out and looked at the label. It was some kind of pale ale from a Seattle micro-brewery. He took another sip, one not so bad, but still bad.

He poured a bit onto his father's head. It fizzed and ran down the side of his face, enough to wake him up.

"Dad," Charlie repeated, kicking him again.

"Huh?" he said, not quite aware.

"Time to get up. It's late."

"Okay, Scharlie."

Charlie helped him and he staggered to his feet.

He took the bottle from Charlie, downed the rest, and handed it back.

"What's for dinner?"

"We already ate, but there's leftovers on the floor."

"Good, I'm starving." He looked up quizzically to the stars, wondering perhaps where his sun had gone. He then wiggled an upside-down "hang-loose" type gesture.

"That's *fat*, Dad."

"Oh."

Susan watched from Katherine Jensen's front porch as Charlie led Roy from the barn and to the house. He was drunk again. Heavy drunk. He ran into the sliding glass door when Charlie opened it for him. He headed straight to the refrigerator.

A cigarette dangled carelessly from Susan's mouth, ready to fall. The orange ember glowed a moment as she inhaled, softened as she exhaled. She sat on Katherine's porch swing, one leg crossed over the other. Her sadness was masked by the darkness, but dried tears glossed her cheeks.

She watched as Roy struggled from the house and to the barn again, another six-pack under his arm.

THIRTEEN

The mirror turns obsidian and the image of his mother fades, revealing the white spherical reflection of Loah, but not Todd. He touches the smooth surface only to find it solid. The floating mirror doesn't even budge, though it appears weightless.

"I must leave you for a while," says the light. "During this time, you will be guided."

So you can protect another?"

"Another's kin."

Where will I be guided?

The light of Loah sinks into black and soon he is alone in the whiteness.

Todd moves around the free-floating mirror, again noting the single word etched into the top of its wooden frame: SPIEGEL. *On the opposite side is another word:* FENSTER. *Instead of a mirrored face, Todd finds a window on the other side, and sees through it to more white. He expects to feel another solid surface as he presses a hand to the glass, but his hand passes through. Startled, he pulls back. Ripples form in the white like droplets of rain over a placid pond and stretch outward until the surface stills. Todd reaches through a second time and peeks around the frame. To his amazement, Todd's hand does not pass through it, but disappears; the opposite side remains black and featureless. He pulls back and watches the water-like effect until the ripples vanish.*

Left behind in the middle of the window is a hint of red, a soft,

274

cloudy sphere that lightly pulsates.

"Come with me, Todd," says the light, "You are to be guided."

Where?

"To one in need of protection."

How do we get there?

"Step into this world," says Nuveli. The red light begins to weaken.

How?

The voice of Nuveli is far away, barely audible. "You have already tested the waters," and then the voice is gone, along with its light.

Todd hesitates, but realizes what it is he must do. He feels for the frame, an invisible sill to this strange window or mirror or whatever it may be, and hoists himself onto it, his body half in and half out. In front of him awaits the brightest of whites. He teeters on the ledge, and slips into an early morning cold.

The sky turns dark, speckled with stars. Todd's is falling through the clouds, the ground miles below.

Nuveli is falling to the earth as well. The red light flickers.

Chilling air flurries around Todd as the outlines of farmlands take shape: a blue river snaking around them with leeches of irrigation, lines of fencing, square rooftops, the green mushroom caps of oak trees, an orange fire burning in the mountains. Just as he panics, Todd hears the soothing voice of Nuveli.

"Open your mind."

The horizon gives birth to a rising sliver of yellow light. Below Todd the farmlands broaden, the rooftops enlarge, the trees sprout from the ground. And then he remembers his conversion from before with the one whose name means Death.

I am Thade, the balancer.

"What do you balance?" Todd had asked.

I balance life.

"How do you balance life?" Todd had asked.

How are you a bat?

Todd unfolds his wings—for a while they flutter hard against the wind—and takes control. He glides downward in a spiral.

Below is Nuveli, floating gracefully ten feet ahead of Todd, pulsating at a much slower pace than before.

Todd glances to his wings; they stretch five feet to each side.

He and Nuveli circle down, the single house below them now more defined. A wooden fence separates it from a neighboring home.

"We watch from here," says Nuveli.

The sky around them is morning blue, the sun not yet above the mountains. The crisp air is refreshing.

A flickering streetlight on the sidewalk casts a white triangular light from its bulb. But Todd discovers is not a bulb at all. It is Loah.

Who is Loah here to protect? Todd wonders.

They circle above like hawks, watching, listening, waiting.

Below them a sliding glass door opens and then closes. A young boy in pajamas, maybe five or six, walks out from under the patio covering in the back yard. His hair is brown and ruffled, flattened on one side as if he just got out of bed. His bare toes squish in mud. He walks to the good-neighbor fence. The fence is weathered. Some of the wooden planks are rotted and holey.

A massive canine growls on the other side, its head low to the ground, ready to pounce.

The light from the streetlight blinks vibrantly. The child mocks the animal, even growls.

For an instant there is nothing but silence, and then the canine bursts through a section of fence. It pins the boy down, goes for the throat, the chest, the wiry arms trying to fight back. Shards of wood lay around them. The boy is thrown around like a rag doll within the creature's mouth.

A soft white hemisphere of light surrounds them both. It is Loah protecting the boy. The light becomes brilliant before it implodes and is absorbed by the lifeless body beneath the hound. A woman still in her nightgown runs out from under the patio covering and attacks it with a shovel. The beast yelps and flees back through the hole in the fence from which it came. The woman joins the boy in the mud and rocks on the balls of her feet as she cradles him in her arms. She rises to her knees before lifting him up and walking him into the house. A pool of reddish-brown stays behind.

Todd looks for the canine, but everything turns white. They are back at the floating mirror / window and he can again see right through the face marked FENSTER.

The voice of Nuveli asks, "Do you understand?"

Todd doesn't answer.

The red light floats out of the white and moves around to the other side, to the black reflective face marked SPIEGEL.

Todd joins the light.

He looks into the black and sees an older reflection of himself signing to someone who is hidden by the wooden frame.

Follow, *say the hands.*

FOURTEEN

Cindy sat with Charlie on the couch watching *Andy Grif-fith* on Channel Thirteen. There were Saturday morning cartoons to watch, but *Andy* was better. Charlie turned up the volume to drown out a lawnmower outside. The theme song whistled on the tube. Cindy finished her cereal and placed the bowl of soggy Cocoa Pebbles on the coffee table in front of her. Then she saw Todd at the top of the stairs. He held an index finger to his lips.

Follow, he signed.

Cindy looked to Charlie, but he was entranced by Don Knotts. She didn't' sign back to Todd; she simply got up and followed her little brother.

At the top of the stairs she shrugged and signed, *What?*

Here, he signed, and led her into her own room. Todd's hair was cut short and she saw the scars clearly, some a quarter of an inch wide. His head was sectioned in lumps where his skull had broken. He looked pieced back together like the glued chunks of a broken vase. The right side of his cranium—a term she had learned while Todd was in the hospital—was a little larger than the left. His walk was more of a waddle, like a penguin.

When they got to her room, he pointed to her desk.

What? she signed again.

Card, he signed and then mocked writing with pen.

"Huh?" she said. *Why?*

He pointed to a collection of stationary, and extended all five fingers of his right hand, resting his thumb onto his chin. *Mother*. He then signed *birthday* by tapping his middle finger against his chin and then to his heart.

Cindy signed the S-word by grabbing her right thumb with her left hand and then dropping it out like a turd.

Bad, he signed, and smiled.

Where Mother? she signed.

Sleeping.

Dad forget?

He nodded. *And Charlie.*

Dumb Charlie she signed. "We should make her a card."

Cindy rummaged through her stationary and found some thick off-white cardstock. She folded a piece in half. On the front, in block lettering, she wrote HAPPY BIRTHDAY, and filled the letters with pink. *Favorite flower?* she signed.

Todd shrugged.

She didn't know signs for specific flowers, so she spelled out *daisy* and raised her palms in the air.

He shrugged again.

She spelled out *rose* and raised an eyebrow.

Todd's eyes lit up. He nodded with both his abnormal head and with his hand.

Cindy couldn't help but smile. Even with all the railroad track scars running along his face, and the offset nose and eye and slack-jawed chin, she couldn't avoid the happiness on her little brother's face. It was beautiful. His goofy face was beautiful.

"Roses," she said.

For the next fifteen minutes, she drew her mother roses.

At commercial break Charlie took his bowl, along with Cindy's, to the kitchen to rinse them out. Dad passed by the window above the sink, the lawnmower motor rumbling. It was not even eight in the morning and he already had a beer in hand as he rode the John Deere across the yard. As he rinsed the bowls, Cindy barreled in.

In a quiet voice she said, "We need to find something for Mom."

"Like what?"

"Like a birthday present."

"Already?" Charlie checked the calendar next to the phone. It was the twenty-third of the month. The number was circled.

"Well, I only have two or three bucks, and Dad's not going to take us anywhere to buy her something."

"I made a card," she said. "Look."

She held it out to show him. HAPPY BIRTHDAY was written on its face in neat block lettering, and below it, a red rose. Charlie took it from her and opened it.

"It's blank inside."

"Yeah, I know. I thought we could all sign it or something. And then maybe find something to give her."

"We can't just sign it. We need to write something else."

"Such as …"

"I don't know. How about 'Happy Birthday, Mom'."

"It says 'Happy Birthday' on the front. And we're giving it *to* mom."

He looked at the front of the card again. "Write something about a rose. "Like, 'Petals whither and fall, but you are always in full bloom.' That's probably stupid."

"No, it's perfect." She grabbed the card from him.

"Is that from one of your love letters?" She smiled and signed her name.

"No." Charlie signed his name next to hers. "It's from a fortune cookie."

"Should we tell Dad?"

"Tell him what?"

"That it's Mom's birthday."

Charlie looked outside and thought hard about it. "No. Let him figure it out. So, what do we get her?"

Cindy checked the cabinets. Charlie watched as she pulled a box of Bisquick from one, a bottle of Aunt Jamima's from another. "I'll start breakfast. She's still in bed, so we can bring it up to her with some orange juice, the card, and flowers."

"What flowers?"

"The flowers you're going to pick before you help with breakfast." She eyed the back of the box for directions.

It was a good idea. There were some places in the backyard, behind the barn, where some pretty wildflowers usually grew. He could put together a bouquet. Mom would like it. Breakfast in bed, fresh flowers, a homemade card; what more could she ask for?

Cindy pulled a carton of eggs from the refrigerator and set them next to the mixing bowl on the counter. The pancakes required only eggs and water and / or milk. This would be a snap. She was about to start cracking the eggs when she remembered the card.

"Todd?" she called, not loud enough to wake Mom.

She turned around and he was at the kitchen table, staring at the ceiling. Sometimes he'd do that. He'd just stare at nothing for hours.

"Do you want to sign the card?"

There was no response. He couldn't sign the card.

"Here, I'll sign it for you."

Cindy was right-handed, but gripped the pen with her left, her whole hand around it. In a scribbled, oversized font she spelled his name, made the "t" lowercase, and the other letters uppercase, how she thought he would have done it.

Like all other mornings, Katherine Jensen got up at six. She made a small pot of coffee—the cheap kind that came in a container like a paint can. A cowboy was riding off into a red sunset that wrapped around to the nutritional information on the back. She scooped enough into the coffee maker for twelve cups, which was really three normal cups. She drank them black as she sat on the porch swing out front, getting up only for refills. She liked the morning routine, liked her feet bare against the cool wooden deck, liked watching the Kenseth's only remaining horse walk in the pasture.

They had named him Spirit because of the mark between his eyes, like a boy dressed for Halloween with a white bed sheet covering him as a disguise. The rest of the colt was a reddish-brown like its mother, Joey Bean. No one ever rode him. It was sad. You could tell he wanted riding by the way he pranced around kicking dirt everywhere. It would cloud around him and he'd whinny and run some more.

Every morning Katherine drank her coffee on the porch

and watched the colt. Every morning she remembered that dreadful night. It had changed her neighbors' lives.

They had decided to keep the horse, but sold the others, such a waste for so much wonderful property. Most of it had overgrown these last years. Only the one pasture stayed clean because of the horse. The other two were forgotten.

The barn had seen better days. The middle support beam had rotted through and was sinking into the ground. The roof sagged, the shingles were covered in moss and weathered away to nothing. Beneath it was junk needing to be taken to the dump. Roy would never dump it, just as he would never try to fix up the place.

He barely cared for the colt. He and Susan only held onto him for the kids. Charlie and Cindy refused to let either of them sell him when they were selling the other horses. Neither rode the colt. No one ever taught them how, and Katherine was too old herself to try and teach them. She couldn't live with herself if one of the kids ever fell. They treated Spirit like he was the last of all horses, brushed him almost daily, fed him oats they bought with their own allowances—Roy provided the alfalfa and walked him around with a lead rope every once in a while. They loved him like a brother. And Todd …

Bless his heart. Katherine couldn't help but think of that awful night and what the Kenseths must have gone through. She sat on her porch every damn morning drinking her coffee and thinking about it. "Todd got kicked in the head by the horse," Roy had said, or something similar. What a horrible feeling to hear those words. She'd never forget it. Susan holding Todd like one of Cindy's dolls. Roy scrambling with the others. Katherine watching them for the night as Susan left in the ambulance, Roy trying his darndest to follow behind. Katherine felt sorry for not being with them that night. She could have kept an eye on Todd if only she'd known it was Joey Bean's night to give birth. She hadn't even woken from the shot. Katherine remembered not feeling well that evening and catching sleep earlier than usual. She remembered reading in the paper there'd be a meteor shower—the Perseid—and regretting she'd miss it. If only she'd chosen the more difficult path in life, and not the simple other, maybe everything would have turned out fine for all of them, maybe the pastures would all be pastures and horses would fill them; Joey Bean would have died, but Katherine could have been watching Todd, and Roy would have put the mare down easily; Charlie and Cindy and Todd would be riding in the fields and Roy putting fresh coats of paint on the barn and Susan with him, slapping paint onto Roy's jeans, maybe getting a little red paint on herself, laughing like so little she laughed these days.

But life doesn't hand you oranges, her mother used to say, or something like it, it throws them at you, and you either catch them, or let them hit you.

Katherine watched as the colt left the water bin and searched for food on the ground. She'd had enough remembering for one day, got up from the porch swing, and headed inside to rinse out her mug. She decided she'd finish her routine by putting on some proper clothes and visiting the colt a while. She'd bring a carrot or an apple, or melon rinds she sometimes kept in a grocery bag in the fridge. Spirit always came to her. She'd pat his head and let him eat right out of her outstretched palm. She'd talk to him a while. Let him know he's special. Let him know his mother was

something special, too, that it wasn't his fault all this had happened.

Sometime later Roy would be out there to throw alfalfa over the fence. Then he'd do some mindless work around the house before he'd start his drinking. Such nasty habits he and Susan had developed following the accident—Roy with his drinking, Susan with her smoking—as if killing themselves slowly would make the world go away. God doesn't take vacations, her mother used to say.

Roy tossed alfalfa to Spirit, who was waiting to be fed. Katherine was there as well, brushing out burrs. Katherine had to be pushing eighty yet every morning on the dot she'd be out there with an apple or a carrot, brushing his mane or simply staring into his eyes.

"You know, the kids should be doing that," he told her.

Roy put his hand through the fence to pet him, but the colt was set on the alfalfa and in moments the square of green was a three-foot flattened circle.

"I don't mind none," she said. "He's beautiful, ain't he?"

Roy looked the horse over. "He is."

"Looks a lot like his mother," said Katherine.

"Yeah." Roy stared at his boots, tapped one against the fence. He turned and started toward the barn.

"Susan turning forty-two this year, or forty-three?" It sounded more like information than a question.

Roy did some quick math. Susan was a year behind him.

"Forty-two."

"That's today, right? The twenty-third?"

It was. He had forgotten her birthday. It hadn't even

crossed his mind.

"Yeah," he said, and continued to the barn.

"What'cha gonna get her this year?"

Roy stopped, his head to the ground. "I don't know. Ideas?" It was probably too late. He checked his watch. It was only a quarter after seven. Susan wouldn't be up for another hour or two. Maybe he could run down to the store to pick up some flowers.

"The colt looks like he could use some ridin'," said Katherine.

"You think?"

"He's been led around enough. It might be time for a saddle. And a gift doesn't have to be something bought."

Roy thought it over and turned back to Katherine. He looked the horse over as it picked through the food. Katherine worked his mane with the brush. Spirit seemed to shy away from Roy, but had no problems scooting in closer to Katherine.

"Suse could use some ridin', too," said Katherine. "I mean on the horse. Doesn't have to be today. Maybe the two of you could spend some time together out here, maybe try the saddle, walk him around wearing it. Neither of you have taken much interest these last few years. Maybe it's finally time. It'd make a fine present."

Somewhere in the barn was a saddle that would fit him. Spirit was Joey Bean's size, maybe be a hand taller. Maybe her old saddle would work.

"What do you say, Roy?"

"I think I'm lucky you're around sometimes."

All the flowers behind the barn were either dead or withered. As Charlie searched, he remembered picking flowers for Mom when he was much younger. She'd always be amazed when he'd find her the smallest flowers amongst the grass and weeds growing around the property. He'd find all colors and varieties—some no larger than the head of a sewing pin—and he would bundle them into mini bouquets. She had always loved flowers, no matter the size. Today he couldn't find a single bloom.

Dad was inside the barn moving the mower out of the way to get something stored high in the loft. Charlie had gone in to say hi, but his father barely recognized him as being there at all.

"What are you looking for?" Charlie had asked. "Can I help?"

He didn't even turn to look at Charlie, just said a single word, "saddle," before climbing the ladder. He hadn't answered Charlie's second question, so he just let him be.

Charlie walked out of the barn and nearly knocked over Mrs. Jensen. She had dropped a lead rope and a halter, so Charlie kneeled down to help her. The lead rope was tattered. The leather straps on the halter were cracked and the metal hoops rusted. They would work though, he guessed.

"Sorry, Mrs. Jensen."

"That's alright, Charlie. What're you up to?"

"Not much." He handed her everything in a wad. "You taking Spirit for a walk?"

"Nah. I figured your father might. He hasn't used these in years. Probably forgot where they were."

"*My* father?"

"Yep."

"But he hates Spirit."

"Your father doesn't hate Spirit, he just hasn't spent much time with him."

A loud thump made them both turn to the barn. The saddle had been tossed down from the loft. A plume of dust and hay surrounded it on the floor.

"Is he going to ride him?" Charlie smiled widely. Dad hadn't ridden since before Joey Bean got pregnant.

"I don't 'spose so. Might just walk him around a bit wearing it. Spirit's never seen a saddle before."

Mrs. Jensen was silent a moment as they both watched his father try to manage himself down the latter while holding a beer.

"He might surprise us. You 'member it's your mother's birthday?"

"Yeah." Charlie sighed. "I was looking for flowers before I came in here."

"Flowers are nice."

"We're making her breakfast in bed. Pancakes. Cindy made her a card and I was looking for flowers but couldn't find any. They're all dead."

"The whole works, huh? Your mother'll love that. You check the pasture over there," she said, and pointed to one of the overgrown fields.

You could barely tell it was once a horse pasture. Some of the red and green fence posts were bent over, the barbed wire nearly to the ground in places. Charlie remembered the field well.

"There might still be some roses out there," she said. "Those things never die."

Charlie remembered the rosebush. He had forgotten all

about it until Mrs. Jensen brought it up. He remembered him and his father trying to think of a way to move Joey Bean into the field after she died. They planted a rosebush over the grave so they'd always remember what happened that night.

"Thanks, Mrs. Jensen," Charlie said and ran to the field.

"Find her a pretty one."

It took him some time to find the rosebush. Most of it was infested by surrounding weeds. One of its thorns found his hand as he tried to clear them away. Three main branches sprouted from the stock. Smaller yet lengthier ones jetted out in every direction—sunlight-seekers, Charlie guessed—which were greener and less barbed than the others. The plant looked gray and dead except for a few vines, and at the tip of one, and only one, bloomed a single crimson flower. It was small, but beautiful. Its bright red petals were edged in black, as if it had pulled its vibrant bloodlike colors from what was buried underneath.

Dad was busy drinking his breakfast, so Cindy made only enough pancakes for Mom. She had just flipped the last one when Charlie returned holding a single rose. He sucked at the tip of his finger.

"*Some* bouquet," she said.

He gave her a dirty look. "It was the only flower on the entire property. You done with breakfast?"

"Just about."

Cindy had set out a lap tray with a plate stacked with nine pancakes, the bottle of Aunt Jamima's, a glass of orange juice, and a set of silverware. She took the rose from

Charlie and placed it in a vase from under the sink. She set the card next to it.

Cindy let Charlie carry the tray.

She saw Todd at the top of the stairs waiting with his crooked smile. He signed *pretty* after seeing the rose.

Roy hid the halter behind his back, but the metal clicking together gave it away. He managed to corner the colt against the fence and held a carrot. The colt eyed Roy suspiciously, snorted, and stamped his feet. He took the bait, which was all he needed to get the halter over the ears and around its long snout. Roy clasped it as pieces of carrot landed near his boots.

"Good boy," he said, and patted the ghost-like marking on his brow. He snapped the lead rope to the harness and the colt reared.

"Easy."

Roy walked him around the pen, clockwise, and then counter-clockwise.

Katherine stood near the gate. "You're doin' just fine."

"Might do okay with the saddle. He walked him around, barely having to pull the lead rope. "He likes the rope."

"That's 'cause it's all he's ever done."

Walking the colt for Roy was like taking a step back in time. He remembered the first time he had ever walked a horse, how it had walked *him* around the pen. The first time he saddled up, Roy had put his foot into the stirrup, and had hoisted himself up and all the way over the other side of the horse, toppling to the ground. It hurt his knees, but his father was there to pick him up and make him try again. The

second time he made it and felt proud sitting so high, feet dangling a good six inches higher than the stirrups. It was one of the few times he could remember his father smiling.

Roy led Spirit back to the gate.

Katherine held her hand out flat to offer another piece of carrot. The colt took it within its giant teeth and flapping gums. Three loud chomps and it was gone.

Roy unclipped the lead rope and let himself out of the gate. The colt stayed close, and wasn't as affected by the saddle as he had been with the halter. Roy picked it up from the ground and draped it over the fence. Roy grabbed a saddle pad from Katherine before heading back into the corral.

Suse bought him the pad years ago, back when it was soft and off-white, and the bright colors in the Aztec pattern along the back and sides had yet to fade. Now it was old and dusty. The last time he had used it was with Joey Bean. It still had some of her hair stuck to it and even smelled like her. Roy brought it to his face and took a deep breath. He loved that smell. He set the pad over Spirit's back.

"Brings back memories, don't it?" said Katherine. She smiled, her hand going over the saddle.

Roy lifted the saddle from the fence.

Spirit didn't flinch as he brought it closer. He simply looked into the distance with those giant marble eyes. Roy couldn't help but remember the scared look in Joey Bean's open eye as she had lain on the ground, panting, staring at the light of the moon as if were there to take her away from all the pain. Spirit turned to Roy as he placed the saddle on his back, and then looked to Katherine for assurance.

"It won't hurt you none," she said.

As if understanding, the colt let out a heavy breath from its snout. It lowered its head to anxiously eat grass at its feet.

Roy secured the buckle near the horse's belly and pulled the leather strap tight. He fixed the reins to the halter and grabbed them tightly within his left hand, and then used that same hand to grab the horn at the front of the saddle. Like the colt, Roy let out a deep breath.

"Here goes nothing," he said and put his boot into the stirrup.

Roy hesitated before hoisting himself up, and then he was on the horse. Like riding a bike, except with reins for handlebars and stirrups for pedals. It felt good to be on a horse again, almost natural—if only for this moment.

The colt turned to look up at Roy and then jerked his head around, nearly yanking the reins free. Roy held to them tightly and balanced himself, one hand on the cantle, the other on the horn.

"Whoa," he said and pulled back on the reins.

The colt was stronger and ripped them free the second time. Roy grabbed the tuft of hair at the base of its neck and pulled hard. "Easy," he said. He checked his footing to make sure his boots weren't set deep into the stirrups. If he put his whole damn boot through and was thrown, his foot might stay there and his leg could snap like a twig. It felt like Spirit might try to throw him off.

"You be careful up there, Roy." Katherine backed away.

The colt reared and for a moment stood upright, Roy hugging its neck to keep from sliding. On all fours again, they turned, Roy's leg smashing against the fence. The colt jostled to the middle of the stable and reared again, but this time Roy was ready for it. What he wasn't ready for was the sudden buck. Spirit's back legs shot outward, his head bent to the ground. Roy somersaulted over the horse—head over heels—and saw the ground for only a second and then the sky as he landed on his back.

The colt steadied. It snorted, as if laughing at him.

FIFTEEN

The mirror turns black as the red light of Nuveli moves around to the other side of the frame, to the window through which he had earlier passed, and disappears into it.

Todd hoists himself up once again and follows the light, unafraid this time. He plummets through a dark sky. A crack of lightning breaks the rushing wind as they fall toward an old cemetery where light fog blankets the ground. Headstones push out like rotted teeth. Todd extends his bat wings and catches air as Nuveli races to the ground— just a small bead of rapid flickering red. A deafening bolt of electricity shoots past the light and burrows into the ground.

Near the impact is a rosebush much like the one on his parent's farm, the one in the pasture where they buried Joey Bean. Smoke ignites the dry branches. The red within the plant is Nuveli, barely noticeable under the flames. Leaves of three and five whither, blister, burn and peel. They turn to ash and fall and soon the rosebush is a stump of charred black. Smoke wisps from the tips of each blackened branch.

Todd lands on the rooftop of the mortuary and waits.

A crow perches on a headstone that reads: HILLCREST. *The first name is worn away and covered in shadow; the rest reads:* BURN FOREVER IN HELL *above an indecipherable date. The crow caws. Bluish moonlight reflects from its beady black eyes.*

The red light of Nuveli emerges from the hole, circles around the bird and then joins Todd on the mortuary rooftop.

A dozen meteors stripe the sky. Monstrous thunderclouds float motionless like gray battleships in a salty sea of dark blue as lightning strikes around them. The earth around the grave begins to shift as the ground violently shakes.

"As with the living," says Nuveli, "there are times when the dead require guidance, sometimes between worlds, sometimes between whens. One cannot bring the dead back to life, but one can guide it to life."

The crow atop the headstone flutters away, but lands near enough to watch what is happening. The disturbed earth sprouts a hand. Blackened fingers reach the sky like the burnt bush next to it. A reanimated corpse pulls itself from the grave.

Why guide the dead?

"Not all can rest," says the red light. "With life there must come death, and with death, life."

From the ashes arose.

The dead man is nothing more than cauterized skin over a skeletal frame. He stands on wobbly legs, his joints no longer connecting properly. His right femur cracks as he takes a step. The broken bone sticks out like a snapped tree branch.

Next to the corpse, the rosebush sprouts lively green and purple leaves from its thicker, lifeless branches, as if a stop-motion film. Leaves of three turn to leaves of five and from the middle of the five grow buds and from the buds blossom black-edged crimson flowers.

From the ashes a rose.

The crow caws as if calling for this dead man named Hillcrest. It looks to the corpse with glowing blue eyes. More bones crack as he takes another step forward. The bird is merely ten feet away, but the journey seems treacherous for him. The wretched body presses on, each step more strenuous. When he reaches the bird he falls to his knees.

The crow flutters, but stays.

"What you see is Thade."

The bird squawks, wings twitching. Intense light glows from

within its body. It stares up at the kneeling, charred remains.

"If one must be guided, another must live, and if one must live, another must surely be balanced."

A set of broken and bony gray hands reach for the crow—Thade in this strangest of forms—and the bird is sacrificed; blood drained. The dead drinks life from the crow until the crow is nothing but a hollowed shell. The light behind its eyes fade and return to glossy black.

Hillcrest sets the bird down gently and, with hands a little more filled with life, he digs a small grave and buries the bird. He stands with legs that have developed new flesh, new muscle, new skin. Life spreads throughout the rest of his body, the blood of the bird flowing through the vine-like growth of veins and arteries. His torso and neck fill with color. His face takes shape beneath a mop of hair. In his changing form he walks back to the rosebush next to his tombstone and pulls a single rose from it. He walks the flower back and rests it on top of the mound covering the bird.

Todd is about to ask about the sacrifice, but remembers his confrontation with Thade.

"What do you balance?" Todd had asked.

Life.

"How do you balance life?" He remembered having many questions, but had asked only one: "Are you Death?"

With life there must come death, and with death, life. That is the balance in this world. The pure shall not leave in death, but be guided to other worlds. If one must be guided, another must be protected to live, and if one must live, there must surely be balance with death.

Todd imagines this triangle: protection, guidance, balance; held together carefully. Life sacrificed for death. Death sacrificed for life.

He looks below to the mound of dirt covering the crow—the blue light of Thade no longer there—and to the red light of Nuveli next

to him on the roof of the mortuary. He searches for the white light of Loah. He looks to the moon and to the stars.

"Loah is with another," says Nuveli. "Below us, under the roof of this very mortuary, is a child in dire need of protection. An evil child, trapped inside by those he hurt."

Inside a mortuary?

"Inside a coffin," says Nuveli. "He will live, but with complications. The lack of air he breathes now eats away what blackens his soul, but this boy is not yet ready for balance."

Todd turns his attention to the dead man standing naked and dirty, but is otherwise lively as any thirty-something man wandering a graveyard. He is no longer grotesque, nor decrepit, no longer decayed. By the time he makes it to the cemetery gates, his body starts to fall apart. For a long while he simply stands there and lets it happen, and then another crow caws and flutters onto his shoulder. He looks to the crow with empty eyes and then to Todd—or perhaps to the red glowing light next to him—with glowing blue eyes of his own.

And then all turns white.

Back at the floating wooden frame, Todd reads the word carved above the black mirrored face: SPIEGEL, and is nearly blinded by white light reflecting off the surface. Nuveli is no longer with him; instead it is Loah this time.

"Do you understand?"

Todd says nothing. He is unable to justify a response.

"Come with me to the other side," says Loah.

They both move to the other side of the wooden frame, the side marked FENSTER.

At first Todd only sees through it to more white and then, as if peering through a window, he sees his mother crying on the shoulder of another.

SIXTEEN

Susan wiped her tears as she left Katherine's shoulder. The porch swing creaked gently as Katherine rocked them with her bare feet.

"We're so distant."

"I just can't see Roy doing that to you, Suse."

Susan pointed to the empty space where Roy normally parked his truck. "The sun's down, has been for hours. The kids are asleep in bed. Where's Roy? He never even tells me where he's going anymore. Sometimes he's not home until three in the morning."

"You know where he is, most the time."

Susan knew. She'd smell it on his breath when he'd stagger into bed. What bothered her most was wondering each night whether or not Roy would make it home at all. She'd be in bed imagining Roy driving drunkenly down that dark stretch of highway, dodging oncoming headlights and playing Pac-Man with the reflectors in the center divide.

"Maybe someone at the bar wore that stanky perfume, sat next to Roy," said Katherine. "Maybe they's just passin' the time."

"He should be passing time with me, or at least with the kids."

"Maybe the barkeep's the one with the stanky perfume."

"Why does he need to go out for beer at all?" Susan

was done crying, her sadness turned to anger. "He drinks enough here!" She sat up, reached for the pack of menthols in her shirt pocket. She shook the pack, but it was empty.

"I don't know what I'd do if I ever found out Roy was seeing another woman," Susan said.

"I'd slap him. Beat the living tar out of him."

Susan started to laugh, but it merged with a coughing fit, deep and guttural.

"It's them cigarettes you're smokin'. Those things'll kill you if you're not careful, Suse. Kill me, too. Eighty-somethin' years old and all the smokin' I've ever done's from sittin' next to you. Nasty habits. The both of you."

"I only smoke when I'm upset."

"Must be a lot you're upset about. You smell terrible."

"At least I'm not drinking."

"Maybe there's a lot Roy's upset about, too."

"I don't even let him drive the kids. I take them everywhere so he doesn't wrap them around a tree." She shook the empty pack of cigarettes again and looked to it nervously, hoping she had overlooked one hidden in there.

"What you and Roy need is to sit down and talk."

"I wouldn't know where to begin."

"Say what you say to me. That you need to talk things through. Ask him about the perfume. Straight up ask him. Never know unless you ask him. Let him know you miss him. Tell him that the family's fallin' apart and things need to change."

Susan coughed and stood from the porch swing. She looked at Katherine and then to the house.

"I'm going inside for another pack." She thought of the young lady at the hospital who had first offered her a cigarette, wondered what kind of life she lived, why she needed to smoke. She remembered coughing when she took that first drag. Since then the cough remained. Julie, her name had been. Julie with the piercings and the tattoos. She was just a kid, but she had a daughter, a paternity test, a cigarette. *Maybe if I just stand by her*, Susan had thought back in the hospital waiting room. She remembered watching Julie through the entrance window before going out. *I'll just stand by her a while and take in some of that magic stress relief.* "Fresh air" her father used to say.

"I'm going inside, too. Take care of yourself, Suse."

Susan nodded and headed to the house.

Roy rode Spirit across the main yard and to the stable. Todd waved at him—one of the few signs Roy understood. Todd stood at the gate with his shoulders slumped, his head tilted a little to the side. His uneven eyes winced against the sun as he signed another word Roy knew well: *drink*. He looked to the reigns and then to his beer.

"Don't worry, Todd, we're on private property, and we're not on no road, so I don't suppose it's considered drunk driving. If riding a horse is driving at all."

Todd signed a word Roy didn't recognize.

Roy took a drink.

"'anger'us," said Todd. His face held disgust. The word took effort. He held his hands above his face to block the light, which seemed to brighten the closer Roy got to him.

"You should talk more often, Todd. Charlie and Cindy know quite a few signs, your mother and I only a handful."

Todd made an unrecognizable gesture.

"Sorry," Roy said, and shrugged. He couldn't help but squint at Todd. It was as if light was coming directly out of his sad face. But he couldn't look away from the scars as he walked the horse closer.

Todd signed again, this time more frantic, and then he blurted out, "'ar."

"Are what? I don't understand you, Todd." For a moment he thought Todd might have meant *bar*. Roy had already gone to the bar.

His son struggled and made a painful expression as he tried to force the word out. "'ar!" He followed with a sign.

"Don't use your hands," said Roy. "I don't understand your hands."

Todd's face grew incredibly bright. Roy could barely look at him, like looking at a sun, not a son.

Todd rolled his eyes and grimaced trying to say a word his father could understand. For a moment, all that came out of his mouth was a moan, and then Todd managed to blurt it out: "Car!"

The light was blinding.

Far in the distance, Roy heard a horn blaring.

Todd held his hands out as if grabbing a steering wheel. He looked upward as he moved his hands back and forth to mimic driving.

Roy was almost to him.

The light was overbearing and so was the sound.

Car?

Then he snapped awake.

Roy jerked the wheel hard and to the right. The oncoming car swerved with its horn blasting. The small space between the two vehicles rocked the cabin of his truck.

He had fallen asleep. While driving.

A few times in the past he had nodded off, just long enough to let his body know he shouldn't be driving, but never in his life had he ever fallen completely asleep. Roy put his hands to his chest and felt his heart pounding. It would take a tranquilizer to put him out now.

How long was I out?

Roy glanced to the clock on the dashboard. It was an hour off because of the time change—he had never taken the time to fix it—and read 1:21. He could barely remember the bar, but remembered leaving around five past one, so he was about halfway home, he figured. The sky in front of him was black, the highway horribly lit. It spun around him, but he was able to straighten it out enough to drive. The passing yellow reflectors on the road were hypnotic.

Drive was the last sign Todd had used in the dream, as easy as driving a car.

Roy vaguely remembered the rest. He was riding a horse. Todd was at the gate. It faded quickly. Soon it was gone completely from his mind and he found himself pulling into the driveway. The only light came from the can light on the front porch. Susan always left it on for him.

Cindy found the last remaining border piece of the jigsaw puzzle she was working on when Dad woke up. It was two in the afternoon. The piece was solid black and shaped like someone doing the splits. The bags under Dad's eyes were about the same color. He staggered down the stairs; the unfinished puzzle looked more together. She pressed the piece in place to complete the frame. The other scattered pieces—nine hundred, give or take—all looked the same. Somehow they were supposed to come together to make a farmhouse with a stallion in the foreground.

Charlie joined her at the table. He plucked a piece and set it in place at the top-right corner. Out of nowhere he said, "You think Mom's gonna leave Dad?"

Cindy found the piece that fit next to the one Charlie placed. She twirled it in her fingers. "You mean divorce?"

They both searched the table.

"I guess so," said Charlie.

Cindy began collecting horse-colored pieces. She found three that joined to make a head and mane. "You know Michael Johnson from school? He's in my class. He thinks his parents might get a divorce. He says they used to fight a lot, but now they mostly don't fight. He says his mom is never home anymore, and when she is, they hardly say anything. He says it's okay, though, because nowadays most parents get divorces."

Charlie struggled with a piece that wouldn't fit where he wanted it to fit and said, "Most of the kids in my class have split families. Jimmy Wilson lives with his mom and two sisters. Tommy Bower lives with his dad 'cause his mom stabbed someone. Jenny Pointrich, I think, is with her Grandma. And there's another kid in my class with two moms."

"Mom and Dad never talk," said Cindy. She was about to add something else, but her brother said it before she could get it out.

"Ever since the accident."

"Yeah."

"You think if it never happened they'd be okay?"

"Probably," said Cindy. "Mom talks to Katherine Jensen more than she talks to Dad."

"Yeah, and she doesn't *sleep* with Katherine Jensen."

"Gross."

"You don't think they sleep together. Mom and Dad?"

"Well, they sleep together, when Dad's not passed out on the couch, but I don't think they do anything else."

"Like each other?"

"Gross." Cindy scrunched her face and threw a few pieces at Charlie.

"He stays out a lot and—"

They both got quiet as their father walked through the room and into the kitchen. The sound of the sliding glass door told them he was going outside, most likely to the barn.

When the door closed, Charlie continued, "—and he spends all his free time in the barn. Drinking."

"I saw him walking the horse."

"But that's what, once in the last how many years?"

Since the accident, Cindy thought. She knew her brother was thinking it too. "You think they will?"

"What?"

"Get a divorce."

Neither said anything for a while; they simply searched for the missing puzzle pieces and for places to put them. Cindy couldn't help notice the similarities between their family and the incomplete picture.

"Life is a jigsaw," she said.

"You mean 'jigsaw puzzle'?"

She thought for a moment. "No."

Susan grabbed two beers from the fridge: a bottle of Bud Light and a bottle of Fat Tire. She hated the taste of beer almost as much as she hated the smell of beer. Old beer. The last forgotten sips at the bottom of a sun-warmed brown bottle. She'd throw them out and the smell would stick to her hands. She would always smell her fingers after recycling them, but had no idea why. Susan looked at the labels and decided—from the label only—on the Fat Tire. It was a twist top—both were—but she used a bottle opener anyway. She popped both tops and watched the white wisps from each of the openings. She smelled the Bud Light first, and then the other, scrunching her nose. She took a sip of the Fat Tire and grimaced. It was probably a good beer. To Susan it simply tasted like any other beer.

When she made it to the barn, Roy was in a fold-out lawn chair watching the horse pull up grass in the field.

Susan held out the Bud Light.

Both avoided eye contact.

"Thank you," said Roy. He downed a third of it.

Susan took another awful sip of her own.

Spirit rubbed against an oak tree.

"Since when do you like beer?"

"I don't." She took a drink and forced it down before searching for another chair.

"There's one hanging on a peg next to the ... by the shovels," he said, pointing to the wall.

Susan set it up next to him. Roy had finished his beer by the time she sat. They both looked ahead into the field, avoiding conversation that could only lead to argument.

It took Susan nearly an hour to finish her Fat Tire, the last bit warm and bitter. For some reason, she felt she had to finish and set the empty bottle next to Roy's on the ground.

"How can you drink this stuff?" she asked, breaking the long silence.

Roy shrugged. "I like the taste. It's acquired, like with you and your wine. You like the taste of grapes. I like barley and hops."

"I share a bottle on rare occasions with friends. You drink beer like you have a hole in your stomach."

"I guess I'm well-acquired."

"If you're so well-acquired, why can't you stay home and do it? Why do you have to go out?" Susan started to shake. She felt red in the face, and knew it wasn't the beer although her head had started spinning. She searched her pockets for a cigarette.

"Sometimes, Suse … sometimes I need to get away from the world, to step out of life. I don't know … drown it away."

"You can't just step out of life, Roy. Some of us are still in it."

She found the pack in her front left pocket and fished out a cigarette.

"Since when do you smoke?"

Susan stopped. "You're kidding."

"No."

Her eyes turned frantic as she lit up, took a drag, and released a plume of smoke.

"Damn it, Roy! 'Since *when* do I smoke?' *How* far out of life have you stepped? I've smoked as long as you've …" she could not say it, "since the hospital."

"I guess I never noticed."

"Because you're too busy noticing other things, like

the ends of bottles." Susan was about to continue, but she started coughing.

"Since the accident, our lives have turned to horseshit." Susan kept coughing.

"I don't know what's real anymore. Every time I start thinking about you and the kids, and how we can fix things, all I want to do is drink. I'm thinking about it right now."

Susan was able to control her coughing for a moment.

"You're an alcoholic, Roy."

"I'm not an alcoholic. I just like to drink."

"And I'm not a woman. I just have all the female parts. You need to look into AA."

"I don't need AA. I'm not an alcoholic, and I don't want to be anonymous. I *like* to drink. Do you like to smoke?"

"This has nothing to do with what we're talking about."

"It has *everything* to do with what we're talking about. Do you like to smoke?"

"It calms me," she said, suppressing another cough.

"Well, drinking calms *me*. I step out of life with alcohol. You step out of life with nicotine."

"I stay *sane* because of these." Susan reached into her pocket for the pack and then threw it in his face. "I'm trying to hold this family together, Roy, *by myself*, and you're out each night doing God-knows-what with God-knows-who. Todd didn't break this family, Roy, *you* broke this family. You and your damn drinking." The coughing returned, hard this time.

Roy didn't say anything. Tears welled in his eyes.

Susan's eyes held tears as well, but because of the coughing. She was too upset for sorrow. She coughed hard in her hand, and wiped it on her jeans. When the fit mellowed, she asked a question she had been meaning to ask since she grabbed two beers from the refrigerator: "Why do you smell like perfume sometimes when you come home?"

Finally, the question was out there, although now, it seemed not so important.

For minutes, they both just sat there.

And then he said what she hadn't expected him to say. Something that scared her more than anything. What he said wasn't a finality, only self-acknowledgement that he indeed had a problem and needed help.

"I don't know."

She could tell by his voice it was honest and sincere.

Susan let him cry, and then noticed the red smear of blood on the left leg of her jeans from what she had earlier coughed into her hand.

The following morning, Katherine Jensen oddly missed her morning coffee. Roy expected to see her on the porch swing sipping coffee from her mug, smiling that old leathery smile, or maybe feeding the horse oats from the palm of one hand while the other patted the white ghost between its large marble eyes.

Roy dreaded this morning more than any of the others in his life. He had promised Susan to call AA after his morning chores. He'd quit drinking if she'd quit smoking. He knew he could prolong his duties, but the longer he tried, the longer it ate at the pit of his stomach, much like the drink already calling for him. One last beer. A farewell. One last round before jumping on the wagon, or off the wagon, or whatever the hell it was called.

A friend at work—Brian—was in AA. He showed Roy his tokens once in a while: one month, one day, one hour—something like that. Brian rarely made it a week sometimes. He could always tell when he'd given in to alcohol because he'd stop showing Roy the tokens.

It was ironic, now that he thought about it, that it took Susan drinking with him the night prior, handing him a beer, to realize alcohol had consumed *him*.

Susan helped him dump all the alcohol in the house. Beer, mostly, and some wine and hard alcohol they both rarely touched. They poured it all down the sink; it was the only way. The kitchen counter was covered in empty brown bottles. Charlie would have a field day with the recycling.

He thought of Charlie running down the stairs and coming to a complete stop at the edge of the kitchen—dollar signs in his eyes—as he counted the bottles and their worth. Cindy would probably put it all together. She was a smart girl. He thought of Todd as he walked to the barn, but could only replay the night of the accident: Todd kicked by Joey Bean, the rifle, the ambulance as it sped away without him, the deer smashing into the truck, blood everywhere. He thought of Susan holding Todd together, her being alone at the hospital, and the long conversation they'd had about Todd and pulling the plug.

Roy stopped at the barn entrance and looked over his shoulder to the house. The entire family was asleep. He looked around for Katherine, but she was nowhere to be found. Maybe sleeping in for once. Turning back to the barn, Roy spotted what he had come for—a horse blanket covering two unopened cases of Bud Light.

He pulled them free from their hiding place, opened

one of the boxes, and removed a single, night-chilled bottle. His mouth watered enough for him to have to spit. He rolled the bottle in his hands. Read the label. Completely. It felt right in his hand, the neck of the bottle fitting perfectly within the circle of index finger and thumb, the base heavy and cool against the cusp of his hand.

A noise behind him sent his heart racing madly in his chest as he turned on his heels. Charlie.

"Dad?"

"Hey, Charlie."

"What're you up to?"

Roy knew Charlie had heard enough the night before.

"You want one," he said to his son, half-jokingly.

"Do *you?*"

This was the question of all questions.

More than anything. The more he thought about twisting the top and chugging down a beer, the more it calmed him. Roy stared at the label again, mesmerized.

"No," said Charlie, breaking the trance. "I don't."

Roy looked from the bottle to Charlie and smiled. He placed it back in the case with the others.

"Neither do I. This stuff is terrible."

Charlie smiled, and after a shared silence asked, "Are you gonna pour it out, like the ones in the kitchen?"

"No. It would be a waste to pour out two cases of beer."

As easily as Charlie's smile formed, a frown developed.

The phone rang and Cindy picked it up. She watched as her mother filled paper grocery bags with the empty bottles from the kitchen counter.

"Hello?"

No one answered. Cindy assumed it was a telemarketer, but she stayed on the line to make sure. A few noises came from the phone, some scratchy sounds.

"Hello?"

"Hang up if no one's there, Cindy," said her mother.

Cindy set the receiver down and grabbed an empty bag.

"Did you and Dad have a fight?"

A couple clangs of bottles and then, "Your father and I had a long talk."

"A fight?"

"An argument."

"Why'd you dump out Dad's beer?"

"It was mutual. Your father helped."

"What's this?" Cindy asked, holding what looked like an oversized crystal perfume bottle.

"Brandy. Well, it *was* Brandy. Don't throw away that one. We'll keep the bottle. It was a wedding present."

"Dad doesn't drink Brandy. I've never seen him."

"It was mine."

"And *you* poured it out?"

"Yes."

"But you're not the one with the drinking problem."

"I do have a drinking problem: your father."

The sound of a gunshot silenced them both.

Brown glass shrapnel and fizzy beer blew in all directions as the bottle exploded. Roy stared down the barrel to the dozen or so Bud Lights they had lined up in front of a dried-up bale of alfalfa behind the barn. He pulled the gun away and felt a little remorse for the fallen soldier. He reloaded the 30'06, aimed, and fired again, missing his target this time. He couldn't help but think of the last time he had fired the rifle. He had missed Joey Bean with the first shot—the shot that had changed everything—and it took a second shot with the rifle to finally put her down.

"You want to try one, Charlie?" Roy asked, holding the wood-stocked rifle out to his son.

Charlie managed to hit three with his first three shots.

Susan stopped outside just as Roy fired a second time, which for some reason settled her nerves. She made her way to the barn and saw them: Charlie and Roy playing shooting range behind the barn. For a moment there was silence, the wind blowing gently. All wildlife had stilled from the gunfire. Faintly, Susan heard the phone ring behind her. Charlie fired and a little brown bottle exploded in the distance. The first gunshot she heard from the kitchen had startled her. The first idea that had sprung to her mind was one she had forced herself not to let play out completely—such a horrid thought—but now, seeing Roy brutally destroying his problem—she couldn't help but smile. She watched Charlie obliterate two more bottles before returning to the house.

Cindy stood at the screen door holding the cordless.

"Who is it, Cindy?"

Cindy put the phone to her ear and then pulled it away.

"I don't know. It's just someone breathing."

Susan took the phone.

"Hello?"

At first she thought the line was dead.

"Is someone there?"

She was about to hang up because of the silence, but heard what sounded like a deep inhalation.

"Please don't call again. I won't hesitate to call the police if—"

And then the inhale turned into an exhale, and what she heard next turned her flesh white. In the quietest, raspiest of voices came her own drawn-out name, "Suuuse."

Katherine.

Susan ran out the back door with the phone to her ear.

Cindy followed, but Susan stopped her.

"Cindy, find my purse."

Into the phone she said, "Katherine, hold on." She covered the headset and yelled to the barn, "Roy!" She turned to Cindy. "In my purse is my cell. Dial 911 and give them our address. Do you know Mrs. Jensen's address?"

Cindy nodded.

"Give them Mrs. Jensen's address." She yelled out again to the barn. Roy must have sensed the desperation in her voice. He hastily made his way to the house, rifle in hand. Charlie ran behind him.

"Can you do that, Cindy?"

Again she nodded.

"Hold in there, Kath," she said into the phone. To Cindy she added, "Once you get them on the line, keep them on the line and meet us at Mrs. Jensen's. Don't hang up."

Cindy ran off to find the cellular.

Susan left the house once again. She didn't even think to close the sliding glass door. She met up with Roy and Charlie in the yard, the phone still pressed to her ear.

"Katherine's hurt," she said through tears.

Charlie put the rifle in the safe and hurried back to see if he could help. Mrs. Jensen looked dead as she lay on her kitchen floor. The phone from the wall was in her hand. Her eyes stared blankly at him, but somehow not at him at all. He knew she was still alive, though; he saw the slight rise in her chest each time she breathed. She looked like Joey Bean right before Dad put her down.

Cindy asked, "What's wrong with her?" She held Mom's cell phone at her side.

His mother held a glass of water to Mrs. Jensen's dry lips. "The ambulance will be here soon," she said.

Charlie could only stand in stupor. He looked around for Todd and found him standing directly behind Mrs. Jensen. He smiled at Charlie with his ruined face and signed something Charlie didn't recognize.

Susan coughed blood into her hand as red light broke through the windows.

SEVENTEEN

A faint red glow fills the floating mirror as Todd steps back from it.

Not my mother.

"Not your mother," says Loah, joining him. The red in the mirror turns white. "Nuveli is there for another."

Mrs. Jensen.

"She has lived a long life. It is time for her guidance."

You will protect my mother?

"From the blackness that eats her lungs. I cannot stop the disease; I can only protect her from it while another is balanced."

Protection. Guidance. Balance.

"There must be three."

The mirror turns obsidian as Loah fades into its surface. Todd admires the heavy wooden frame and the letters carved into it.

"Follow me," says a different voice.

Todd recognizes it as Thade, but the blue light is nowhere to be found. The mirror remains empty black, the room around him empty white. He listens for the voice, but is met with silence, and then he remembers the monstrous floating object in front of him is both a mirror and a window. Blue light waits for him on the opposite side. Todd climbs the sill once again, reaches through the rippling face, and is pulled inside.

He lands on all-fours as a wolf with matted fur and sharp claws, his hind legs ending in a ruffled tail—a character from one of the stories his mother used to read to him before bed. Through canine eyes, the world is a mixture of black and white. The full moon overhead shines bright and slightly blue, and from it drops a creature of shadow.

A black silhouette joins him: an ever-changing form both vast and free-flowing, as if created by weightless silk cloth. Twice the height of an average man, the rough night wind noiselessly passes around it as if not there at all. The shape is varied shades of black with luminous glowing eyes; they sparkle like captured blue suns. It is Thade in the most horrific of forms. A mouth—near what should be its head— opens wide and ready to feast, a mess of black spiraling razor teeth. The creature is completely silent, as if it exists only in Todd's mind.

His first thought is to run and he oversteps his legs—not yet used to the four—and stumbles to the ground, but he quickly rises and bolts through the field. Sharp stalks slap against his face and snout and poke his long ears like the foxtails back home. Looking back, Todd leaves behind a flattened trail.

Thade is in his wake—blue eyes swimming through a fluttering sea of darkness.

Ahead lies nothing but gray wheat that is taller than Todd in this wolf form. Overshadowed, he runs, no longer wishing to look back. He cuts through the field, his ears back, and his heart beating madly. His lungs burn as he pants to cool them down. He runs until the wheat stops hitting him in the face.

And then he realizes the crop hasn't stopped at all, but is flattened underneath him. Heads of wheat point counterclockwise and flush against the ground in what appears to be an impression over a hundred feet across, as if something large, a spacecraft perhaps, landed within the field and abruptly left. The perfect spiraling circle glows abnormally bright.

Todd vulnerably enters the open space. Thade seems to have vanished, the only thing chasing him is the tunnel of wheat from which he came ... whether led, or chased, it's uncertain. He sticks to the rounded wall at first and follows it around, his eyes constantly drawn to the center, head down and body hugging the ground.

A backpack sits in the middle of the formation.

Someone made this place.

Todd pokes his snout around and pats at the pack with his paws. It looks a lot like the backpack Charlie used to take to school. The bag is zipped shut and there's not much he can do but sit next to it and admire the spectacle surrounding it. The moon directly over him.

Crunch, *the sound is distant, but startling.*

The bag is his only protection in the open. Todd cowers next to it.

Crunch, *then two voices masked behind the wall of untouched wheat.*

Todd considers sprinting in the other direction, but remembers he may have been led to this place to watch as he had with the boy at the fence and again at the cemetery. Directly ahead of him the wall of wheat shimmers and falls as a young man smashes it flat and enters the formation. Behind him is another. Their conversation is soft, but it carries easily across the field as they high-step through the crop and into the open.

"Probably anything *that sucks blood: fleas, ticks, mosquitoes, bats.*"

"Bats don't suck blood. They eat mosquitoes and other small bugs. It has definitely kept the fleas down, though. I've hardly found any on the dogs since I sprayed the yard."

"It's got to be the smell or something."

The two young men admire the formation from just within it.

The taller one takes a drink from a water bottle, then says, "Doesn't it make your yard smell like garlic?"

"Not really. It smells a little strange at first, but it's diluted."

"This thing is freakin' huge."

"I know. I can't help but keep staring at it."

They both look around in silence. Todd wonders if they might just leave, and then one of them says something that makes the hair near the base of his tail stand on end.

"Where'd you leave the backpack?"

"I put it in the middle of the big circle so we could find it."

The taller of the two clicks on a flashlight and points the beam to the center of the circle.

Directly into Todd's eyes.

"Jesus!"

The flashlight clicks off.

"What?"

In a whispered voice: "You see that?"

"What, the bag?"

"Shh … yeah. Something next to it moved. Listen."

Todd is frozen in place, eyes closed. It is silent for close to a minute.

"I don't hear anything. Shine the light back over there."

Todd hears the flashlight again, but refuses to open his eyes.

"You see the backpack?"

"Yeah."

"Look just to the right of it."

"I think you're paranoid from last time. It's probably a shadow. Whatever it is, it's not moving."

A heavy object lands a few feet away from him. Todd continues to play the role of Backpack's Eerie Shadow. He acts quite well until a rock pelts his side and he lets out a yelp and opens his eyes into a beam of light and rises partially from the ground to step back.

"What is it?"

"Look at the eyes! I've seen green eyes and red eyes, but what is that?"

"Throw another rock at it," says the one with the flashlight. "If it's a coyote, it'll probably run away. Maybe coyotes have eyes like that.

Maybe it's for night vision. What if it's not a coyote? Why are the eyes so damn bright? Like the deadlights from It *or something."*

"Just shut up and let me think for a second." A hint of laughter behind his voice, but it's not humor; it's fear. "Should we run?"

"We can't leave our backpack in the middle of a crop circle!"

Another rock lands a few yards in front of him.

Todd takes another step back, not because of the rock or the young men, but because of the blue eyes and black shadow approaching from behind them in the field. He tries to warn them, but the only thing that leaves his maw is a menacing snarl.

"I think it's a coyote. It'll probably run if we start walking toward it. Want to?"

The silent shadow looms over them as Thade draws near, changing shape. Drooping appendages fall from the top half—arms stretching outward in parabolas each as long as the creature is tall. They silently reach outward.

Todd rushes them, howling wildly, and stops midway. The fur along his spine puffs as he reveals the fangs in his snarling mouth.

The shorter of the two bolts to cut through the wall of wheat next to him. The other turns around to run, but is captured in the blue lights of the giant black shape. He stands paralyzed as Thade wraps around him like a blanket and squeezes until there is nothing left but swirling black. In seconds, he is gone and all that remains is Thade. The glowing blue eyes look to Todd, and then to the path left behind in the wheat field by the one that got away.

Todd runs after him, hoping to chase him to safety, and makes it to the opening just as Thade turns in a fluid, stealthy motion. And so starts a three-way chase.

A beam of flashlight violently moves across the night ahead like the brushstrokes of an angry painter. Todd follows the light at first, and then tracks the scent as he gains on the scared young man. He soon hears snaps of wheat under feet and heavy gasps for air—a simple pounce away. A scared face looks back and then straight ahead to the edge of the field not far away. Soft triangles of yellow from street posts reveal a road. Only a few headlights and taillights cross in perpendicular streaks of red and white. Further in the distance is the rotating lamp of an airport watchtower. Todd chases him through the wheat and into the open. The crunching of stalks turns to the crunching of gravel and finally to the young man gasping as he looks back one final time, not to see the eyes of Todd staring him down, but much higher, to the blue vacuumesque gaze of Thade. The young face transforms from panicked to disarray as he runs blindly into the road and against the weathered truck that smashes into him.

Everything slows as Todd witnesses the skull as it crushes and deforms the front right fender of the truck. Red mist surrounds a bright crimson flower of blood as the rest of him crumples over steel. His body is thrown far ahead into a dark ditch. Todd watches the vast yet elegant form of Thade as it spreads those black curtain wings; they wrap around the body and swirl until there's nothing left but the gore on the beaten truck.

A middle-aged man shakes in the cabin of the truck with the white light of Loah surrounding him. It is Todd's father. The light intensifies until the truck is no longer distinguishable and Todd's surroundings are engulfed by rays expanding from the windows.

Todd's monochrome world fades until there is nothing but the whiteness.

And the floating wooden frame.

"You must have many questions," says the voice of Loah.

The white orb reflects in the glass. Todd's own reflection is not cast back, but Todd knows he is no longer a wolf. Questions flood his mind: why was his father in the truck; what happened to the two young men in the field; why a wolf? He knew his father was protected, and the two men in the field balanced, but who needed guidance? Since two were taken, did that mean a second was protected, and thus two required guidance?

"Do you understand?"

Todd does not.

"Every question has an answer; every answer a question."

Why a wolf?

"That is the form you chose, such as earlier when you chose a bat."

Why my father?

"Without my protection, my light, your father would have crashed into the ditch upon seeing whom you chased into the truck's path."

Thade—

"—was there for another—the first in the field. Only one was supposed to be taken, not two. If one must live, another must be guided, and if one must be guided, another must surely be balanced. There must be three."

None of this makes sense.

"Life falls into place, like pieces to a puzzle."

Other worlds. Other whens.

Todd thinks of the crow and the burning rose and the man wrought from its ashes.

How can the three of you handle this chaos?

"We three are made of many."

Like pieces to a puzzle.

"Existence is the puzzle. There are many pieces, but two remain to be placed: one needs protection, the other guidance."

Who?

"One is your mother; the other is you. Do you understand?"

No.

"Take one last look through the mirror."

EIGHTEEN

Charlie sat with his sister in the Brenden Memorial patient waiting area. "I read somewhere a baby is born every six seconds, or minutes, or something like that, and that someone dies every ten, or maybe twenty seconds. I can't remember. It was close to two-to-one, though."

Cindy ignored him, or hadn't heard him. She flipped through a *Highlights* magazine and then turned it to the back cover to look for objects in the cartoon picture that didn't belong. Charlie leaned back in his chair so he could see it. He found a bird flying upside-down in the sky, a tree with a saxophone as one of its branches and a bunny in the grass wearing sneakers on its back feet. Someone had circled a few of the oddities with a ballpoint pen.

Dad sat a few chairs down. He held a paper called the *Brenden Daily*, but hadn't turned a page. It lay in his lap like a wet jacket. On the front page was a black and white photograph of the mortuary where Charlie's friend's father worked. Charlie couldn't make out the caption. It was partially covered by an arm.

They all sat as if bored at church.

Mom was outside smoking. The hospital didn't let you smoke inside. There were signs everywhere stating so. She had been out there for the last half hour. He could see her through the window. Sometimes it was hard to tell if it was warm air or smoke leaving her mouth. Maybe it was both. She paced, peering through the windows every so often to check on the family.

"You shouldn't say things like that," said Cindy. She tossed the magazine on the table and grabbed a new one.

"What?"

"You shouldn't talk about people dying," she said. "This is a hospital. It's not right."

He thought of a comeback—her face not right, or something—but decided to let it go. She was right. Hospitals served two purposes: to bring life into the world, and to take life out of it. Like a doorway to wherever it is you go when you die.

The last time Charlie remembered being in the hospital was when Mom brought him in after he had stuck part of a stick into his eye while playing on the property. He was ten, or maybe eleven. He remembered leaning down to pick something up from the ground—a rock, perhaps—and the tip of some dead and dried-out twig jammed into the soft tissue around his right eye, the part next to his nose. The tip of the branch, or whatever it was, snapped off, and stuck out from the socket. He had pulled it free, but couldn't see from that eye much, which stayed reddened and teary until the doctor examined him, flushed his eye out, and gave him overly expensive eye drops to apply every few hours. His eye was fine, but he remembered waiting just like this. The same room.

It wasn't right to talk about death in a hospital waiting room.

Charlie looked out the window a second time and Mom was still smoking. Orange amber brightened at the tip of her cigarette as she inhaled. She held it in her hand like a single chopstick, the way she always did, nervously shaking. Her eyes seemed so empty. He couldn't help wonder what it had been like the night she brought Todd to the hospital.

The red on her jeans had turned brown. Roy had asked her about the stain on the drive to the hospital. Susan avoided talking about it by changing the conversation to Katherine's condition. He'd probably bring it up the moment Susan stepped back into the waiting room. That was one of the reasons she'd gone out for a smoke, to avoid Roy. She knew she should tell him. But what did it matter? She took another drag from the cigarette, and then held it in front of her like it was trash she had picked off the ground. It couldn't be the smoking. She tossed it to the ground and snubbed it out with the tip of her shoe. It was too soon for lung cancer. No one got the big C smoking only a few years, and there were no cases of the disease anywhere in her bloodline. Her sister Jill had had a scare a few years back, but the tests from a biopsy from one of her breasts came back benign. Susan self-consciously felt her breasts, but put her hands to her sides as she realized she was standing in front of the waiting room windows. No one seemed to notice.

Susan had no idea what she'd do if anything bad happened to Katherine. She remembered back to one of her conversations she'd had with her about cancer. Katherine diagnosed with cancer all those years back, telling the doctors it was a bunch of hogwash. Maybe now it was finally claiming *her*. Susan hoped not, praying it was age playing havoc with her body, a mild stroke, perhaps, or something

a little oxygen tank could help control. She imagined Katherine trolling a tank behind her, cussing over the tubes and reasoning constantly why the oxygen wasn't needed. Strong as an ox, she'd say, *I don't need no breathin' tubes.* Susan smiled. Katherine sure was a stubborn old bat.

She pictured Katherine on the operating table—or wherever it was they had her—looking at the doctors with distrust. Maybe they had her anesthetized and her body was lifeless, like Todd the night Susan arrived at the hospital covered in his blood.

She looked down to her jeans. The smear no larger than a gum wrapper. On that horrid night with Todd, her jeans looked like she had just finished painting the barn; her entire front covered in Todd. She had changed into a different set of clothes after realizing there was nothing else she could do for her son. The hospital let her take a shower. She remembered the red swirl of Todd circling her bare feet as it murmured down the drain.

You need to stop this, she told herself. *What happened, happened.* She closed her eyes, but Todd was there in the ambulance, in her hands. *Stop it!* She slapped her face. The image of Todd changed. He lay still in her hands, but the gore was gone, and in its place, scars in jig-jag shapes cut across his face. His head ill-proportioned, his forehead a little more massive on one side than the other. His smile was crooked, but it was a smile. A pair of offset brown eyes looked up at her.

"Stop it!" she yelled aloud. She slapped her face again., which probably left a handprint.

This launched a series of coughs. Susan covered her mouth, but the fit broke through. The tickles were deep inside her lungs. She coughed until it hurt. Air difficult to catch. She fell to her knees and vomited blood.

"Hello. My name is Roy, and I'm an alcoholic." That was all he had to say. He had to stand in front of a group of strangers to admit it, but it was all he needed to say.

All I want to do is drink, he had said to Susan. *I'm thinking about it right now*. It was true then. It was true now. He'd give anything for a longneck. *To drown this all away*, he thought.

"What do you think, Todd? Can I do it?"

Todd held up a fist that nodded. Roy knew the sign. Todd smiled with a crooked mouth.

"Tell me I can do it, Todd. Don't sign it."

After a brief struggle, Todd managed, "Nes."

"Good. Now say your name."

Another painful expression.

"Say it. It's easy," said Roy. "Todd."

"… 'odd!" It came out like a gunshot.

"Todd."

"'odd."

"With a T. Tuh-odd. Todd."

"… 'odd."

"We'll do it together," said Roy. "You'll help me quit drinking. I'll help you annunciate. Sound like a plan?"

Todd looked to him with disappointment. He signed something Roy didn't understand at first, but it looked like it was "I can't" by the downtrodden look on his face.

"Sure you can. Say *T*, and then the *rest* of *odd*."

Todd's attempt started as a long slur, then tumbled out. "Thee … 'death of 'odd."

Roy smirked at how literal Todd had taken him.

"It's morbid, but a good start. We'll work on it."

Todd gave the sign for drink, and then pointed at Roy.

"We'll work on me, too."

Roy thought of his own father's drinking problem. Every night after work he would come home and sit in the den, pick up the book he never seemed to finish—*David Copperfield*—and pour himself two fingers of scotch. No ice, just the scotch. He always read next to a candle. When his glass emptied, he'd fill it again.

He was an angry drunk, and had backhanded Roy once, still holding the drink, hard enough that the glass shattered. He never told anyone. Back then, fathers were hard on children. School talk often included stories of belts and paddles and open hands. Stories that started with "My old man …" with each story topping the next. Today children could sue you just for raising your voice. The backhand wasn't right, but his father wasn't right, either. Alcohol was driving him. Possessed him. There were few things Roy remembered about his father. This was one of them. Shooting the horse was another. Being there with his mother at the front door the day the police told them your husband your father your piss-drunk role model had wrapped himself around a tree with the Dodge earlier that morning was yet another fond memory. Roy remembered the rain. It poured. Liquids— rain and scotch—took his father's life.

Roy swore never to grow up to be like his old man, yet here he was. Alcoholic. Horrible father. Shot the family horse. He couldn't imagine ever hitting his children, but he couldn't remember ever *not* doing it, either, and that's what scared him most. Somewhere along the way he had lost his own trust. Since the accident with Todd, he let drinking take over his life to forget what had happened. There was always something of Todd to remember. There wasn't enough alcohol in the world to drown it all away.

Roy looked at Todd, at his scars, the irregularities, the sad expression that always haunted his face.

"I'm sorry, Todd."

Todd stared back with a half-smile. He made two signs. The first Roy didn't recognize. The second sign was *Mother*.

Roy turned to the window in the waiting room. Susan was no longer there.

Lightheaded and short of breath, Katherine reached for the wall-mounted phone and fell. Her breath wasn't there for the catching. Fingertips met plastic. Somehow she managed it in her hand, the coil of cord stretching, as she towed it with her to the floor. As the cord reached its limit of elasticity, the base of the unit split apart. Some of it dangled above her in pendulums. She held the receiver close to her chest as if she were going to cross herself with it. The *beep-beep-beep* of busy signal yapped at her to hang it up.

She wanted to laugh, but could only do it in her head. She was like one of those helpless old ladies on the tube advertising medical help at the touch of a button. *I'm one of them 'fallen and can't get up' decrepit ladies. I've still got laundry to do, and a horse to say mornin' to. I gotta get up off this floor and talk some sense into Roy.* But she couldn't get up off the floor. She was a turtle on her back. A turtle with a phone.

Katherine took a painful breath and let it leak out with a wheeze. She'd call Suse. Suse wouldn't make her feel like she was going nuts. *Suse'd help. Suse'd …*

The next breath was more difficult. She *was* one of them old decrepit ladies, or turning into one. She dialed the Kenseth's and pulled the cord for more slack. Part of her wanted to sleep. Cable ripped from the wall. The base dropped six inches and smacked hard enough against the wall to make the bell clang inside.

She let it ring three times, then Cindy's voice: "Hello?"

Nothing but strain left Katherine's mouth. She tried again for air. It wanted nothing to do with her.

"Hello?" said the small voice a second time.

Katherine drew in more air, but was unable to respond. Just a wink of sleep, and then she'd try the phone again.

Just need some rest is all. Count some sheep.

Distant, she could hear Susan telling Cindy to hang up.

Hey, Suse, Katherine carried on in her head. *It's Katherine. You won't believe it, I'm sure*—another painful breath—*but I'm on the kitchen floor, unable to talk, but somehow talkin' anyhow. I'm tired, Suse. I know it's not yet even seven or eight or—I can't see the clock from here—but I'm tired none'less. Thought I'd nap on the 'noleum a while.*

Susan wasn't in the mood to talk, though, because the line was beeping again. She shushed it with her palm and listened to it muffle as she took a long breathless breath. The mouth of a goldfish short on water.

If Suse was in no mood to talk, maybe Roy might be. She hung up. Pressed the redial button. It rang twice.

Roy.

The other end said hello. It didn't sound like Roy.

Is that you? Another breath. *Suse ain't mad at me is she?*

The other end said hello again.

I already said my hellos, Roy. But if you ain't payin' attention, I'd rather not bother talkin' to you at all. Listen …

She took a breath and shut her eyes. It took three seconds for them to reopen.

The other end of the line swooshed like a screen door.

I've been thinkin' bout the horse. Maybe put some weights on the saddle when you walk him round next. Get him used to somethin' heavy on his back, and slowly add—

"I don't know," said the phone from far away, "It's just someone breathing."

Roy …

"Hello?" It was Susan. She sounded ill-tempered.

You're not mad at me, are ya, Suse?

The kitchen had gotten darker, as if a large cloud had passed in front of the sun. Katherine let the ceiling spin slowly above her. It spiraled downward.

The phone said something again, but Katherine lost it in daydream. Her lungs filled with air. She counted to five. She no longer held onto the phone. It rested peacefully like a rose under both her hands. She had loved the roses at the Kenseths. Somehow they had reminded her of Todd. She didn't know why. Maybe it was the thorns. When Todd was a couple days over two he'd tried plucking one, cutting his palm in the process. Katherine saw him do it but wasn't able to warn him in time. It scared him more than anything. She had him hold onto a wet washcloth to take away the sting.

Most of the bushes were dried up and dead now. Some still bloomed in the springtime, but the flowers were always flatter and smaller than they could be. They were Susan's roses. After Todd died, Susan had let the roses die.

Katherine exhaled Susan's name, and gave in to sleep.

Cindy was supposed to be in bed all those years back but she had heard them arguing and put her ear to the door to listen and heard her father scream, "We had to pull the plug, Suse!" as they yelled at each other about Todd being dead and how they'd never ever see him again and she had jumped away from the door when Dad said it was Mom's fault and Mom said it was Dad's fault and then they said it was neither of their faults and she fell onto her bed crying into her pillow because she and Charlie never got to say goodbye and Todd was dead and gone forever and so was Joey Bean.

She was alone in the waiting room and she sat in her chair, feet on the seat. She hugged her legs, cried into her knees. She sniffed and looked up for a bit, but she was alone because Dad had left to check on Mom and Charlie was looking for a vending machine and Mrs. Jensen was probably dead, too. She looked up because sometimes Todd was there. Sometimes if she thought about him hard enough he'd be there. They'd sign together like it was a secret code they shared. Charlie took sign language classes with her, too, and she wondered if Charlie ever saw Todd, or imagined him the same way with train track scars covering his face, sometimes staring up at nothing, sometimes sharing secrets, sometimes offering guidance. To her, Todd had always tried his hardest to smile. Maybe he was there to protect her like a guardian angel and maybe he protected Charlie, too, or even the whole family. She was always afraid to ask Charlie if he ever saw him.

Mom and Dad fought all night that night and Cindy had

heard it all from her bedroom through the blankets over her head but she couldn't block out all the sounds and heard them say that Todd had suffered enough and it was none of their faults Todd died even though they both thought they'd killed Todd before the doctors tried to make things right, but all they did was put together an incomplete puzzle; the parts still missing were the pieces of Todd that gave him life—the parts that made him Todd, and her parents pulled the plug on Todd's body, not Todd, and neither accepted that. Her parents had fought hard, and cried hard. They destroyed themselves over time and it often showed like the time Mom threw the garlic bread across the kitchen table when Cindy mentioned Todd because she had seen him.

Cindy rocked in her chair. She looked again for Todd. Sometimes he was there. Sometimes he wasn't there. She couldn't find him, so she rocked. Cindy knew she'd never see him again.

Susan opened her eyes to blurry white ceiling tiles. She was on her back, wore a light blue hospital gown, and was covered partially by white linen bedding. Oxygen tubes ran from her nose. An IV transfusion stuck from her arm. A contraption on her index finger fed her pulse to the bulky machine next to her.

She remembered coughing blood outside the waiting room but that was it. The last time she saw Todd, he was in a similar bed, unconscious, with the same type of gadgets. Gooseflesh covered her arms as she sat up. Roy was with her; he stood up from a chair and walked toward her. He held her hand, smiling, but somehow not smiling.

"What happened? Where are the kids?"

"Charlie and Cindy are fine," Roy said. "They're in the waiting room reading magazines and drinking hot chocolate from the vending machines. I gave them each a few bucks for snacks. I couldn't see you from the window so I went out to check on you and you were—"

Susan could tell he didn't know what to call it.

"—you were having an episode. I didn't know what to do. You were shaking and coughing and there was blood on your blouse and on your face and hands. You gave us quite a scare, Suse. I ran back inside and grabbed a nurse and she paged for help. Two guys came rushing out. I told the kids to stay put when they carted you away. You were having trouble breathing, Suse. They had to put a tube down your throat and squeeze air from a big plunger-looking thing." Roy was in tears. His hand shook hers. "I've spent the last hour filling out forms. I didn't know what to put in some of the boxes."

Susan's throat was sore. Her words came out hoarse.

"How's Katherine. Do they know what's wrong?"

Roy looked to the door, then back to her hand. "I'm sorry, Suse. Katherine passed away almost four hours ago."

They shared silence for a long while.

Susan cried on his shoulder until she was out of tears.

"Do the kids know?"

"Yeah. Cindy didn't take it too well. Charlie seemed to know it was coming before the doctor's told us. Every time we come here …"

"Roy," said Susan, almost in a whisper.

Roy looked into her eyes.

"Did the doctors tell you what's wrong with me?"

"No." His eyes were honest. "They took blood for tests. They won't know for a while. One of the doctors said they wanted to run a chest X-ray. An MRI or CTscan or something later. They don't know much. We should be lucky they got you breathing on your own again. It's probably those damn—"

"Roy," Susan interrupted. "I need to tell you something."
He listened intently, still holding her hand.
"Something is wrong with me. Something terrible."
"Don't think that, Suse. The doctors will—"
"The doctors will tell us it's SCLC. I looked it up last week on the internet. I'm sure it's what I've got. I fit all the symptoms. I've been coughing this way for months."
"It's probably just pneumonia or—"
"I've been coughing *blood* for months. I was too afraid to say anything. It's Small Cell Lung Cancer."

NINETEEN

"Do you understand?"

Everything is captured within the floating frame in front of Todd before it turns black. Three deaths: Mrs. Jensen, his mother, himself. Counting Joey Bean, there are four.

The red light of Nuveli says, "There must be only three; one must live."

One is in need of protection, the other guidance.

The white light of Loah joins them and says, "Sacrifice is the greatest gift one can give to another."

Both orbs circle round to the opposite side of the mirror and beckon Todd to follow.

Todd finds himself staring through a window.

He sees the farm and he is three again and he is carrying a heavy bucket of water with a bar of soap floating within it. The night Joey Bean gives birth to Spirit. The night his father puts her down. The night Todd is kicked in the head. The night his mother rides with him to the hospital, holding him together. Todd watches through the floating frame as she holds his fractured skull like the shell of a cracked egg. They are riding to the hospital where he will be pieced back together only to become a vegetable on a medicinal salad, a body kept alive by machine, and after a long fight between his parents, a decision will be made that will tear them apart, a decision that will ultimately turn his father to drink, and his mother to smoke.

A mother will pull the plug on her son and a father will pull the plug on his son and by signing a form they will cease life support on his body and then they will slowly begin destroying themselves and each other.

Understanding what he must do, Todd passes through the window and joins his mother in the ambulance.

TWENTY

"Tell me he's going to be okay," Susan said to the paramedic.

She stood at the rear of the vehicle and smacked her head on a storage bin when the van lurched forward. She balanced with outstretched arms until she was sure they were off the gravel driveway and onto the road. There was one final bump as the ambulance tires connected with the asphalt. She sat onto the red vinyl seat and stared at Todd. He was looking right at her, but somehow looking past her as well.

How could he even have so much blood?

The white gauze applied by the paramedic quickly turned red. Susan was sure he was doing his best to stop the bleeding, but wondered how it would even be possible to apply pressure without injuring him further. She watched his eyes bounce from monitor to monitor as he checked the various numbers and pulsing lines that meant absolutely nothing to her.

Susan closed her eyes and clasped her hands together. She had not prayed for years, but said the following under her breath: *If you are there … Look after my son. Help him live through this. Send him an angel. Help him pull through this. Save Todd.*

She opened her eyes and found the paramedic staring at her; it was a somewhat hopeless expression. "How long till the hospital?" he asked the driver.

"Twenty minutes. Maybe more."

Susan could barely hear him over the engine.

"We won't have that much—" the paramedic said, cutting himself short.

"Improvise," said the driver.

The man standing over Todd bit his bottom lip and nodded. He looked again to Susan.

"Your son is losing a lot of blood."

Susan rolled up her sleeves.

He pointed to a small refrigeration unit and said, "We've got plenty. We're one of the few ambulances carrying blood. Do you know your son's blood type?"

"AB Positive," she said.

"Good. Put on a pair of rubber gloves; they're in the small drawer behind you."

Susan pulled them over her bloody hands.

The paramedic held out compresses with his free hand. It was an inviting gesture.

Susan scooted closer, took it from him, awaiting instruction.

The paramedic switched gauze, somehow never removing pressure from Todd's skull, and made sure Susan paid attention.

"I need you to hold these bandages, exactly like this, while I get blood ready. Can you handle this? If not, I need to know."

Susan nodded.

"You're going to need to apply some pressure, but not a lot. You'll get the feel of it. Try to avoid movement as much as possible. Pretend you're holding a vase full of water. Do this until I can relieve you. I'm sorry to have to ask you—"

Susan interjected not with words but by rushing between Todd and the paramedic and by putting her hands in place of his and applying pressure as he slid his larger hands from underneath and looked to the monitor displaying his pulse and she could feel his pulse and it was hot and she couldn't keep it inside because the vase was beginning to spill over as blood quickly rushed to the gauze and out through her fingers and Todd was dying and spilling out onto the gurney and onto her shoes while the number on the monitor lowered until it reached zero and became flat as the line began to blur and the van began to blur and it all started to fade away with the life of her son.

Epilogue

"What does that signify to you, William: 'from the ashes arose'?"

Dr. Milton's eyes were drawn to the tattoo.

"*A* rose," said his patient. "Not arose, *a* rose."

"What does that phrase mean to you? What is its significance?"

Hillcrest sat in his metal folding chair rubbing his neck. His white T-shirt and pants matched the room. It made the bruises, and the scars on his forearms, purple under the fluorescents.

"From the ashes a rose," Hillcrest said. "Have I told you about my problem?"

"Yes, you have."

"You see, I have this problem."

"Tell me about the rose."

"I can't seem to remember things one day to the next. It's like I wake up each morning not knowing what I did the day before. As if—"

"As if you are reborn."

Hillcrest looked to Dr. Milton as if *he* were the crazy one and scratched the bruises around his neck. Six days prior he had twisted a ripped section of bed linen and wrapped it around his throat until his face turned blue. He only succeeded in cutting off circulation of blood to his head and simply passed out. One of the nurses found him on the floor and reported the incident. At their next session, Dr. Milton didn't ask him why he did it. It was much too soon. It was safer to discuss past incidences with suicide patients than to bring up recent attempts.

Since he wasn't getting anywhere with the rose, now was that opportunity.

"Tell me about last Wednesday, William. How was last Wednesday different from the others … the paperclips in the razorblade box, the sugar candies in the prescription bottles, the Mike & Ike's in the revolver? How were those attempts different than when you tried to choke yourself?"

His patient rocked in his chair like a child.

Dr. Milton clicked his pen on and off as he waited for an answer.

"Sometimes it burns."

"Sometimes *what* burns?"

Hillcrest covered the red and black rose tattoo.

Chills ate his spine, for he had earlier drawn a rose on his notepad, and added flames underneath it as the session progressed.

"The best way to put out fires is to smother them. Fire breathes oxygen. You have to smother a fire to kill it. You have to drown a fire to kill it." Hillcrests eyes were terrifying. He brought his knees to his chest, hugged them as he rocked in the chair. "Sometimes it burns, doctor. Sometimes it burns and the only way to put out the fire is to smother it, or drown it. To keep it from spreading. You have to stop it from destroying—"

"William."

He had to keep his patient from breaking down entirely.

It was the most difficult part of his job sometimes. With Hillcrest, he had to use assertion.

"I don't remember doing these," said the patient. Hillcrest held out his wrists. "I don't remember doing a lot of things."

Letting a patient self-explore was often beneficial.

"I had a lucid dream last night. I could still smell the smoke when I woke up this morning."

The feeling of déjà vu returned, as if he were somehow in a recursive nightmare of his own, as if he woke up with a blank notepad on his lap and in each interview he got the same answers to the same questions, but in each of their sessions the variables somehow changed, such as the breakdown moments ago.

He looked through the blank pages as William carried on about the dream—the one about waking up naked in a cemetery wearing only a silver necklace with some kind of charm. He had heard the dream before, at least twice, word for word, it seemed.

"It wasn't a crucifix; that was my first thought. It was a little silver revolver. I wouldn't have noticed it—"

But it was burning against my chest, thought Dr. Milton.

"—but it was burning against my chest."

He had heard it all before, but decided to let Hillcrest tell his story. He looked once again to his drawing of the rose with the fire blossoming beneath, the fire just scribbles. A couple lines resembled numbers. He had somehow randomly inked 196 beneath the stem. The little hairs on the back of his neck stood on end.

A previous patient of his had repeatedly tried killing himself both at home and under Dr. Milton's care. He had once—jokingly at the time—told Dr. Milton about his viewpoint of the cross and its symbolism. He remembered something about if Christ had been shot rather than crucified, how most of the Christian faith would today be reading bibles with guns printed on their covers, wearing necklaces with guns instead of crucifixes. The number 196 had come up with another of his patients, a man who had taught him about palindrome sums; a man claiming to be God on vacation.

"I broke the chain when I pulled it from my neck. The glowing gun burnt into my hand."

Hillcrest held out his right hand. An L-shaped blister stood out on his palm.

The burns were new. They wouldn't be in his notes if he could find them, nor were they mentioned on the tapes. He must have found a book of matches left by one of the nurses, or inflicted the wounds earlier in the morning by grabbing the radiator in the patient lounge. He made a note to follow-up.

"At first, I couldn't let go."

"But once you did, the pain went away," said Dr. Milton.

"Have I told you this before?"

"I'm sorry, William. Please continue."

"And then the pain went away. The necklace fell to the ground, but kept getting hotter. Dry leaves under it started to smoke, and the next thing I knew, all the trees around me were on fire—the whole mountainside."

His patient touched the rose tattoo.

"Sometimes it burns."

"The design on your neck, or the bruises around your neck?"

Hillcrest didn't appear to hear the question.

"Everything in the dream seemed so real. I can still smell the smoke—"

His eyes bounced from Dr. Milton to the wall, as if pondering whether or not he had told him this before.

"No matter which direction I fled in the dream, I found fire. It burnt me alive. I remember being unable to run, unable to breath—smoke filling my lungs. My skin peeling and turning black. The smell of my hair catching fire. My body turning to ash. I can remember every last one of these horrid details as if this dream were not a dream at all, but some kind of penance I must suffer for something I can't remember ever doing."

"Take a deep breath, William."

Hillcrest held the sides of the metal folding chair, knuckles white. Sweat soaked his collar. He breathed in deeply and let it out. It took him three times doing this before loosening his grip on the chair. The rocking stilled.

Dr. Milton clicked his pen and jotted notes about the dream. The vivacity of Hillcrest's nightmare intrigued him, especially the smells and the bold words he used to describe certain things. The mention of *penance* …

"In our third session, William, you mentioned other dreams."

"You are mistaken, doctor. This is our second session."

"Tell me about the dreams you had before our *previous* session."

His patient admired the white tile flooring, polished so that faint images of both men reflected from it.

"Sometimes I wonder about dreams," said Hillcrest. "What if, when we dream, we are really going someplace

else—to another dimension, or another plane of existence—and what we do when we dream plays out wherever
it is we go, and consequences follow our actions … Like my
dream of lycanthropy."

"You felt your stomach churn for blood when you were
in wolf form," said Dr. Milton.

He had filled three pages worth of notes on the dream
about werewolves.

"The blood tasted like dirty change. It felt real. What
if I killed all those people? What about the consequences?
What if I have it all wrong? What if *we*—you and me—*are*
the consequences? What if we are simply someone else's
dream? Somewhere, some *when*, a person could be sleeping,
and dreaming about a doctor and a patient discussing this
very conversation."

"A recursive reality," said Dr. Milton. "Interesting."

"What if that person dreaming is a little boy—three,
maybe four years of age—and his creative imagination is
the foundation for our very own being? Maybe God is just
a child in a coma."

It was starting to come together for William. His dreams,
his attempts at taking his life, the tattoo on his neck—they
were intimations to a paradoxical condition.

"I had a patient a while back. He had a condition
not unlike your own. He was first brought to me after he
attempted suicide."

Hillcrest leaned in closer.

"His wife came home to an empty house and found a
note on her pillow. According to the police report, he tried
to kill himself in front of a mirror with a revolver. He said
a demon lived inside him and that he was trying to kill the

man in the mirror, not himself. During our sessions, he had many questions. What if when we die we are waking somewhere else? What if when we look into the mirror it is not our reflection staring back, but a different being altogether? What if we are someone else's reflection? What would it take to kill the man in the mirror? Those types of questions. As I discovered, he wasn't trying to commit suicide at all. He was trying to kill the demon inside him, the man in the mirror. Luckily, he shot his reflection, not himself. He cleaned up the mess, but forgot about the letter and the—"

"The letter and the what?"

He was caught breathless.

"He forgot about the rose. Next to the letter for his wife, he had placed a single red rose."

"Interesting," said William Hillcrest, as if their roles had reversed.

"A week after he was put under my care, I gave him a task to test his progress. I told him to go into the restroom, to turn off the lights, and to face the man in the mirror. He attacked his reflection and cut himself, badly. The last time I saw him, his arms were bandaged from wrist to elbow. Abrasions on his face and neck. He nearly bled to death by the time our nurses found him."

They sat in silence, each leaning forward in their chairs.

It was Dr. Milton who spoke first.

"Earlier, William, you said something that caught me off-guard. We were discussing the time you found the candy in your revolver instead of cartridges. You asked me to imagine pulling the trigger of a gun pointed at my head, thinking each time that *this* could be the one, *this* could be the one that ends my life."

Hillcrest began to shake.

"You said 'from the ashes *arose*.' You said each time you die you are born again … like a phoenix. What does that mean to you? What does the rose tattoo signify?"

"From the ashes *a* rose," said Hillcrest.

"William …"

It was too many questions. Dr. Milton lost control.

The patient grabbed his knees and rocked.

"Have I told you about my problem?"

About the Author

Michael Bailey is a multi-award-winning author, editor and publisher, and the recipient of over two dozen literary accolades, including the Bram Stoker Award, Benjamin Franklin Award, Eric Hoffer Book Award, Independent Publisher Book Award, the Indie Book Award, the International Book Award, and others. His novels include *Palindrome Hannah*, *Phoenix Rose* and *Psychotropic Dragon*, and he has published two short story and poetry collections, *Scales and Petals*, and *Inkblots and Blood Spots* (illustrated by Daniele Serra, with an introduction by Douglas E. Winter).

He is also the founder of the small press Written Backwards, where he has created psychological horror anthologies such as *Pellucid Lunacy*, *The Library of the Dead*, four volumes of *Chiral Mad* (the fourth co-edited by Lucy A. Snyder), and a few dark science fiction anthologies such as *Qualia Nous* and *You, Human*. He also served as the co-editor of both *Adam's Ladder* and *Prisms* (with Darren Speegle). Most recent publications include *Oversight*, a collection of novelettes including *Darkroom* and *SAD Face*, and the standalone novelette *Our Children, Our Teachers*. He lives in forever-burning California.

You can follow him on social media at twitter.com/nettirw, facebook.com/nettirw, or online at www.nettirw.com.